# MORE MYSTERIES FROM THE
# BERKLEY PUBLISHING GROUP...

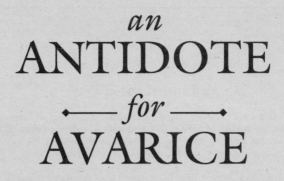

# *an* ANTIDOTE ◆—— *for* ——◆ AVARICE

*Caroline Roe*

BERKLEY PRIME CRIME, NEW YORK

## AN ANTIDOTE FOR AVARICE

A Berkley Prime Crime Book / published by arrangement with the author

PRINTING HISTORY
Berkley Prime Crime edition / December 1999

All rights reserved.
Copyright © 1999 by Medora Sale.
This book may not be reproduced in whole or in part, by mimeograph or any other means, without permission.
For information address: The Berkley Publishing Group, a division of Penguin Putnam Inc., 375 Hudson Street, New York, New York 10014.

The Penguin Putnam Inc. World Wide Web site address is http://www.penguinputnam.com

ISBN: 0-425-17260-0

Berkley Prime Crime Books are published by The Berkley Publishing Group, a division of Penguin Putnam Inc., 375 Hudson Street, New York, New York 10014. The name BERKLEY PRIME CRIME and the BERKLEY PRIME CRIME design are trademarks belonging to Penguin Putnam Inc.

PRINTED IN THE UNITED STATES OF AMERICA

10  9  8  7  6  5  4  3  2  1

*This book is dedicated to*

DEBORAH SCHLOW

*to whom, in so many ways, it belongs*

I would like to express my heartfelt thanks to Alain Duffieux, whose knowledge of early cookery and Mediterranean foodstuffs fills all these books. The road to Tarragona and back would have been longer and more arduous, except for the graciousness of so many who answered queries, large and small, on questions of travel in the Middle Ages. I could never have finished it without the unstinting help of Harry Roe, both in research and travel, and of my editor, Gail Fortune.

# CAST OF CHARACTERS

Avignon:
  Gonsalvo de Marca, a landowner from southern
    Cataluña
  His Holiness, Pope Innocent VI
  Norbert, a Franciscan friar
  Rodrigue de Lancia, a gentleman from Cataluña
  Tomas de Patrinhanis, ambassador from Ancona to the
    Pope

Girona:
(Church)
  Arnau de Corniliano, canon, canon vicar in
    Berenguer's absence
  Galceran de Monteterno, Pere Vitalis, Ramon de Orta,
    canons
  Fortunat, Galceran's nephew
  Vidal de Blanes, Abbott of Sant Feliu

(Call)
  Daniel, a young glove maker, Raquel's suitor
  Salomó des Mestre, Yusuf's tutor

(Town)
  An eight-year-old girl from Sant Feliu
  Marc, the eight-year-old's uncle
  Mother Benedicta, a tavern keeper
  Romeu the joiner, a shipbuilder

The travelers:
  Agnete, an erring nun
  Andreu, a traveling musician
  Berenguer de Cruilles, Bishop of Girona
  Bernat sa Frigola, his secretary
  Elicsenda, Abbess of Sant Daniel
  Enrique, the youngest of the Bishop's guards
  Felip, a traveling musician
  Francesc Monterranes, Berenguer's adviser and
    confessor
  Gilabert, an injured young gentleman
  Ibrahim, Isaac's houseman and porter
  Isaac, physician of Girona
  Judith, Isaac's wife
  Marta, Elicsenda's nun
  Naomi, Isaac's cook
  Raquel, Isaac and Judith's daughter
  Yusuf, Isaac's apprentice

Barcelona:
  Pedro of Aragon, Count of Barcelona and King
  Eleanora, his queen
  Francesc Ruffach, canon vicar of Barcelona in Miguel
    de Riçoma's absence
  Mordecai ben Issach, a physician

Tarragona:
  Dinah, Judith's sister
  Joshua, Dinah's husband
  Ruben, Joshua's nephew
  Sancho Lopez de Ayerbe, Archbishop of Tarragona

Dwellers by the road:
  Emilia, wife of the castellan at Castellvi de Rosanes
  Lluisa, her incompetent nursery maid
  Fernan, Gilabert's uncle
  Benvenist, a servant
  Miró, a servant
  Tavern keepers, monks, lords, ladies, and their servants

# HISTORICAL NOTE

In the spring of 1354, when *An Antidote for Avarice* takes place, the pope, like his immediate predecessors, was living in Avignon, driven there by political unrest in Rome; Pedro IV (a.k.a. Pere III of Cataluña, known as the Ceremonious) was King of Aragon; Aragon was preparing for war against one of the King's subject states, Sardinia.

The war was an administrative headache. Pedro had to raise huge sums of money in taxes and loans to fight it, as well as find reliable people to govern while he and the Queen were in Sardinia. Their absence in a foreign war could offer his political enemies an ideal chance to seize power.

As well, the archdiocese of Tarragona was calling its bishops to a General Council, an undertaking almost as complex. Moving a bishop from city to city was rather like going to war, since he was expected to travel with a small army of retainers and guards for safety, dignity, and comfort.

The background events and most of the characters in the book are drawn from the copious writings of the time. Pedro left us a chronicle of his reign, filled with people, politics, and glimpses into his married life with Eleanor of Sicily, his confidante and adviser, a shrewd and fearless woman who traveled everywhere with him, even into combat on his warships.

Papal records are a rich source. For centuries, the papal courts had functioned as an international court, acting as arbitrator in disputes between countries. A papal letter written to resolve one of these lies behind *An Antidote to Avarice*. Enraged merchants from the city of Ancona had accused five ship captains from Cataluña of piracy, claiming the loss of valuable ships and cargoes belonging to them. The Italians pursued the Catalans into the papal courts, only to come up against the hard fact that it is easier to get a judgment than to have it enforced. Ancona's pirates were Aragon's loyal fleet.

Berenguer, bishop of Girona, traveled to the council on the Via Augusta, that magnificent Roman road from the Eternal City to the southern coast of present-day Spain. The road is still there, although obscured in places by later construction.

Historians have assumed that Berenguer was involved in the King's preparations for war, and give that as a reason why he left no record of his presence or absence at the General Council in Tarragona in 1354. *An Antidote to Avarice* offers a few alternate explanations.

The bishop of Girona, Berenguer de Cruilles, existed, and the records attest to his friendly relations with the Jewish community. His blind physician, Isaac, is only a partial fiction. Half a century before, there was a mystic philosopher and Cabbalist, Isaac the Blind, revered for his wisdom and his uncanny ability to "see" illness and the approach of death. His students carried his religious and philosophical teachings south, particularly to Girona. If Isaac the Blind had had a descendant who came to the city as a young man, and if that descendant possessed his ancestor's powers, he might have studied medicine, married a woman like Judith, been Berenguer's physician, and lost his sight. Jewish physicians were highly regarded and counted among their patients both the upper clergy and the ruling classes.

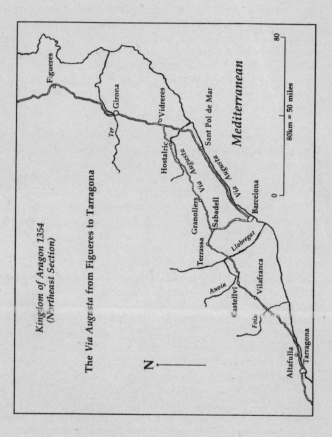

Kingdom of Aragon 1354
(Northeast Section)

The *Via Augusta* from Figueres to Tarragona

N

Figueres

Ter
Girona
Videreres
Sant Pol de Mar
Hostalric
Via Augusta
Granollers
Via Augusta
Sabadell
Terrassa
Barcelona

*Mediterranean*

Anoia
Castellvi
Vilafranca
Foix
Llobregat

Altafulla
Tarragona

0    80km = 50 miles    80

# PART ONE

# ONE

## Girona

*March 10, 1354*

"I don't care what you say, Isaac. I'm coming with you."

The physician turned his face toward his wife, as if he were studying her with his sightless eyes. "No, Judith," he said briskly. "It is not possible. Now, if there is any more of that most excellent lamb, I would be pleased to have it. Raquel and I walked a great distance this morning, did we not?" he asked, turning to his daughter.

"Yes, Papa."

"Certainly," said Judith. "Naomi, give Master Isaac more lamb." As soon as the cook went back into the kitchen, the physician's wife returned to the attack. "Don't change the subject, Isaac. I am going to Tarragona with you to see my sister. I haven't seen Dinah since her marriage."

"Judith, you must be sensible," said Isaac calmly. "It will be a long journey and His Excellency the Bishop is an impatient man."

"That is nothing to me," replied his wife. "Let him be impatient."

"Mama," said their daughter. "The twins are still at the table."

"Then they may leave," said Judith angrily. "And Yusuf as well."

"Judith, you must understand that the Archbishop of Tarragona is angry at His Excellency," said Isaac. "I will not add your unreasonable demands to his other troubles."

"I don't care if the Pope of Avignon wants his head," said Judith. "I'm coming to Tarragona."

"You'd care soon enough if he lost his position," said her husband.

"He can lose it tomorrow. It won't bother me."

"And we'd go down with him, I assure you. He's been a good friend to us—and a powerful protector." One of the twins reached for his cup and knocked it over with a soft thump. Isaac turned one ear toward the children. "Judith," he said firmly, "this is neither the time nor the place to discuss such things."

"There never will be a time or place with you, Isaac. You refuse to talk about anything that displeases you, and Raquel is always there to help you out. I'm sick of it. And I told you two to go," she snapped. "You, too, Yusuf."

The seven-year-olds scrambled hastily off the bench and raced out, followed by Yusuf, the physician's apprentice, who made a dignified exit, closing the door firmly behind him.

"Extra people will slow him down," said Isaac, with a slow emphasis he only used when angry. Raquel pushed aside her plate and began searching for an excuse to follow the younger ones out. "No one comes with us who is not absolutely necessary," added her father. "And I assure you that I do not accompany him for my pleasure. I will be working, and will have no time—no time at all—to amuse you."

"Nonsense. The Bishop may suffer from a few trifling complaints, but he is never ill," said Judith. "You will have nothing to do for that whole long trip and back. I'm coming with you. And I'm bringing Raquel." She stood up. "I shall ask the rabbi to write a letter for me to tell Dinah of our plans. Raquel, come into the sitting room. I want to talk to you," said her mother.

"Wait here, Raquel," said Isaac, pushing aside the extra plateful of roasted lamb with garlic and savory herbs that he had asked for. "I want to talk to you."

Judith glared at her daughter and swept out of the room.

"Oh, Papa," said Raquel. "Please. I don't want to go to Tarragona. Mama and Aunt Dinah are still trying to marry me to her husband's nephew."

"Don't worry. We won't be taking any women," said her father. "His Excellency is determined to travel as quickly and as lightly as possible."

"Are you sure?"

"Absolutely sure, my dear. I promise you, you are safe from whatever young man your aunt has decided on for you."

"Thank you, Papa," said Raquel, with relief. For although her mother could be astonishingly stubborn, Raquel was confident that her father was as immovable as a mountain on those occasions when he intervened in household affairs. "But I was wondering . . ."

"About what?"

"Wouldn't you think that the Bishop, with all his wealth and importance, could afford to travel slowly and in the greatest comfort? Especially if he is ill."

"His Excellency may have a few aches and pains, Raquel, but he is a vigorous and healthy man. As you know perfectly well."

"Why is the trip to be so very hurried, Papa?"

"My dear, we must be considerate. Things are difficult for His Excellency. He is in disfavor with the Archbishop and with the King. Even your mother is now talking of the Pope. And if your mother has heard of it, that means the rumors that the Archbishop is sending someone to Avignon to complain to the Pope are widespread indeed."

"But surely none of this is true. I mean, people always say terrible things, and they're almost never right."

"Nonetheless, the world outside Girona appears to hold our good Bishop in rather low regard right now," said Isaac dryly.

"I would think His Excellency could ignore most of the world outside Girona," observed Raquel.

"Perhaps. But His Majesty is preparing for war with the Sardinians—"

"I know, Papa."

"Of course you do. But when there's talk of war, people start seeing traitors hiding in every shrub and doorway. Remember that my lord Berenguer, the Bishop, failed to deliver that nun—the one who was involved in kidnapping His Majesty's daughter—"

"She has a name, Papa," said his daughter, if only to remind her father that she, too, had been a victim of that failed scheme. "Sor Agnete. And it was the Abbess Elicsenda who was supposed to send her to prison. Not the Bishop."

"But as bishop of the diocese, he is seen to be responsible, Raquel, and his failure to act has angered His Majesty and started rumors of treachery. And he wasn't supposed to send her to prison," said Isaac, since his daughter was in a mood for accuracy. "Only to Tarragona, to be tried. And that, of course, means the Archbishop is also angry with him."

"Why don't they send her off and have done with it?"

"You would have to ask the Abbess and the Bishop that one, my dear. I do not know. Except that it has something to do with the security of the travel arrangements."

# TWO

## Avignon

**March 12, 1354**

"How do I know you will pay me once you have heard?" said the angelic-looking page in the velvet tunic.

Rodrigue de Lancia untied his purse and handed over a coin. Then he grasped the boy by the arm and gave him a shake. "Now—what happened in there?" he said.

"Your cousin is to hang, signore."

"On which charge?"

"Piracy. And all his goods confiscated."

"I must go," muttered Rodrigue. "I must return to Empuries and let him know before—"

"But, signore, it is far from over. Did your advocates not tell you?"

"I was told nothing," he said. "Nothing of any use. What now?"

"The problem must be placed before His Holiness," said the boy. "Then it will be considered in great secrecy with his closest advisers."

"And is one of those advisers to be your master?" he asked.

The page boy raised his hands in a helpless gesture.

"When is this secret meeting?"

"Tomorrow, my master says," he said, holding out his hand. "And tomorrow your friend's case comes to trial. I will meet you in the grand courtyard at this same hour and tell you about both."

"Him? He's no particular friend of mine." A look of sardonic amusement briefly altered Rodrigue's somber face. "But no doubt he will be here. He can pay you himself," he added, and walked away from the papal palace. Behind him, great shouts went up as the architect directed the stonemasons in the placement of a another block of finely worked pale stone into a new section of the papal palace at Avignon.

Tomas de Patrinhanis, ambassador to the papal court from the city-state of Ancona, was ushered into the Chambre de Parement, where the privileged few waited for a private audience with His Holiness, Innocent VI. Lord Tomas's pale and angelic-looking page, dressed in a blue tunic as fashionably cut and as expensive as his master's red-and-gold velvet one, had abandoned his newfound friend Rodrigue and rejoined the ambassador's retinue. Lord Tomas and his secretary warmed themselves at the fire that was close to the steps leading to the Pope's bedchamber. The rest of his attendants chatted in subdued tones at the other end of the room.

The little page seized his chance; armed only with his curls and his enchanting smile, he left, darting through a small dining hall and into the Pope's private kitchen, evading the servants as he went. Emerging triumphant into a maze of narrow corridors and stairways, he threaded his way expertly through the complex back passages, until he reached a nook with a deep window seat. It was right next to Innocent's bedchamber, but on the opposite side of it. His mission had been successful. He was thirty feet away from where he had started, and alone. He settled down to wait.

The ambassador from Ancona was ushered into the grandeur of the bedchamber originally constructed for Clement

VI, Innocent's predecessor. The fifty years that the Popes had lived in Avignon—after Clement V's most unhappy embroilment in civil strife in Rome—had seen much time, thought, and gold spent turning a modest abbey into something suitable for the princes of the Church. Even Lord Tomas, who had been received in this room before, was noticeably subdued by his surroundings.

"This is not the first time the Holy See has had trouble with Aragon," said the Pope. "We had hoped to avoid these clashes, but we cannot condone one Christian sovereign state preying upon another at sea."

"The people of Ancona would be most grateful if Your Holiness would intervene on their behalf," said the ambassador. "They are being impoverished by the cruel and unprincipled disregard—"

"Yes, yes," said Innocent. "We have seen and noted the submissions from Ancona. We will draft a letter," he said, with a nod to his principal secretary, who looked at the scribe, who in turn dipped his pen in his ink, "to His Majesty Don Pedro of Aragon, demanding the return of the ships."

"And their contents?" prompted the ambassador.

"And their contents—and anything else they took," he added impatiently.

The secretary murmured in his ear.

"The pirates to be hanged for their misdeeds, all this under pain of excommunication. We will discuss the precise wording at a later time."

The bitter wind that swooped over the thick walls of the palace did its best to deny that spring had arrived. It swirled around the grand courtyard and probed under the arches, impudently lifting the tunics of those less privileged petitioners who waited outside under the cold eyes of the guard. Someone in a furred cloak rode through the principal portal, dismounted under the arches, and threw the reins of his glossy beast at a lackey who had appeared from nowhere. He ran up the broad staircase and the men who waited narrowed their eyes in envy.

"He's going to the private apartments," said a round, pale man, dressed in the gray habit of a Franciscan friar.

"I doubt it, Father Norbert," said a priest in clerkly black beside him.

"I hear they're filled with treasure," said Friar Norbert. "Gold, and rubies, and silk robes."

"What good are silk robes in a north wind?" said the priest. "I'd exchange them all for young Lord Moneybags's furred cloak right now." He stopped to rub his cold hands. "But what brings you here, Father?" he asked, as if suddenly conscious of his brusque and unfriendly manner.

The friar reddened and stepped back as if struck with a sudden blow. "Nothing, really, Father." He stumbled over his words and broke into a sweat. "A minor thing."

Standing near them in the doubtful shelter of the pillar, Rodrigue de Lancia waited with an older, burlier gentleman. The older man glared at the friar, causing the unhappy creature to blush scarlet and turn his attention to the admirable stonework of the floor.

Rodrigue looked inquiringly at his companion.

"Priests and magpies," said the older man. "Never silent and never a sound you'd like to hear." He shifted impatiently from one foot to the other. "I wonder how long we'll have to wait here," he added. "It is not a pleasant day."

"Not long, I hope, Don Gonsalvo," said Rodrigue.

"That excellent young lad of yours assured me the case would be decided this morning," said Gonsalvo. "And I am most grateful for him. Without your assistance I would not have known where to turn."

"It was not worth mentioning," said Rodrigue politely.

"Not at all," said Gonsalvo heartily. "It was a most extraordinary kindness on your part, Don Rodrigue, and good fortune on mine that I should happen upon a fellow countryman so far from home. And one so much more skilled than I in the ways of the papal court."

"Pray, Don Gonsalvo, speak no more of it. It was nothing," said Rodrigue irritably. "I gave your name to a boy who is now fleecing both of us for his very paltry assistance. I would have done the same for any man."

As if his words had been a signal, the doors swung open. The page came out surrounded by a dozen or so men, talking loudly among themselves. He nodded at Gonsalvo, and began to drift to the edge of the crowd. By the time everyone had passed the gate, the page was walking beside Rodrigue.

"Well?" asked Rodrigue. "What have you to tell us?"

The page covered his black curls with his cap and smiled conspiratorially. "The scullery lad in the lower kitchen was telling me that His Holiness has his very private apartments newly painted with pictures of beautiful naked women and wonderful scenes of great depravity. But I don't know that I believe him. He's never been in the private apartments, but he says he heard it from—"

"What did they say in there?" hissed Rodrigue. "Before I pull your jesting tongue out of your mouth."

The page shook his head. Obediently, they followed him in silence to the street below, straight into the crowds of noisy buyers and sellers of every description, jostling each other, screaming, bargaining, and thrusting wares in their faces. He pulled them through a doorway and into the back of a dark tavern, as far from the smoky fire—and the other customers—as he could. It seemed as quiet as an empty forest after the tumult of battle. "Order something," he said.

Gonsalvo ordered a jug of wine. The page reached out his hand in silence. The burly man took a coin from his purse and placed it on the table. Rodrigue added another. "The rest when you have spoken," said Gonsalvo. "I would like to assure myself that you have something to say."

"I know very little but scraps of gossip I pick up from time to time," said the page with mock humility.

Silence fell over the group as the taverner's wife slung a jug and three cups down in front of them and waited for payment.

"But I will tell you what it is," said the page as soon as she was out of earshot again. "My noble master the

ambassador, Lord Tomas, had a private audience with His
Holiness. He asked him to intercede with Don Pedro of
Aragon on behalf of the most loyal and Christian people
of Ancona to ensure that the condemned man and his fellows—''

"We know what he wants," said Rodrigue. "What did
His Holiness say?"

"He assured them that a letter would be written—a
strong letter—demanding restitution of Master Nicolas Polluti's stolen ships and goods. My master asked His Holiness's secretary on what terms the demand would be made.
The secretary assured them that His Holiness would demand the utmost penalty of the law for the pirates, this
injunction to be laid upon Don Pedro of Aragon on pain of
excommunication."

"Who told you this? Or were you present at the audience?"

"No one," said the page, "and I wasn't."

"Then how do we know—"

"I was sitting outside a door waiting for my master to
finish speaking to His Holiness. By some strange chance,"
he said demurely, "the door was open a little. I could hear
it all quite clearly."

"When is this letter to be written?" asked Rodrigue.

The page shrugged his thin shoulders. "In God's good
time, I suppose. His Holiness didn't say."

"Good. Certainly no letter will be dashed off tonight and
sent off tomorrow," said Rodrigue thoughtfully.

"I heard one of the secretaries say that before the wording could be decided on, many other issues must be considered," said the page.

"What did he mean by that?" asked Gonsalvo.

Rodrigue shrugged. "I would suppose that His Holiness
must decide how much he wishes to disoblige His Majesty
in order to satisfy the city of Ancona."

"The kingdom of Aragon is larger than the city of Ancona," said the other. "It is not, after all, as though Innocent's saintly mother were pleading the case for the city.
Of course, it's an ambassador against a crowd of pirates."

"Be careful, sir. You speak of my noble cousin, a loyal captain of Don Pedro's fleet."

"And a pirate. You admit that he is."

"He faces losing everything he has. And possibly a shameful death by hanging if Don Pedro bows to the papal decree."

"Enough of this. What about my case?" said the burly man, grasping the page by his thin arm before he could dart away. "When is it being heard?"

"Your case? Oh, that one," said the page. "The judges heard one of the witnesses, said they had several depositions to hand, and then declared that there was neither time nor need to hear more. The decision will be sent to the diocese of Barcelona in due course. And to the Archbishop of Tarragona as well, I think."

"No time?" said Gonsalvo in anguished tones. "You are saying they had no time to hear my case? Those were my witnesses. It cost me much gold to bring them here. Which one gave testimony?"

"A holy friar, signore," said the page. "One Norbert. And a miserable business he made of it, too. But no doubt he will tell you what happened. I most humbly beg your pardon, gentlemen," said the page. "But your cases have both been heard, one way or another. I was there, and reported. And now my master will be looking for me. I have fulfilled my promise, and you have not fulfilled yours."

The burly man raised a hand and cuffed the page on the ear.

"None of that, Don Gonsalvo," said his companion. "Pay the fellow. You received good value for money in him."

Four more coins chinked into the outstretched palm.

"And should you hear any further gossip," said Rodrigue. "From your master, from the servants, from the scribes—especially concerning the time and the precise contents of those letters, there will be more than that amount for you."

"Double?" asked the page.

"Double," he said.

# THREE

Girona

**Thursday, April 10**

Down by the river Ter, in the Girona shipyards, Romeu the joiner set down his polishing stone and ran his hand over the piece of wood he had been working on. It was rounded, almost crescent-shaped, and smooth to the touch. He slipped it into place on the prow of a broad-beamed galiot, tapped it home, and fastened it in.

He was pleased with life. They were working sunrise to sunset, and the pay, even at the regulated scales now in force, was excellent for master carpenters and their assistants. Two more days on the hull and this one would be finished, ready to be shielded in hides for protection. But he had already been guaranteed several weeks more work on the fittings.

The kingdom was preparing for war against the Sardinians and some of the refitting of His Majesty's fleet was being done in the city. Don Pedro intended to sail in full force against the rebellious island to settle the matter, but many of his ships had been battered by weather and enemy action in the past year's naval engagements with the Genoese, and there was little time to finish necessary repairs.

That morning, the careless, unskilled, and lazy workers had been let go, though shipbuilders were scarce; of those who remained, the architect had selected the most skilled and hardworking to carry on until the ships were ready to go downriver to meet the rest of the fleet at Rosas. War may be a terrible thing for some, Romeu thought cheerfully, but it was excellent for men who could build and repair ships.

He had just chosen another piece of wood when he noticed that the light was fading fast. He marked the wood as his and secreted it away before bundling up his tools and saying good night to his fellows.

"Come and take a cup of wine with us, Romeu," said one.

"My wife expects me at home," he said. "And I'm as hungry as I'm thirsty."

"One cup to celebrate our good fortune, and then we'll go home to our suppers."

The tavern nearest to the shipyard was small and unpretentious. When Romeu and his fellow celebrants came in, it was already filled with men who had been there for a while, and were still absorbing the unpalatable news that, for them, the work was finished. A hush fell over the room as the newcomers walked in; they nodded to their ex-workmates and sat down on a bench in the far corner.

"Look on it this way." The speaker was addressing a wiry little man. "It's Holy Week, isn't it? You'll have time to ready your soul for Easter. Since I haven't noticed that your Lent has included much fasting."

"Do you accuse me of not fasting? Here? I've lived on Mother Benedicta's raw wine and thin soup for weeks now."

"They feel like a penance," grumbled another.

"Why, this mouthful alone has spared me at least five hundred years of purgatory," said the wiry little man, draining his cup.

"We'll have plenty of chances to fast now that the work has dried up," said a short, square man, balding and red-faced. "They all moan there's nobody to work, but when you're free, do they hire you? No There we are—out on the street, our children hungry, our wives complaining endlessly. Something should be done about it.''

"If you hadn't ruined more good wood than you fitted into the hull of that galiot,'' observed a neat, spare fellow, "you might have been kept on.''

"Oh? And what about you?'' said the square man.

"I don't do much, everyone knows that, but what I do is good,'' the thin one replied with a lazy grin. "I enjoy the money while it comes in, but I'm never surprised when they let me go.''

The square man lurched to his feet and stood swaying sideways. The table edge pressed against the top of his thighs, keeping him upright. "You're saying I don't know my trade.''

"That's right,'' said the thin one, yawning. "You don't know your trade.''

The square man straightened up, reached across the trestle table, and grabbing his former workmate by the tunic, dragged him to his feet. The narrow table tipped, spilling a great deal of wine. The thin one kicked back the bench behind him, bent down his head, and butted his erstwhile friend in the stomach. The square man folded and fell, tipping three people off the bench on his side of the table. "And you can't fight,'' added the thin one.

In the background, Mother Benedicta squeaked, and rubbed her hands in distress. No one noticed. She moved ponderously back to where the wine barrels were arranged and extracted a sizable wooden club from behind them. "Out,'' she yelled. "I won't have fighting in my tavern. Out before I smash you on the head.'' She raised the heavy club as if it were a wooden spoon and waved it menacingly in the air.

"You're upsetting Mother Benedicta,'' said another voice. Its owner rose tipsily to his feet. "Outside, friend. You want to do good works? Let's go to the *Call* and baptize some Jews.''

They poured out into the street, laughing heartily.

Romeu looked at his companions and shook his head.

"I'm leaving," he said, pushing away his half-finished cup of wine.

"Joining them?"

"I think not," he said soberly. "Nothing good comes of these things."

He stepped out into the cool spring evening, but instead of going straight to his tidy little house in Sant Feliu, he headed into the city and strode up the steep hill to the Bishop's palace.

There was no question that young Salomó des Mestre should not have been outside the *Call* that evening. All Christian festivals had the potential for violence, but Holy Week and Easter week were always the worst. All doors and windows in the walls were to be kept locked and barred or shuttered, including the postern gate with its permanent gatekeeper.

But Salomó was in love. That morning, he had decided to buy a present for his beloved the minute his duties as tutor to the physician's apprentice, Yusuf, were finished for the day. He knew that a peddler in the city had new ribbons temptingly displayed, some of them broad and of a clear, deep red that would look enchanting in her hair. He told himself that he would be back long before the city stirred itself from the quiet of the afternoon.

He had not reckoned on the stallkeeper's uneasiness. When he arrived, he found the ribbons packed up and the stall closed for the day. It took Salomó considerable time to convince the man that it would be worth his effort to find the bewitching trifles, set them out, and come to some sort of agreement over price.

He left the stall in triumph with a packet of ribbons tucked safely in his tunic, turned the first corner of his return journey, and stopped. His way was blocked by a group of some six or seven shipyard workers, laughing and weaving about in various stages of inebriation.

"A Jew!" yelled one.

"Grab him!"

"Take him to the river and baptize him," counseled another.

"To the river!"

Salomó was neither a weakling nor a coward, but seven against one was clearly foolhardy for an unarmed man. He turned on his heels and ran.

Salomó was fast, young, and completely sober. His pursuers were much slowed by too much wine, and a certain vagueness of purpose. He was leaving them well behind him when he turned another corner and stumbled into a stack of broken baskets left in the street.

Romeu also moved quickly. He arrived at the quarters of the Bishop's guard just as the men from the shipyard started their uncertain march past the gates and through the city. By the time a patrol reached the drunken band, they were carrying a struggling Salomó des Mestre onto the bridge across the Onyar River. At the sight of the guard, the most sober among the workmen dropped the prisoner and bolted; the remaining three, too dazed and unsteady on their legs to consider escape, were arrested; Salomó, bruised, embarrassed, but essentially unharmed, his purse and his ribbons intact, was escorted back to the postern gate of the Jewish Quarter.

"Where were the guards?" asked Berenguer, Bishop of Girona, when the incident was reported to him.

"The city guards were rolling dice in front of the gates to the *Call*, and finishing a skin of wine," said the captain. "Our guards—one patrol—were in another part of the city. Clearly more patrols are needed. I shall double them."

### Girona, Friday, April 18

"My dear sir," cried a prosperous-looking corn merchant to his friend who dealt in fleeces. "I am just returned from my travels. What news?"

"Little that does not already come from Barcelona," said the wool merchant. "The shipyards are buzzing with work and the mood in the city is good. I trust your negotiations went well.''

''Well enough. Between shortages and surpluses and government controls on prices, it's not easy to make a decent living in the corn trade,'' he said. ''Does the Bishop still plan to travel to Tarragona?'' he added. ''Before I left, some question remained of whether he would go.''

''He does, unfortunately.''

''When is he leaving?''

''Tuesday, at first light, I hear,'' said the wool merchant. ''And taking Master Isaac, his physician, with him. I am not pleased about that.''

''Why should he stay behind?''

''Because Master Isaac is my physician as well. And the road to Tarragona is long and mountainous. That journey is not made in a day. We will not see them for a month or more. Much can happen in that time.''

''Perhaps he will leave his beautiful daughter here to look after us.'' The corn merchant gave his friend a conspiratorial grin.

The wool merchant was not given to lascivious amusement. ''He takes his wife and daughter with him,'' he said stiffly, ''along with the apprentice. We shall have to hope that we stay well until he returns.''

''Who is left to handle the affairs of the diocese? Monterranes?''

''No. Don Arnau de Corniliano.''

''Impossible,'' said the corn merchant, with something of mixed anger and disbelief in his voice. ''I cannot believe you.''

''Why do you say that? It's odd, but not impossible.''

''He detests His Excellency. And he is so frail I am astonished anyone would consider him.''

''I remarked upon that to Father Bernat,'' said the wool merchant. ''And the good friar observed that he will be asked to sign documents, not finish building the cathedral, and that his strength is up to that.''

''But why appoint your worst enemy as your vicar?''

''Why not? It means he will be too busy to do the Bishop

any harm. And His Excellency Is in even worse trouble now than he was when you left, friend. Or so the rumor is.

"I'm not pleased to hear this, my friend. In addition to being unpredictable, Don Arnau must argue fourteen sides to the question before he can agree with himself to take breakfast. I have some business coming before the episcopal court—this could cost me a pretty penny."

"We must all suffer, my friend. I lose my physician, you wait for judgment."

And the two men, confident in their prosperity, strolled across the square in the warm spring sunshine, cheerfully heading for the certainty of an excellent dinner, complaining all the while.

The north wall of Girona city towers high above the Galligants River and the suburb of Sant Feliu; the cathedral church of Santa Maria, scorning the shelter offered by the wall, rises higher still from its hilltop foundations. Just outside the city, the church of Sant Feliu stands alone, lifting its sharply pointed spire in bold challenge to the overwhelming presence of the cathedral. And no great distance to the east and north sits the heavy symmetrical grace of the Benedictine Abbey of Sant Pere de Galligants.

The three towers slumbered in the quiet of afternoon. But within the triangle they formed, the Abbot of Sant Feliu, by nature impatient, ambitious and restless, paced back and forth across the plaza in front of Sant Pere, oblivious to the peace, the beauty, or even the oppressive weight of stone that surrounded him. If he had been stripped of his robes and tonsure, and arrayed in well-fitted hose and tunic, with his glossy brown hair dressed in a modern fashion, Don Vidal de Blanes could have been an ornament to the court. On a spirited horse, with a sword in his hand, he could have led a regiment of seasoned troops. But in spite of his noble ancestry and martial nature, Don Vidal had been destined for the Church, and now belonged entirely to the Cloister. He was an unyielding and combative churchman in every drop of blood and every ounce of bone. And at that moment, to judge by the expression on his face, all that combativeness in blood and bone was rising to the surface. Don Vidal was not pleased.

"He does not deserve the name of bishop. The man is a disgrace. To the city, to the diocese, to Holy Mother Church herself," said a gray friar who stood meekly by the church steps. He glanced over at the Abbot to assess his reaction to the statement and dropped his eyes again.

Don Vidal stopped pacing. "No," he said at last. "You are not the first to come running to me with such tales, but it does not help Mother Church to add lies and false reports to an already unfortunate situation. The Abbess has acted foolishly, but I do not believe she has forgotten her vows. The Bishop is rash, and reckless, and sometimes careless, but he is not an evil man, nor has he brought disgrace upon the Church."

He frowned and turned away from the friar. A dog trotted toward the bridge, intent on his own concerns. A workman somewhere close by began to whistle rather mournfully. Suddenly the abbot started rapidly across the square in the direction of a small cemetery. "We will walk," he called back. "Give me your report once again, Father, but consider what you say, and this time strip it of the trimmings of malice." These last words came faintly to the ears of the panting friar as he tried to catch up with the man ahead.

Bishop Berenguer picked up the skull he had inherited from his predecessor and looked into its empty eye sockets. "Rest assured, Bernat," he said to his secretary, "I understand the situation. I have heard the rumors, and as wild as they are, I know they can do me no good. Nor can they help the Abbess. But I cannot believe they are being spread by Don Vidal." He shook his head.

"No," said Bernat sa Frigola. "I doubt that any of them originate with Don Vidal. But now that he is in a position of great power, all who seek to curry favor with him are running to him with these tales. And he is genuinely indignant that, as he sees it, you have done nothing to persuade the Abbess Elicsenda to turn Sor Agnete over to justice. As you know, he has written to His Majesty and to the Archbishop on the matter.''

"I have told the Abbess of Sant Daniel what she must do. She is preparing to deliver Sor Agnete to the mother house in Tarragona. These arrangements take time.''

"Ten months?" said Francesc Monterranes, one of his closest advisers. "May I remind Your Excellency that His Majesty is seriously displeased? I suspect he named Don Vidal as his procurator for Catalonia to remind you of his displeasure.''

"You think so, Francesc?" said Berenguer. "I confess that the thought had entered my head as well, but I assumed that His Majesty made the choice because of Don Vidal's administrative competence.''

"Of course," said Francesc smoothly. "But there are others in the province with equal administrative competence.''

"I think," said Bernat, "that you must consider stopping in Barcelona on your way to Tarragona to speak to His Majesty. Assure him of Your Excellency's loyalty and your determination to see the nun duly tried.''

"Nonsense," said Berenguer. "That would add at least two more days to the trip." He stood. "It is time for me to have a friendly conversation with the good Abbot.''

"Are you sure that is wise, Your Excellency?" asked Bernat.

"Certainly. My physician said that I am in need of mild exercise. I shall stroll from here to Sant Feliu. You may accompany me, if you like.''

"My lord Berenguer," said the Abbot cordially.

"Don Vidal," replied the Bishop. "I hope I find you well.''

"You do indeed.''

"I have come to seek your assistance in a matter of some importance," said the Bishop easily. His secretary repressed a desire to catch hold of his spiritual lord and whisk him forcefully out of the room before he said something truly unfortunate. "Because of the costs incurred during the disturbances in Holy Week, the council of the city wishes to reduce the number of guards protecting the Jewish Quarter, *and* double the tariff charged against it for protection. This means, as you can see, that both the King's Jews and the bishopric's Jews will pay much more to the city and be at greater risk if problems occur. I realize that you have not as yet taken up your post as His Majesty's procurator, but—"

"I understand you. I am here and, in some sense, responsible. Have you spoken to them?"

"I have, most forcefully."

"As their spiritual leader. Then I shall speak to them, as it were, in place of their temporal leader. This is a mean-spirited attempt to divert to themselves taxes owing to the diocese and to the crown. In direct contravention of law and customary usage, my lord Berenguer."

"It is indeed, Don Vidal."

"Especially now, when His Majesty is raising money for refitting ships—to the great benefit of the city, I might add. And those guards they have been supplying are useless, to say the best that one can say of them. Can you guarantee to supply extra men . . ."

And the two titans bent over specific long-term plans to organize security for the city.

# FOUR

Outside Figueres, on the Via Augusta

*Monday, April 21*

The inn that lurked beside the road at an inconvenient distance from both Figueres and Girona was no palace. It was small, dirty, and noisy. But it was cheaper than most, and the old road built by the Romans that led eastward over the mountain passes to Perpignan, Montpellier, and Avignon passed right by its door. On that Monday, its main room was crowded with local farmers, travelers, and sundry less easily classified visitors. A musician was playing something loud and lively in hopes of coaxing a penny or two from the crowd, or at least a free drink. Most of the clientele seemed to share a common desire, however, to pour as much of the landlord's wine as they could afford down their own throats, and paid little attention to him.

At the end of one of the long trestle tables, close to the fire, three travelers sat in silence—Rodrigue de Lancia, Friar Norbert, and an elegant young man of no more than twenty. The friar's round face was thinner and more haggard than it had been a month before in Avignon. The young man and Rodrigue looked up from their supper of bread and cheese at the noisy entrance of a new guest and his three hulking attendants. It was Gonsalvo. Don Rodrigue smiled icily.

"Don Rodrigue," cried Gonsalvo, hurrying over to join them. "I heard you were on the road ahead of me, and spurred my poor horse unmercifully to catch up. Madam! A cup of wine and some of this excellent-looking cheese."

"Good evening, Don Gonsalvo. You seem in good spirits."

"And well I might be," he said. "The closer I am to home, the happier my disposition. Are you by any chance riding to Barcelona, Don Rodrigue?"

"Alas, no," said Rodrigue, looking far from sorrowful at the prospect. "I am on my way to see my cousin. I leave you tomorrow at dawn."

"And have you further news of your cousin's case?" asked the newcomer, loud enough for all to hear.

"Until the judgment is in His Majesty's hand, we cannot know," he answered stiffly.

"The result of my case is also being sent to Barcelona right at this very moment," Gonsalvo whispered, leaning forward. "Every time I see a horse gallop by I wonder if his rider carries it with him. That is why I go there instead of directly home."

Rodrigue made no response.

Gonsalvo raised his cup and saluted the friar. "To you, Father," he said cheerfully. "We met last at Avignon, did we not? In a bitter chill wind, as I recollect. This bright fire is much kinder on the fingers."

The friar looked up and nodded, and then returned to contemplating the untouched food in front of him.

Gonsalvo turned to the elegant young man. "And you, señor, are you also a traveler? Did I not see you at Avignon as well?"

"I was there, almost twelvemonth back. If you were in the city then, we may indeed have passed each other. I spent the months between in Montpellier, señor," he said politely. "Improving my store of wisdom and emptying my purse. I travel from Figueres to Girona to visit my uncle."

"You have not traveled far today then," said the burly

man. "You would make a slow traveling companion, sir," he added with a robust laugh. "At that rate it would take me a year to reach home."

"I was much delayed in my departure, señor, and preferring not to ride at night, thus have chanced upon your company. Fortunat is my name," he said, with a slight bow and a wry smile, as if he enjoyed the jest in it.

"And I am Gonsalvo. No doubt you have already met Don Rodrigue, and the good Friar Norbert. We three have all come from Avignon."

"But not together," said the friar, and lapsed into silence again.

"Not together until now," he said, "although I would be delighted to have company on the road besides my servants. They are useless louts when it comes to merry songs or amusing tales."

The friar signaled for more wine.

The innkeeper's stout and hearty wife—always a patient and good-tempered woman when she saw profit to be made—hurried over to fill their cups, and then carried her fast-emptying jug of wine over to a bench in the other corner by the fire to fill up the last empty cup in the room. The thin, wiry man who sat there staring into the glowing embers looked much the worse for drink. She paused.

He couldn't be. She knew him well enough; he passed this way often, and she had never seen him drink himself past a certain level of quiet cheerfulness. She set down the jug.

"Hola, señor," she said. "Are you ill? You look not like yourself."

He raised his head and looked blankly at her.

She clapped a hand on his forehead and cheek. They burned under her touch. Quickly, she pulled back his tunic and scanned his upper chest for rashes or marks. There were none. He clasped his belly with one hand and shook his head mutely.

"Here, Johan," she said sharply to a big man sitting close by. "The messenger has been taken bad. You and Pau, help him up to the chamber at the top of the stairs.

Quick.'' She watched until they were on their way and sought out her husband. ''Look after the room, you lazy hound,'' she said, sounding more preoccupied than annoyed. ''The messenger is in a bad way—I'll see to him.''

''But—''

''You want him to die down here? That won't do our business any good, will it? Besides, he's always been a quiet, cheerful gentleman who pays up without complaint. I'll do what I can for him.''

And she gathered up water, towels, and brandy, ordered the drudge in the kitchen to carry up some broth, and taking candles and a lantern, moved swiftly up the stairs with her load.

His pain worsened, and his fever mounted. The innkeeper's wife did what she could, but cool cloths, brandy, and broth were of no use to him. For a while he seemed to drift into sleep and then opened his eyes wide and blinked. ''Fetch me a priest,'' he said. ''For the love of God, woman, please fetch me a priest. I have silver here—''

''Keep your silver,'' she said roughly. ''I'll not take money for that.'' For she had her superstitions, though not many of them, and this was one. To demand money from a dying man for fetching a priest was sure to bring terrible misfortune. In addition, it was not going to be difficult to find one. ''There's a friar downstairs,'' she said. ''I better get him while he can still stand, and understand what you're saying.''

She was just in time. The friar was raising his fourth large cup of wine and was about to pour it down his throat in his earnest search for oblivion when she reached out her hand and snatched the cup from him. ''Father,'' she said. ''There is a dying man upstairs who cries out for a priest.''

He looked up at her with an expression of bitter sorrow on his face. But in spite of his drunken misery, he stood up, brushed the dust from his gray habit, and pulled himself together. ''Take me to him,'' he said with a certain dignity.

He washed his face and hands in cold water, dried them, and sat down by the bed to offer whatever help and consolation he could to the dying man, who wavered between raving and lucidity, one moment clearheaded, the next unable to tell where he was, or why. The innkeeper's wife retreated to a far corner as a compromise between availability and nosiness and sat down, grateful for the respite from work.

The murmured conference between the priest and the messenger went on for some time, and the wife was nodding off to sleep in her corner when Norbert called over to her. "Leave us for a few moments, good woman," he said.

When the room was empty, the dying man whispered, "Any man may hear my sorry sins—I do not mind—this is different."

"Something worse?" asked the friar gently.

"No," he said, and paused for breath. "A charge. A solemn charge, Father. Come closer—your ear."

And he bent over until his ear was close to the man's mouth.

When the wife was summoned, the dying man seemed close to his last breath. The friar stood up, but the man's hand reached out and grasped his sleeve. "Swear you will take it to him yourself, Father. You may have my horse. She's the small gray."

The friar's countenance, still reddened from wine, paled until he looked as sick as the dying man.

"Swear."

"I swear," he said hesitantly.

"Pray for me."

The friar sat down heavily in the chair again and laid a hand on the man's chest.

When everyone had gone home, and the rest of the travelers could be expected to be asleep in their beds, Friar Norbert sat downstairs by the dying fire with a candle. He took paper, pen, and ink from his pack and wrote steadily in a neat, well-trained hand for as long as it took to fill up two sheets, pausing now and then for reflection. He read over his work, making a few small adjustments to it. He folded it carefully and firmly and looked helplessly around the room. He had no sealing wax. The only candle was tallow, and its grease would make a miserable seal. Instead he took a length of ribbon from his pack and tied the sheets together. He reached into his sleeve and took out a package wrapped in leather and sealed in red. He started to undo it as though to slip his letter inside, and seemed to change his mind. He slipped the package back into his sleeve and tucked the letter under his sash. Picking up his bundle, he went out to the stable to find the messenger's gray mare.

When the first light of dawn came, the innkeeper's wife looked at the dead man on the bed, yawned, murmured a paternoster, crossed herself, and left him, reckoning that his soul was safe, now that it was light. As soon as she was settled in the kitchen, Gonsalvo and Rodrigue entered the dead man's dimly lit room. Gonsalvo snatched up the messenger's pack from its resting place on a bench and untied it, dumping its contents on the bench. "A change of linen," he said, "and a wool hood—that and a few trinkets."

"Those documents won't be with his possessions," said Rodrigue sharply. "They'll be in his official pouch. He'll have kept it by him." The men looked at each other uneasily. Then Rodrigue stepped forward and ran his fingers under the mattress and through the bedclothes, before beginning a search of the body itself. Almost at once, he straightened up, a good-sized sealed pouch in his hand. He handed it Gonsalvo, and then with great care composed the dead man's limbs in a seemly manner once more. He straightened the bedclothes, took up his own pack, and headed for the stables without a glance at his companion.

From a window in the inn overlooking the stables, the elegant young man watched their progress.

The two men rode a mile or two toward Girona before pulling up by the side of the road. "I must leave you soon, Don Gonsalvo," said Rodrigue. "Let us see what we captured in there."

Gonsalvo dismounted and unhooked the messenger's bag from his saddle. He sat down on a large rock and sighed heavily. "I have found this a tiring night, Don Rodrigue," he said. "I am not as young as you."

Rodrigue crouched in front of him and opened the bag. He started to search through its contents, and then, frustrated, dumped them out onto the ground. They were some dozen pieces in all—letters and other documents; they unsealed each one, scrutinized it in the strengthening light of day, and tossed it aside. Gonsalvo picked up the last one and unfolded it.

"What is it?"

"It appears to be a list," he said dully. "They're not here. Neither one of them."

"May all the devils in hell take that confounded messenger," said Rodrigue. "He told the serving wench at the last inn that he carried them. He had a good head for wine, poor wretch, but a weakness for women."

"Perhaps someone took them before we got there," said Gonsalvo.

"Very likely," said Rodrigue. "His horse was gone. And there was only one person who—" He stopped at the sound of a horse approaching at a steady pace.

"Look. It is young Master Fortunat," said Gonsalvo.

"Yes, it is," said the young man. "And why do you sit by the road surrounded by papers and parchment?"

"We borrowed the messenger's sack," said Gonsalvo.

"Since that is our private concern," said Rodrigue angrily. "We—"

"We were looking for documents destined for us," interrupted Gonsalvo. "It seemed foolish to ride off and leave them behind. The poor soul died in the night, you know."

"No, I didn't," said Fortunat. "May his soul rest in peace," he added, crossing himself. "And did you find your documents?"

"No," he said. "He must have entrusted them to someone to deliver when he felt his illness coming on him. And his gray is gone from the stable."

"I was awake in the night myself," said Fortunat. "And saw the friar departing before it was light. On a light-colored horse."

"He arrived on foot. That's what they said. He has taken them, Don Rodrigue," said Gonsalvo, grabbing him excitedly by the arm. "And ridden off on the horse. May he rot in hell! I could cut his treacherous throat. What I would not give for a look at those things," he added. "One look."

"How much would you give?" asked Fortunat, looking at him with considerable interest.

"How much?" said Gonsalvo, taken aback. "Well—I'd give five *maravedis* to see the result in the case that interests me."

"I beg you to excuse me, gentlemen," said Rodrigue coldly, "but I have already spent enough time and money over the exact wording of one papal letter. My men wait for me at the crossroad. I bid you farewell. And a pleasant journey home." He mounted his horse and rode off.

"And I must return to the inn," said Gonsalvo, "to stir up those louts who work for me."

"Then you are no longer interested in your document?" asked the young man.

"How would you get it?" asked Gonsalvo. "You can't expect the friar to drop conveniently dead the way the messenger did."

"No. But if I catch up to him, no doubt he can be persuaded with a little gold to give me a glimpse of what he carries. He seemed fond of wine and the good things of life. After all, what is sealed can be unsealed and sealed again," he said. "As you know." He looked over at the contents of the sack blowing about in the morning breeze. "But you must decide quickly, for he is getting farther and farther ahead of me on the road. Where can I find you to tell you the results of my search?"

"In Barcelona. I will be in Barcelona for some time. Stay for a moment and we will talk about it."

# FIVE

## The First Day

*Tuesday, April 22*

The baggage mules had been hitched to the wagons and were waiting to set out; one of the guards, the chief cook and his assistant, and a kitchen lad—His Excellency would not be deprived of an adequate midday meal if his staff had anything to do with it—were standing about gossiping. The chief groom was standing by, in his supervisory capacity, watching his assistant, who would be traveling with them, direct two burly but awkward helpers as they loaded the carts. The first wagon was stacked high with baggage; cooking pots, sacks of provisions and other oddments had been slung from the slats that formed its sides. The second was much more lightly loaded, but the floor of the cart had been strewn with a thick bed of straw, and that was covered over with a heavy rug and some cushions, to form a comfortable resting spot for the weary, saddle-stiff, or footsore.

The Bishop's household servants formed a loose and cheerful confederation at the head of the line. On the north side of the square, a small group of convent servants huddled together. Toward the east, not far from the gate of the *Call,* the Jewish Quarter from which they had just come, the physician's family and servants had gathered together. His wife, Judith, stood rocklike, disapproving, as if she were being dragged to Tarragona against her better judgment, even though it had been she who insisted on coming. Naomi, their cook, and Ibrahim, their houseman, stood glumly by, having only just realized from the size of the crowd that they would be walking with the rest of the servants.

Judith and Isaac's seven-year-old twins, Nathan and Miriam, stood in the gateway, partially hidden behind a plump, motherly-looking woman. Judith had decided—most reluctantly—to leave them behind with her capable friend, Dolsa, the glover's wife. Miriam glared mutinously and Nathan looked stricken with disappointment as they watched their mother and sister, about to leave for the unimaginable delights of Tarragona.

Raquel stood near her mother, looking like a brown parcel, wrapped in veils to protect her from prying eyes. She was no happier than her brother and sister. The evening before, Daniel, the nephew of Dolsa and Ephraim the glover, and the most charming and pleasant young man she knew, had come to wish her a good journey. In the midst of his cheerful farewells, he had abruptly and earnestly demanded that she not consent to a marriage in Tarragona. Startled, she had snapped back that her marriage was none of his concern. He had reddened, bowed, and left without a word. She had lain awake most of the night, raging at his presumption, and then furious at her own lack of courtesy, but mostly trying very hard not to think of that word, marriage. Her eye fell on Dolsa, who was dealing so well with the unhappy twins, she blushed with shame and guilt, and heartily wished she could leave the city this very moment and not return.

In the Bishop's palace, Isaac was closeted with Berenguer, examining His Excellency's painfully swollen knee. "It should be better as the day progresses," he observed. "Yusuf is preparing something that will help with the pain and swelling. Are you not, Yusuf?" he asked his apprentice, a

Moorish boy from Granada, clever and quick, but thirteen and inexperienced.

"Yes, lord," murmured the boy. "It is almost ready. At the moment it is still too hot to drink."

"Before we join the others," said the physician, "I would like to express my great sorrow at burdening Your Excellency with my wife and servants. I am well aware that they will slow us down."

"Do not think of it for a moment, Master Isaac," said the Bishop. "Once I received word from the Archbishop that I was to bring all those nuns with me, the trip was doomed to be slow and cumbersome. Your wife will not add a second's delay, I assure you. And your excellent daughter could well be of great use, should someone fall ill."

"As soon as Judith heard that the Abbess and two of her nuns were traveling with you, she would not rest until you had given permission for her to accompany us."

"I hope she enjoys their company, Isaac, for she will have to spend many nights with them, I suspect." The Bishop laughed wholeheartedly, drank the infusion that Yusuf had prepared, called for Francesc and Bernat, and the five of them headed out to join the others.

The grooms appeared with the riding animals for the cathedral party and the physician's family. Judith clambered rather grimly onto her mule, Raquel hoisted up her skirts and flung one of her long legs over hers with more determination than skill; Isaac swung himself up on his with ease. Yusuf, who would be walking, looked with envious longing at the captain of the guard's elegant white horse. In a flash of self-pity he reflected that if his father were still alive, he, too, would be riding, and on a better horse than the captain's.

A clatter of hoofbeats announced that the last group had arrived. The Abbess of Sant Daniel, followed by two nuns and a priest, and accompanied by two members of the Bishop's Guard, joined the group. Lady Elicsenda greeted Berenguer and then drew her veil across her face. Sor Ag-

nete, ignoring him, dug her heels into her mule. The startled
animal broke into a trot; the two guards, whose only task
was to ensure that Sor Agnete arrived in Tarragona fit for
her trial, spurred their horses and came alongside her. The
procession, whether it wanted to or not, started on its way.

Isaac's mule looked at the activity and broke into a trot.
Ibrahim, who was leading his blind master's animal, yanked
at the rein in a panic, causing it to stop as suddenly as it
started, and then pulled it forward again.

"Gently, Ibrahim," said the physician. "She is a mule,
with feelings, not a cart, stuck in a hole."

"Yes, master," said Ibrahim in tones of misery.

"What was the cause of all that?" asked Isaac.

"It was Sor Agnete, Papa," said Raquel. "She gave the
Bishop a poisonous look and clapped her spurs into her
mule."

"It should be an interesting journey," murmured her father.

An hour later, when the April sun had climbed high enough
to take the morning chill off the air, an eight-year-old girl
carrying an earthenware jug came across the meadow outside Sant Feliu, heading along the river path to fetch water.
She was dawdling, lost in a daydream, when she heard a
deep groan coming from the long grass beside the path.
She stopped, clutching her jug to her breast, and battling
with her first instinct, to run. Already in her short life she
had learned that investigating strange adult behavior usually
led to trouble. But to flee meant to leave without water,
and certain trouble when she reached home. There was another groan.

"Who's that?" asked the girl.

"Help me," said a voice, very weak, but deep and def-
initely male.

It was just what the magical creatures in her aunt's tales
cried out in their distress. She was caught now between
fear and curiosity. Prudently she set down her jug—for ease
of flight—and slipped through the grasses to peek at whatever it was that had spoken.

It was a man. He was lying on the ground, and there was blood on his head and all over his chest. He was a friar, she knew that, like Father Bernat, who had visited her mother once about something very important, and had given her a farthing for her very own as he was leaving. "Did someone hurt you?" she asked.

He opened his eyes. She couldn't tell if he was looking at her or not, and she was now even more frightened. He reached out and caught her hand and held it. "Take this, and give it to—" He was shaken by a spasm, and then a fit of coughing.

She saw that he was clutching something in his other hand, which he was holding tight against his bloodied breast. "Who do I take it to?" asked the child.

"Who?" His eyes wandered, dull and confused. "The Bishop," he said, gasping for breath. "Into—his own—hand. Swear—you will give it . . ." A little blood seeped from his mouth and he closed his eyes. "Swear, and then leave me here to die as I deserve," he added, with sudden strength and clarity.

She turned and ran, not forgetting to scoop up the pitcher on her way.

She was not so much fleeing, as realizing that she could not help him alone. But of the competent adults she was willing to approach, all seemed to have left their houses and disappeared: mother, father, grandfather, and neighbors. At last she found her uncle Marc, sleeping late after a particularly hard night. He staggered out of bed, sent his wife to find his sister, the girl's mother, and followed the child back to the meadow.

It was too late. The young uncle looked at the dead friar and shook his head. Without a doubt it had been too late before his niece had run off to find help. He bent down to close the friar's eyes, paying little attention to the arrival of the child's breathless mother.

She clutched her new baby to her breast, torn between satisfaction and fear. "I've told you not to go near strangers," she said.

"But, Mama, he's a priest . . ."

"Priests can be strangers, can't they?" she said obscurely. "Still, you did what you could. Who is he?"

"I don't know," said the little girl. "He never said. But he said that what he had was very important and it had to go to the Bishop. He made me swear." She pointed to his hand, which was clutching a letter.

Slinging the baby onto her hip in one practiced move, her mother extracted the paper from the dead man's grasp and looked at it. "It's only writing," she said, disappointed. "All smeared with blood. I thought there might be money in it."

Marc took it from her. "Not likely, sister. Whoever killed him slashed his purse strings and took his money. I'll take that to the Bishop this morning."

"But the Bishop's gone," said his sister.

"Then I'll take it to the one they left in charge," he said. "Was that all he said?" he asked his niece. "They'll want to know."

"I don't know," she said, reluctant to tell them. "I think so. But he didn't speak right."

"What do you mean?" said her mother.

She shook her head, unable to explain further. "I don't know. I could understand him, but he didn't speak right."

"He was dying," said her uncle, shocked for a moment.

"Who are you to judge the speech of holy men?" said her mother, and relieved her feelings by clipping her daughter on the ear. "And I'll warrant you didn't fetch the water. How am I to cook dinner without water?"

"Go to the well," said her brother Marc. "It's much closer anyway."

"She can't get water from the well," said the mother. "The bucket's too heavy for her."

"Then go yourself, you lazy slut," he snapped back.

And the little girl raced home in tears, leaving the adults to bicker their way back after her.

Don Arnau de Corniliano, canon vicar of the diocese of Girona during the Bishop's absence, regarded the crumpled, bloodstained paper in front of him. It was possible to make out the word "excellency" through the stain, and fragments of the word "bishop". The rest was lost in the heart's blood of the man who had written it. The friar's blood had also sealed it closed, almost as firmly as wax. No one had attempted as yet to open it.

Don Arnau had reacted with distaste to the slovenly man who had arrived at the palace reeking of last night's excesses and impertinent with insistence. Even so, he did all the correct things: listening to the message; gingerly accepting the blood-soaked letter; ordering that the friar's body be conveyed decently to the palace. He had been about to instruct his secretary to pry the letter open when he stopped. Perhaps it was intended for Berenguer himself. Opening it would leave traces. He would not do it until he found out who the dead man was. "Tell the man who brought us the letter to wait for us here," he said. "And make sure that he does."

The body lay in a cool, dark room in the lower reaches of the palace. A lay brother stood nearby, waiting for permission to wash and prepare it. The canon vicar gave it a hasty glance, and then a much more careful one. Neither one solved his dilemma. The dead friar was a stranger to Don Arnau and, apparently, to everyone else who had looked at him.

"He must have journeyed from afar," said Don Arnau.

"Perhaps he was a pilgrim," suggested his secretary.

"Excuse me, Father," said the lay brother, "but we found this on his poor body. It is somewhat dirtied with blood," he added apologetically, and with due decorum gave the canon vicar a folded parchment half-soaked in blood.

Don Arnau handed it as rapidly as possible to his secretary, and left the chamber.

"What was it?" he asked his secretary fretfully.

"A travel document, Don Arnau. The name can be read and a few other words. It's for one Norbert. Unfortunately, the rest is badly obscured."

"And he had to be murdered here, within a few paces of the cathedral," said Don Arnau bitterly, as if it were a personal insult.

"More than a few paces, sir. It was quite some distance," said the secretary, then caught the canon vicar's look and fell silent.

Don Arnau was thinking hard. Time was passing, and the Bishop was getting farther and farther away. Should he send a messenger pelting after him? Or should he open the letter and deal with its contents himself?

Or should he seek advice? Because if this letter were connected with Berenguer's quarrel with the Archbishop, Don Arnau's motives in opening it would be very suspect. If it had to do with some urgent but routine matter of diocesan business—a document requiring immediate signature, a permission desperately needed—then it would be ridiculous to send a messenger galloping after Berenguer. Ridiculous and a charge on the cathedral, as well. Don Arnau was noted for his skill in the management of finances, and for his meanness in little things.

"Ring for someone," he barked at the secretary.

The secretary rang. At once.

"I would like to see the canons immediately," he said, as soon as the door began to open. His voice, grating, unemphatic, and dry, filled the room and penetrated into the corridors beyond.

"Excuse me, Father," said the servant. "But most of the canons are out on other business."

"Then get me the ones who are here," he said coldly. "At once."

At mid-morning, Daniel, son of Mossé the baker and heir to his uncle Ephraim the glover, was in the workroom, trying to bring a new design to life in a pair of ladies' gloves. Unfortunately, every time he picked up a glove, he saw Raquel's long, elegant fingers and slender hand gliding into the almost insubstantial kidskin, remembered the humiliating encounter of the night before, and made a mistake. The last one had been fatal. This pair of gloves could no longer be rescued. He dropped them on the workbench in despair.

The Bishop's party had left for the council in Tarragona an hour after sunrise. He knew. He had watched them from the shadow of a doorway. They would now be miles and miles away, drawing closer and closer to Tarragona, and Raquel's loathsome cousin Ruben, whom her mother wished her to marry. She would never return. His life was over. He sighed, picked up the ruined glove, and went to confess his clumsiness to his uncle.

"Does this concern the friar who died this morning?" asked Galceran de Monteterno.

"In a sense," said Don Arnau. "We know from his travel document that he had permission to travel to Avignon. No doubt he was on business for the Archbishop, or even His Holiness the Pope. His name was Friar Norbert."

There was a noticeable increase in tension in the room. "The friar carried with him a letter," Don Arnau continued, pointing to the object on the table in front of him, "that he wished delivered to the Bishop. The uncle of the child who found him brought it to me. It is apparently addressed to His Excellency personally."

"Apparently?" asked Pere Vitalis.

"If you look you will see that the direction is obscured by blood, but one can make out 'excellency' and part of the word 'bishop,'" said Don Arnau. "And the child apparently said that he was quite insistent on that point."

"May I examine the seal?" asked Galceran.

Don Arnau pushed the letter in his direction. Galceran picked it up, turned it over, and looked carefully at it. "I can see no seal," he said. "It would seem to be only one or two sheets of paper, but it is, as you say, badly stained."

"That is the difficulty. It is soaked in blood that has dried. I cannot see if it was sealed and opened, or not sealed at all. But if we try to open it, it will be clear that—"

"We have opened it," said Galceran de Monteterno.

"I hesitate to do that lest it concerns him alone, and not the affairs of the diocese. I seek your advice."

There was not a man there who did not grasp instantly the reason for calling them together. Whatever the letter contained, Don Arnau was determined that all would share in the blame or the praise for opening it. Ramon de Orta, expert that he was in saving his own skin, saw the pit yawning in front of him. "What were the friar's exact words, Don Arnau? It might help if we knew."

There was a silence. "We have only the uncle's word that there is a child," said canon vicar at last. "And his version of what she is supposed to have said."

"The presence of a rather dusty little female on the bench at the foot of the stairs would suggest that there is a child," said Orta. "Why don't we call her in and ask her?"

"She will be too frightened to speak," said the canon vicar.

"Then let the unsavory-looking man seated beside her, whom I take to be her uncle, come in with her to reassure her."

Don Arnau nodded. "I will send my secretary to fetch them both," he said, and left the room to summon the world to his assistance.

"I hope he will not be too long about it," said Galceran. "My nephew arrives today, most insistent that he wishes to see me. We dine together."

"I would not venture to guess how long he will be," said Pere Vitalis impatiently. "But for the sake of us all, pray do not mention your nephew. It will cause him to slow down even more while he ponders the consequences of a canon dining with a nephew."

A low buzz of conversation continued outside the chamber.

"How many instructions can you give to a secretary," said Ramon de Orta, "just to send for a lout and a dirty child? He almost makes me long for His Excellency's return."

And Pere Vitalis tucked that little comment away to pass on to His Excellency when he wrote his next confidential report.

•    •    •

The canon vicar and the little girl, followed by her uncle, arrived one right after the other. She looked at the four men in clerical black seated around the table and curtsied in a composed manner. They were much less intimidating than either of her parents.

"Can you tell us, little girl," said Pere Vitalis, "exactly what you saw and heard this morning?"

"I was fetching water, sir," she said. "And I heard someone groan. I put down the jug and went to look. It was a priest, like Father Bernat, and he asked me to take the piece of paper in his hand to the Bishop."

"There, you see?" said her uncle. "Just like I said."

"Quiet, man," said Vitalis, who had nieces and nephews of his own and was used to children. "I'll warrant you can't tell me his exact words," he said, with a smile. "You've forgotten."

"No, I haven't," she said indignantly. "He said—" She paused and closed her eyes. " 'Take this, and give it to— the Bishop. Into his own hand. Swear—you will give it.' " She stopped at that point.

The four men stared at her in amazement. In that high-pitched, childish voice they could hear the accents, the gasps and hesitations of the dying friar. "And is that all he said?" asked Pere Vitalis.

She blushed scarlet. "He was a nice man and I do not like to say what else he said."

"You may tell us," said Don Arnau with unexpected gentleness. "We will not be shocked or surprised."

"Oh, sir—" Her uncle prodded her in the shoulder. "Your Excellency, he seemed such a good man, I don't want—"

"There now, child. It's important that we know exactly what he said. And there is no need to call me Excellency." But the others noticed that he smiled, a tight smile compounded of pleasure and bitterness, at her use of the term.

"Yes, Your Excellency—sir. He said, 'Swear, and then leave me here to die as I deserve,' all quickly like that, and nothing else at all."

The canon vicar beckoned her to his side and, under

cover of the table, pressed a penny into her hand while
patting her on the head. "You have done well, child," he
said, "very well. And God will reward you for your kindness to a dying man."

"Thank you, sir." She headed hastily for the door.
"Oh—and he talked funny, but I could understand him."

"Wait," said Galceran, his impatience forgotten. "What
do you mean?"

"He didn't talk like people here, Father. He talked like—"
She frowned. "Remember, Uncle Marc, at the fair, the man
who made the sweetmeats and you wouldn't buy me one
because you said they weren't good? But you bought me a
honeycake instead?"

"No," said her uncle truthfully, looking confused.

"Well, you did," she said. "He talked like that." She
smiled, bobbed down in another curtsy, and made good her
escape, still clutching her penny.

"All we have to do now is wait six months for the fair,
and ask the sweetmeat seller where he comes from," said
Ramon de Orta.

"That is not our immediate problem," said Galceran.
"But I think it is clear that this is a very personal letter to
the Bishop, having to do with some transgression on the
friar's part. It would have been more appropriate for him
to send a message to his superior, but that is no concern of
ours."

"Then you think we should send the letter to the
Bishop?" asked Corniliano.

"Yes. It would be safer."

"Safer?" said Don Arnau. "And if it should be diocesan
business that must be carried out at once?"

"Then His Excellency will send the messenger back with
his instructions."

"An excellent idea," said Pere Vitalis, who had his own
reasons for agreeing with Galceran.

"I agree," said Ramon de Orta, and rose. The three canons walked together out of the study and down the stairs
toward the courtyard. At the foot of the stairs stood a young

man, elegantly clad in a blue silk tunic, with sleeves slashed in crimson. He bowed.

"Fortunat," said Galceran. "You are most welcome. I hope you have had an uneventful journey."

"A very profitable journey, now that I have arrived and can see you, Uncle," he said, with a little smile.

"And all is well?"

"All is well."

"My nephew Fortunat," said Galceran to Pere Vitalis and Ramon de Orta. "A fine young man, is he not? I had hoped that he would follow his uncle into the Church, where I would be able to help him to some preferment, perhaps, but he wishes to make his way in the world, without his uncle's aid."

"It is clear that he has done so," said Orta courteously.

"Thank you, Father, but I still have far to go and much to learn."

"We have an hour before dinner," said Galceran. "Perhaps you would like to walk through the gardens of the abbey. It is a quiet and pleasant place for a talk."

"I would be most pleased, Uncle," said the young man. "But I fear I will not be able to dine. I have a pressing engagement to fulfill on behalf of a patron. I won't be able to return before tomorrow or the day after."

"Then let us enjoy these moments while we may," said Galceran. "Orta, Vitalis." He nodded. "Until this afternoon."

"There is a small problem, Uncle," said his nephew. "But I am sure we can work it out." They passed out of earshot, and neither of the canons heard the reply.

"The function of uncles," said Orta, shaking his head.

"To empty their purses for their nephews? I'm afraid it is. That young man was entirely too neat and gracious for someone who has just ridden into town," said Pere Vitalis. "He must be hoping for a very fat present."

By the end of the second hour, the sun had warmed the spring air. Gradually the subdued chatter began to die away and a drowsy quiet fell over the travelers. Even the billowing hills and well-worked fields lying on either side of the road looked lazy and somnolent. "Why are we moving so slowly?" Raquel asked the closest guard. He looked to be younger than she was, and she felt free to treat him like her brother, or Yusuf.

He gave her a charming smile. "Some of them up there—the palace cooks and the like—are not fast walkers. You might as well try to hurry an ox."

"We couldn't be moving more slowly if we tried," she said. "I hadn't thought travel would be so tiresome and boring."

"This is the first time I have gone with His Excellency on one of his journeys," said the guard. "I'm lucky we have such lively company, Mistress Raquel. I am Enrique, and should you ever need anything, I am at your service."

"I cannot imagine what service my daughter would require," said Judith in her most forbidding tone of voice.

Raquel's cheeks reddened. "He meant nothing by it, Mama," she replied.

"I'm sure that such a skilled and lovely young lady has no need of anything I can do," said the guard cheerfully. "But if we run into trouble, I have a strong sword arm to protect both of you."

"We need no protection," said her mother.

"Mama," said Raquel, "you know that is not what he meant. Don't you think this trip would be much more interesting if we were walking?"

"Walking!" said Judith. "Certainly not. In with the servants from who-knows-where . . ."

And having achieved her objective of changing the topic, Raquel stared dreamily over the slowly changing landscape and thought her own thoughts.

They came upon and edged by slow-moving oxcarts, merchants with wagons overloaded with bundles and barrels, and a few other groups on foot. A band of traveling musicians offered to stay with them and amuse them for a very modest fee. They gave them a sample of their skills; the Bishop threw them a few coins and declined. A group of farm laborers in a very jolly mood were walking with their bundles and a skin of wine, going, it seemed, from one excellent situation to three more weeks of work at very good pay.

"But only what the law allows, Your Excellency," said their leader hastily. "It is in the accommodations and the cooking of the farmer's wife—a woman beyond compare she is—that we are more fortunate than most."

The Bishop smiled. Ever since the Black Death had devastated the workforce, laws on allowable wages had laid out stern penalties for masters and workmen who flouted the minutely calculated posted rates for each trade. The chances that this cheerful group of sturdy, competent-looking men and women were to be overpaid were overwhelmingly good, as were the chances that everyone—man, woman, child, and master—would escape the consequences. "I'm delighted that you will be so well fed and looked after for three weeks," said Berenguer. "I trust you will remember the poor in your good fortune."

Their leader winked. "We will indeed, Your Excellency," he said, and tipped his hat once more.

With every hill, and every bend in the road, and every milestone passed, Ibrahim sighed louder and louder. He panted in exertion. He trotted from time to time to keep up to the mule. Now he was limping. "What is the matter with you, Ibrahim?" asked Isaac.

"Oh, Master Isaac," he said. "Your mule walks so quickly I cannot keep ahead of it to lead it."

"Then walk beside it, and hold its head at the bridle," said Isaac.

"Papa, that is nonsense," said Raquel. "Your mule is moving so slowly she may soon fall asleep. And do stop sighing and limping, Ibrahim."

"Yes, mistress," said Ibrahim, limping even more.

"Ibrahim," said a voice that struck terror in his ears, "do as Mistress Raquel suggests. You are perfectly well."

"But, mistress," he said to Judith, turning to her like a cornered rat, "I have a stone in my shoe."

"Then stop and take it out," said Judith.

"Here," said Raquel, nudging her mule around to the

right side of her Father's. "Ibrahim, hand me that rein. I will lead you, Papa."

"Can you do that?"

"Of course."

Ibrahim moved over to the side of the road, took off his boots, washed his feet in a stream he had noted, dried them on his tunic, and reassembled himself for travel. With a burst of speed that no one would have believed possible from him, he ran beside the road until he reached the almost empty wagon. He jumped up and settled himself on the straw bed, right beside Naomi. She was there to guard her pots, which were in the wagon, not to save her feet, which were well accustomed to walking.

The sun was now high in the sky, and the walkers were beginning to complain. About a half mile farther on, the captain of the guard had a brief word with the Bishop and called a long-awaited halt. The Bishop's cook and his helpers went rapidly into action. They built a fire, dragged out pots and kettles, and assembled all manner of ingredients for a substantial meal. Some distance farther off, the convent servants started their own fire and unpacked their own food. Naomi scooped up Ibrahim and set him to work getting her fire ready. The three households all started to cook their dinners.

Isaac set to work on Berenguer's knee—probing, stretching, and moving the leg for him, and finally massaging it with sweet oil. "It feels to be in reasonable condition," he said. "It would be advisable for you to walk for a while. You have been sitting in the same position for too long."

"As long as you have, Master Isaac. Take my arm and walk with me and Francesc." The three men set out over the rocky meadow. "We shall seek the shade of a grove up ahead," he said. "Isaac, I wish you could see what I see now."

"And what is that, Your Excellency?"

"Three groups hard at work on three almost identical dinners, when my cook is willing and prepared to cook for everyone."

"But perhaps Master Isaac's good wife fears that your

cook will serve food that is forbidden to her and her family," said Francesc.

"Then she need not eat it," said Berenguer.

"I'm sure she believes the very worst of your cook," said Isaac. "But I shall have a word with her."

"The nuns have no such excuse."

"I would suggest, Your Excellency, that we ignore it for today," said Francesc. "Later in the journey the groups may come together."

It wasn't until the afternoon sun left the upper reaches of the sky that the pots were gathered up and slung back around the wagon. The impatience of the morning had diminished considerably, and it took some effort to get everyone on the road again. Still, on the road they were, heading south for Tarragona. Raquel had automatically picked up the lead rein for her father's mule. Had anyone thought to look for Ibrahim, they would have found him back in the second wagon, sitting in the shadows behind Naomi.

They passed Caldes, and then the road that branched off to Barcelona. They encountered several more groups of travelers, exchanging friendly words with some and suspicious glances with others. By the time they heard a galloping horse gaining rapidly on them, most of them were too jaded to give it more than a cursory glance. But the horse slowed, and when he reached the Bishop, the rider dismounted smartly, bowed, and presented a thin package wrapped in leather and tied in ribbon to His Excellency.

"Letters from Don Arnau, the canon vicar, Your Excellency."

"Already?" asked Berenguer in astonishment. "Has something happened?"

"Not that I have been told of," said the messenger discreetly.

"Speak, man," said Berenguer. "Why were you sent off hot on my track?"

"The body of a friar was discovered near the river. Outside Sant Feliu," he observed. "It may have had something to do with that. The friar had been murdered, they said, and was carrying a letter addressed to Your Excellency. A Franciscan, Your Excellency, apparently named Father Norbert. But I was told nothing, except that the matter was most urgent, and that the letter must be delivered to you.''

"They?''

"Four of them. Don Arnau, Your Excellency, and three more—Father Pere Vitalis, Father Ramon de Orta, and Father Galceran de Monteterno.''

"Excellent. You have done well,'' he said, rewarding the messenger and turning to the package.

The Bishop broke open the fresh seal and glanced at the letter. A slight wave of the hand summoned Francesc and Bernat to his side. He murmured to Francesc, who beckoned to Raquel to bring her father's mule up beside them. When they were all gathered he turned his attention to the letter once more. "Read this for me,'' he said to Bernat. "It is somewhat stained and difficult to make out.''

Bernat took the pages and scanned them rapidly. When he got to the second page, which had formed the envelope, he frowned. "Some of this cannot be made out at all, Your Excellency.''

"Do what you can.''

"As Your Excellency wishes,'' murmured Bernat. "It begins, 'To His Excellency the Bishop, or his most reverend Vicar. I find myself in a very difficult situation; I beg your indulgence and assistance. I do not know if word of what I have done has reached your ear. If it has, you will understand that, given my great fault—my crime—I cannot bring you these documents in my proper person. In failing to do so, I pile sin upon sin, for I have given my solemn, most holy oath to a dying man that I would deliver them to you. May God forgive my cowardice.

" 'Since I cannot approach you, for fear of hanging, I will attempt to describe how these documents came into my possession. In fleeing from Avignon, I avoided any but the lowest of taverns and inns in which to seek hospitality, and did my best not to linger in towns where I might be recognized or sought. Unfortunately, outside of Figueres, I inadvertently fell in with a group of travelers whom I would have preferred to avoid. One of them was a messenger carrying documents for you and for His Majesty.

" 'Soon after we reached the inn where we all stayed, the messenger fell ill, in great agony. He asked for a priest, and there was no other close by. Drunk as I was, and drenched in the blood of an innocent man, I was fetched to do what I could for him. Just before he died he gave me these two documents, and explained something of their significance. I already knew what they were, but not what was in them. He extracted an oath from me to keep them safe from prying eyes, including my own, and to deliver them into your hands. I have not examined them, but I cannot deliver them to you. I will seek out some honest soul to take them for me.' " Bernat paused. "That is the end of the first page, which is scarcely stained at all."

"And the second page?"

"I will give you what I can of it."

"If he preached at as great length as he writes," said Francesc, "it is no wonder he was murdered."

"First there is a stain that obscures several lines of text," said Bernat. "Then it continues. '. . . seems to me to be strange. I think it likely that the unfortunate messenger was assisted to his death by some vile poison. At least two men who traveled with us had cause to wish to see these documents. I do not know if these were their names, or birthplaces, but they called themselves . . .' And then another section is obscured."

"Read what you can," snapped Berenguer.

"Yes, Your Excellency. The first name is not legible, except that it ends in 'ca.' The second is 'Rodrigue de Lancia.' "

"Lancia," said Berenguer. "That family comes from my part of the world."

"Rodrigue?" said Isaac. "I know only of the other one."

"You mean Huguet? A case has been brought to the papal court at Avignon in which he is named, I hear. This Rodrigue, as I remember, is a younger cousin."

"If the documents concerned Huguet, that would explain his interest in them," said Isaac.

"It would," said the Bishop. "I remember him as a pleasant, fearless lad, Isaac, brave as a lion, and rather lacking in judgment, even for a boy. Completely heedless of the consequences of his acts. And now his daring has landed him in more trouble than he reckoned on. But His Majesty appreciates his participation in retaliatory attacks on the Genoese."

"But it was not the Genoese—"

"No. That, I suspect, was one of his errors of judgment. They should not have preyed on Ancona, with whom we had no quarrel at the time." He turned back to the two priests. "Forgive us. We interrupted you, Father Bernat."

"Think nothing of it, Your Excellency. Now a line is obscured," he continued. " ' . . . is Majesty must receive that document, for it contains a decision that may affect his preparations for war. And you yourself have long awaited the results of the other one.' He ends there, with, 'I beg your forgiveness for my transgression, and your prayers for my soul. Norbert de C.' "

"That will be a judgment from His Holiness on the suit brought by Ancona," said Berenguer. "This letter must be delivered to His Majesty. He will have to know that a judgment exists, and may have been lost."

"Or stolen," observed Isaac. "But what decision is he referring to that Your Excellency has long awaited?"

"I cannot imagine," said Berenguer. "Unless . . ."

"Your Excellency," said Francesc, "perhaps he believes it has to do with the Archbishop's . . ." He paused. "But that little dispute has been quite recent, and surely was not sent to His Holiness, the Pope."

"I do not wish to contradict the good Father," said Isaac, "but let us consider the rumors that fill the city. Concerning the Archbishop sending a complaint to Avignon. I have assumed they are false—"

"But some rumors are not? You do well to remind us, Master Isaac," said Berenguer. "Although 'long awaited' seems an exaggeration. But we now have a decision to make. His Majesty must be told," murmured Berenguer.

"In all likelihood, he knows already," said Bernat.

"Very true," said Berenguer. "But still he must be told."

"He must, Your Excellency," said Bernat. "But by messenger, or do we go in person?"

"In person," said Isaac.

"In person, I agree," said Francesc. "If Your Excellency is willing."

"I am," said Berenguer. "When did we pass the Barcelona road?"

"Captain," called Bernat, "how far are we past the Barcelona road?"

"It is a few miles behind us," said the captain, moving his horse closer to the group. "Two or three. If you must get a message to Barcelona, the messenger would be faster than sending one of us," he added.

They looked at each other. "It may be the ravings of a drunken madman," said Berenguer. "And not worth the paper wasted on it. But I think we must all go, Captain. That is, I must go, and I should not go alone."

"That will add several days to our journey, Your Excellency. We are not moving at any great speed."

"How many days?"

The captain paused to consider. "At least two, Your Excellency. More likely three, in addition to any time spent in the city itself."

"I will do my best to keep that time to a minimum," said the Bishop. "And those extra days will not be wasted entirely. In addition to waiting on His Majesty, there are foundations that I must visit."

"Shall I turn the wagons, Your Excellency?" asked the captain.

"But did you explain to the Bishop that we are in a hurry to get to Tarragona?" asked Judith, trying to deal with the irritation of seeing all her well-worked-out plans destroyed in a moment. Her husband smiled with amused indifference.

"It is a hazard of travel, especially with a Bishop," Isaac said. "There was no need for you to come along."

# SIX

## Near Vidreres

The castellan of the Castell de Sant Iscle, near Vidreres, had received word of the impending visit of the Bishop—and thirty retainers and servants—an hour before the procession arrived.

"What?" he roared at his harassed-looking steward. "What is the Bishop doing here today?"

"If you remember, my lord, you requested his assistance in the matter of that field claimed by the monastery . . ."

"I know what I requested," he said. "But I did not expect him to arrive in person, bringing his entire household with him. How are we to accommodate so many?"

"As best we can," murmured the steward. "The servants will sleep in the attics and the stables, and that means we have beds for . . ." And the two men settled down to the complicated business of offering hospitality to a wealthy and noble churchman.

By the time everyone was seated in the great hall, and an excellent soup, savory stewed beef with sweet vegetables and onions, and cheeses and bread had been brought in, each member of the Bishop's party had been assigned a bed, even if only of thick clean straw in the stable loft. In addition, Berenguer had soothed his host's temper by promising to deal summarily with a certain land-hungry religious order, whose actions had prompted him to request this visit from the Bishop.

Judith sat silently beside her husband. In front of her was a good-sized morsel of bread and a plate of soup. She heard the scrape of a spoon beside her and turned to her husband.

"Isaac," she whispered. "You aren't eating that soup, are you?"

"I am, my dear," he said. "And an excellent dish it is, too."

"But we have no idea what is in it."

"The steward assured me that it was a good mutton broth with vegetables."

"It doesn't smell like mutton broth," she muttered.

"Perhaps the castellan's cook does not have Naomi's skill with herbs and spices," murmured Isaac. "But I assure you it is very good. And I would remind you, my dear, that starving yourself in difficult circumstances, of which traveling is one, is not the act of a virtuous woman. We are instructed to eat what is offered, if that is all that is available."

Judith had long suspected her husband of interpreting the law to suit his convenience, but had neither the skills nor the knowledge to argue the point. She picked up her spoon and took a taste of the soup. She was very hungry and it was, as he had said, delicious. Before she realized what she was doing, she had finished it, and was well into the stewed beef. "That's a ham on the sideboard," she said.

"Then I advise you not to eat it, my dear," said her husband.

"Since we will be in Barcelona at the end of the week," observed Bernat when they had eaten and were strolling in the park attached to the castle, "we cannot very well leave before Monday. It might cause unwelcome comment."

"We shall leave," said Berenguer, "as soon as I have delivered this letter to His Majesty, whether or not he grants me an audience. If we stay until Monday, we will not reach Tarragona in time for the council."

"Should I tell the others to be ready to depart at any time?" asked Francesc. "The Abbess? And the physician and his family?"

"Yes. And tell Master Isaac that I would speak with him."

Lady Elicsenda stood apart from the table in the great hall and summoned her companion with a look that the sister knew of old. Sor Marta did not scuttle—Sor Marta never scuttled—but she did move with most commendable haste to the side of the Abbess. "We will arrive in Barcelona Thursday evening, and will leave Saturday or Sunday morning," said Lady Elicsenda.

"I had thought that might happen, my lady," said Sor Marta. "Do we stay at the Bishop's palace?"

"I think not. We will make our own arrangements."

"Certainly, my lady," said Sor Marta. "The Abbess of Santa Clara would be pleased to welcome us," she said.

"No," said Elicsenda.

"They will not welcome us?"

"We cannot afford to stay with them. There has been talk of worldly conduct—a certain lack of discipline in the convent. I would enjoy seeing the Abbess. She is an amusing lady of great virtue and learning," said Elicsenda, "but . . ."

"She has little control over her nuns," said Sor Marta, "I have heard that."

"And since we are not here for our enjoyment or amusement, I suggest we seek refuge with the sisters of Sant Pere de les Puelles," said Lady Elicsenda briskly. "No one could fault us for staying with them."

"And they are not far from the palace," said Sor Marta.

"That will please the Bishop," said Elicsenda dryly.

"I agree that it would be impolitic at the moment to stay with any but the most chaste of sisterhoods, Lady Elicsenda."

"Isaac, my friend," said Berenguer. "I fear I have taken you from your family this evening. And for little cause, perhaps."

"Are you unwell, Your Excellency?" asked the physician.

"Not at all. I have no such excuse. I wished only to talk to you."

"Nothing could please me better. It is pleasant out here in the gardens, and good company can only improve the occasion."

"Shall we sit down? There is comfortable-looking bench nearby that is tolerably far from prying eyes and ears."

Isaac laid a hand on the Bishop's arm and let himself be directed to the bench. Berenguer sat beside him in silence for a few long moments.

"And these are private matters we speak of, Your Excellency?"

"Why else would I be concerned with prying eyes? Yet I am not sure, Master Isaac," said Berenguer. "You, with your skill in logic, may be able to tell me. Isaac, that friar's death fills me with foreboding."

"Foreboding, Your Excellency? Why? I can understand that any man would feel pity and horror at such a crime, but why foreboding?"

"You heard that letter, Isaac. It was filled with terror before it was drenched in blood. Friar Norbert—and who was he, Isaac?—Friar Norbert was crying out to me in fear when he wrote it."

"You are deceived by eyesight," said Isaac. "The blood the letter is steeped in makes you feel the terror of a dying man, Your Excellency. I, who could not see the blood, heard only the self-serving justifications of a man afraid of being punished for his misdeeds. When he wrote it, whatever he may have said, he feared disgrace and prison more than sudden death."

"You are too cold, Isaac. There was terror there."

"Some. I will allow you a little terror, Your Excellency. You, in return, must grant me a great deal of self-serving justification."

The Bishop paused. "The clarity of your mind gives me comfort. But who was he? A Norbert de C. not recognized by the cathedral canons. He speaks like one who knows me well, Master Isaac. Yet I cannot remember a Norbert who was a Franciscan, with a family name beginning with *C*."

"That does seem odd," said Isaac. "Your Excellency has a good memory. There must be an explanation, and if we discover who he is, the reason you fail to recognize him will become clear."

"Whoever he was, Isaac, he must be avenged. Whatever his sins may have been, he died carrying out a worthy action. He sought my forgiveness for his wrongs. He considered himself a member of my flock, and deserved my protection. Instead, he was butchered within sight of my cathedral."

"It would be easier to avenge him if we knew who he was," said Isaac.

"True," said Berenguer. "But how do we find that out? Isaac, I am sure it is a simple problem, but I am so weary and so hounded by my enemies that I cannot see what to do next. That is why I need you. Bernat and Francesc are only concerned with protecting me and my interests, and they earnestly desire me to do nothing about this Norbert."

"What do we know of him?"

"Nothing," said Berenguer wearily. "Nothing at all. Except that he was dressed as a Franciscan."

"No," said Isaac. "We know that he recognized Rodrigue de Lancia, he also knew the man whose name was obscured. He may have known Huguet de Lancia. If Your Excellency were to write to this Huguet de Lancia—"

"Not Huguet, I think," said Berenguer with interest in his voice. "I will not trouble him in his difficulties. I have a closer friend who lives nearby. It is an excellent idea. Bernat!" he called. "Oh, and Isaac. Francesc has a message for you from me about our travel plans. Francesc!"

"It seems we must beg shelter for a night or two in Barcelona from an old friend," said Isaac, when Francesc had restored him to his family, who were strolling peacefully through the castle gardens.

"Why?" asked Judith.

"Because, my dear, the Bishop has decided that we will spend two or three days in the city."

"Papa—surely if he is an old friend we need not beg."

"Perhaps not, Raquel," said her father with amusement.

"What's Barcelona like?"

"You will see soon enough. Now let us go in and sit for a while near the fire. There is a chill wind rising."

When they returned to the hall, the travelers within its hospitable walls had increased by two. "A pallet of straw in the stable would be luxury to us, sir," said the first, the taller of the two. "We missed our road earlier, and cannot possibly reach our destination tonight. A night in the fields might not be very pleasant. I can smell rain in the air."

The steward raised a hand and one of the servants arrived with soup and bread.

The two men looked dusty and travel-stained, as well as tired and hungry; relative quiet reigned until they had finished their soup. Then the smaller of the two, who was fair and bearded, and dressed in a short dark red tunic of fantastic if somewhat old-fashioned design, looked around the room as if gathering an audience. "Gentlemen, ladies," he said, "we apologize for intruding on your group. We are most grateful to be here. I am Andreu, and my silent companion is Felip."

"And what brings you on the road to Barcelona, gentlemen?" asked Berenguer with grave courtesy.

"We have come down from the north with a desire to see the world, and to study, and to learn what we can of men and philosophy," said Andreu.

"And to earn our keep as we go," added Felip wryly, proving that he could speak when called upon to do so.

"And how do you do that?" asked Berenguer.

"Honestly, Your Excellency, I vow. We do it honestly," said Andreu. "Felip," he added. "Your instrument."

Felip reached down to a bundle at his feet and withdrew from it a rebec and a small bow. He tuned it carefully, frowning intensely as he worked, and then turned to his companion with an interrogative look. Andreu nodded and Felip began to play a plaintive air, at first unadorned, and then with elaborations; after a while Andreu began to sing, in a light, sweet tenor voice that filled the hall, a song of the sorrow of parting from his native soil. It was a melancholy tune and they performed it well. Then Felip struck a happy chord, and they both sang a robustly comic love song of parting and meeting again. Felip's baritone was not as accomplished as Andreu's tenor, but it had a pleasant sound, and the assembled group was dissolved in laughter by the end.

"And that, Your Excellency," said Andreu, "is how we earn our keep on the road."

"You are musicians by trade?" asked Berenguer.

"Oh, no, Your Excellency. But we sing and play indifferently well, and are pleased to do so when someone is generous enough to share his dinner with us."

"Will you favor us with another song or two?" asked Berenguer. "You are a welcome relief after the tedium of the road."

A burst of appreciation from the listeners signaled the end of a song. They paused for a mouthful of wine to moisten their dry throats. "And where does your thirst for knowledge take you tomorrow, gentlemen?" asked the Bishop.

"As far along the road to Barcelona as may be before night overcomes us," said Andreu.

"Then I suggest that you join our party," said Berenguer expansively. "Your songs and merry conversation would lighten our journey considerably, and in return you are welcome to share our humble fare."

"We would be honored," said Felip.

"And nothing could please us more," said Andreu.

The steward stood at the foot of the stairs like a puzzled stag at bay, facing the Abbess of Sant Daniel, Sor Marta, and the erring Sor Agnete. The guard assigned to watch over Sor Agnete during the night stood impassively by.

"This is not a prison, madam," said the steward. "We do not customarily lock our guests into their rooms."

"Whether it is customary or not is not my concern," said the Abbess. "Is it possible?"

The steward paused for a moment. "Yes," he said, "it is possible. But with such a number needing accommodation, the only chamber where she might be alone is not suitable for a lady of her standing."

"She must suffer its inconveniences," said the Abbess. "The guard will stay outside the chamber, with the key." She turned and swept off to her own quarters, with Sor Marta at her heels.

"It will not be the first night I have spent sleeping against a wall," said the guard philosophically.

"I will bring you something to lie on to temper the cold and discomfort of the stones beneath you," murmured the steward.

"Why did you invite those two to travel with us?" asked Francesc as they made their way to their rather more palatial quarters.

"Yes, Your Excellency," murmured Bernat. "That was the very question I was going to ask. I do not trust them," he said. "Not entirely."

"Do you believe them to be a threat to us?"

"No," he said honestly. "Not a threat. But they are at best common jongleurs or tricksters who have learned to speak as well as their betters."

"Well," said Berenguer, "they are unlikely to try to steal our purses, I think. They look to be a relatively harmless pair, earning small amounts of money as they can. At the very worst, I expect that they cheat in small ways if it is convenient and safe, and are otherwise harmless. They are well worth the cost of their meals in the skills they possess. Did you notice what happened to the group as they sang?"

"Nothing happened," said Bernat. "They sat and listened, and as the evening went on, some began to sing with them. It was to be expected."

"That is why I invited them to join us. I don't like traveling in a group where everyone is at each other's throat.

It makes for a wearisome, and perhaps dangerous, journey.
Even the servants were singing together, instead of glaring
at each other. Good night, my friends. God bring you good
slumbers.''

Rain pounded on the castle roof until dawn; wind tore at
the shutters and howled down the chimneys. Few in the
castle rested well. Only the guard outside Sor Agnete's little
chamber, who tied his wrist to her locked door with a
length of rope and composed himself for slumber. The
steward's pallet was thick and soft, and he slept easily. And
Yusuf, in the great hall, who stretched out on a pallet near
his master, and slept like a tired child. The grooms and lads
who had been given beds in the stable fared better than the
gentry. Its stone walls were as solid as the castle's, and
they, like Yusuf and the guard, were too weary to concern
themselves with weather. Up in the hayloft, they shared the
warmth of the beasts below, which was better than a dozen
fireplaces in easing the raw chill of the wind.

   Others were not so fortunate. In a small room with her
mother and Naomi, Raquel listened to the wind and rain
and prayed to be allowed to stay at home and not have to
marry. Then she thought of the pain she had seen on Daniel's face the evening before and brooded on times when
he had found her unhappy and made her smile with his
sharp wit. She amended her prayer to ''not marry yet.''
The Bishop fared no better. Comfortably settled in the castellan's private apartments, he was too weary and preoccupied to sleep, and passed the long hours until dawn
staring into the future.


*Wednesday, April 23*

The mules were hitched to the wagons in a misty, pene-
trating drizzle. In the courtyard, walkers and riders were
ready to set out. Glumly, they pulled their hoods down over
their foreheads and waited for Berenguer to make his farewells to their relieved host. At last, he clattered down the

steps and mounted. "We begin at once," he said with energy, and his mule, as impatient to be off as her master, broke into a trot.

Over the first hill, the drizzle eased off and the clouds began to thin. A breeze sprang up. At the horizon the sky began to clear.

"I do think," said Raquel cheerfully to no one in particular, "that this is going to be a lovely day after all."

"I'm wet to the skin," said her mother. "And that's a nasty, cold wind."

"The sun and the wind will soon dry you off. Are you wet, too, Papa?"

Her father did not respond.

"Papa. Are you wet?"

"Am I wet?" he asked in surprise. "Not that I notice. I was thinking that this weather is bad for His Excellency's knee, Raquel. He must be in pain after yesterday's long ride."

"It requires little effort to sit on a mule for a few hours, Papa," said his daughter impatiently. "And you know that the Bishop's knee is almost better. Why are you so concerned?"

"Ah, Raquel, you don't understand," said Isaac ruefully. "It's boredom, my dear. I'm not accustomed to having only one patient, and that one as strong as His Excellency."

"Perhaps we could convince some of the servants to fall ill to convenience you," said Judith sharply.

"You are right, Judith," said Isaac, accepting the remark as a rebuke. "I should be grateful for the respite from labor. Even if I didn't choose it. Unfortunately, I'm not, but I wouldn't want anyone ill to gratify my desire for useful activity."

Raquel, bored herself, was not interested in her parents' boredom or lack of it. She sighed. "I wonder when we will see the sea. When do you think we will see the sea, Mama?"

"I don't know, Raquel," said her mother. "I don't ride this way every day. What I do know is that you are beginning to sound like your small brother on a rainy day."

"Sometime around dinnertime, I expect, Mistress Judith," said the sergeant, who had moved up beside them. "Between the rain and the mud in the stable yard, and everyone's bad temper, we were late in setting out."

Then, above them, the sun broke through the cloud cover. From the road ahead, they heard a thin, piping sound. "Listen," said Raquel, and looked up ahead. Andreu and Felip were walking at the head of the procession, surrounded by a small crowd of admirers. Andreu was playing a cheerful dance on a high-pitched pipe, with a spirited accompaniment on the rebec by Felip. "It's Andreu, Papa, playing a pipe. And one of the lads is dancing." She lifted a hand to block the sun from her eyes. "Why is the Bishop's horse saddled today?"

And indeed, the Bishop's glossy steed, saddled, and with an elegant fringed bridle studded with silver bosses, paced gravely behind the carts at the side of the stable boy who had him as his special charge.

"Is it indeed?" said Isaac. "His Excellency must be impatient at our slow progress, and feeling better."

A shout from the front of the procession interrupted the musicians. The Bishop's kitchen lad was waving and pointing to the side of the road.

Berenguer urged his mule to a startled, rapid trot and caught up to the captain of the guard. "What is it, Captain?"

"A man, Your Excellency, by the side of the road," said the captain. "On the rise over there to the right. The groom who went to look says he is alive, but badly injured."

"Have them fetch the physician," said Berenguer, dismounting. "And then come look at him." The captain sent a rider for the physician and followed the Bishop up to the top of a little hillock. In the middle of a tangle of grasses and coarse shrubs, and partly hidden by them, lay a young man. His arm was twisted at an impossible angle, and his clothing soaked in blood. "The lad is sharp-eyed to have picked him out. You would think he had been deliberately hidden."

"It would be unwise to ignore the possibility, Your Excellency."

"Señor," asked the Bishop loudly. "Can you hear me?"

The young man groaned.

"We have a physician with us. He will tend to your hurts."

The young man opened his eyes in fear. "No," he whispered, and blinked. He looked again, trying to focus on the faces in front of him. "Who are you?"

"Berenguer de Cruilles, Bishop of Girona."

"God be thanked," said the young man, closed his eyes, and fell into a faint.

"It is his arm," said Raquel steadily. "It is twisted completely out of its joint and is soaked in blood."

"What else? Can he speak?"

"He is in a swoon. He looks young—perhaps twenty or twenty-five. His face is too gray and sunken looking to judge well."

The physician crouched down beside the young man and Raquel guided his hand to the injured arm. "Cut away the cloth so I can feel it."

Raquel took her silver scissors from the pouch hanging by her side and snipped the laces holding his sleeve in place. "There, Papa."

"Has he other injuries?" asked Isaac, after letting his fingers brush very lightly over the dislocated arm.

"Yes. Wounds. It is difficult to tell how deep they are."

"Yusuf, fetch clean cloths from the cart. How much has he bled?"

"There is a great deal of blood on the ground, Papa," said Raquel, who was cutting away his admirably fitting buskins. "It comes from a wound on his thigh. I am sorry to be so slow, Papa, but the cloth is wet with rain and soaked in blood. It is difficult to deal with. I have cut to the knee and a little beyond. And the bleeding started again when I moved the cloth with my scissors. I think—"

"Ssh. Let me feel, and then you can tell me what you think." Isaac moved his hands down to the thigh, pausing on the injured flesh of a wound and continuing with blood-ied hands down past the knee. "Is Yusuf there?"

"Yes, lord. I have brought the cloths. And the sergeant has come to help if he can."

"Fetch wine and water and a basin." His fingers ran very delicately over the knee again. "When he returns, Raquel, wash the cut with wine and water and bind it up. Then clean up the rest of the blood, for I will need to be able to work without my hands slipping."

"His hands are also very bloody," said Raquel.

"Perhaps he was trying to stanch the wound on his thigh," murmured her father. "But let me feel them." His fingers moved over one hand as lightly as a butterfly land-ing. He frowned, seemed to press harder, and elicited a groan from the half-conscious man. "Do not touch them, Raquel. Where is Yusuf with the water?"

"Here, lord," said the boy. "Hold out your hands and I will wash them."

As soon as they were clean of blood and dry, Isaac stood up. "We must deal with this arm right away." He placed a foot against the man's side to brace him, grasped the arm well above the hand, and with a smooth strong pull, set it back in place.

"Can anything be done with that hand?" asked the ser-geant.

"Perhaps," said Isaac. "But not here. First I must know if there are other broken limbs. What about the other hand, Raquel?"

"Not hurt, Papa."

"I need a board to rest this hand on . . ." And he mur-mured his list of requirements to the sergeant. "Open his tunic, my dear," he said. "We must find out what else has happened to him before we attempt to move him."

"Will he live?" asked the Bishop.

"He has so far. He seems to be tenacious of life," said Isaac.

"What injuries does he have?"

"A sword wound on the thigh, deep and long, from

which he has lost much blood. His body, both on the sides and back, is heavily bruised.''

"Beaten?"

"Most likely. His arm was out of joint and his hand crushed."

"Tortured," said the Bishop. "Caught in a sword battle, captured, beaten, and tortured."

"I can find no better explanation for his injuries. Two ribs are cracked—I have bound those, and we have tied his hand and arm to a cushioned plank. All we need now is two stout men to carry him, and a good soft bed on a wagon to place him on. I will give him something to make him sleep and try to set those fingers.''

"The sergeant and the head groom are the stoutest and least excitable of men I know," said the Bishop, summoning them.

"His clothing is wet with the rain and he is shaking with cold. We must then get him dry and warm. Until all that is done, and we see how he is," said Isaac, "I cannot say how long it will take him to recover. Since my daughter tells me that Naomi is already settled in the cart, she can look after him. When he awakens again, Your Excellency, you can question him.''

"I bow to your superior knowledge, Master Isaac. If we can save him, we shall, no matter which one of God's creatures he may be—friend or foe.''

The injured young man was gently placed on extra bedding set on top of the thick straw and carpets already laid down, with a soft pillow under his head. Raquel took a cup of wine and water into which she had stirred five drops of a thick bitter distillate and held it to his lips. "Drink this, señor," she said firmly. "It will make you feel much better.''

"Are you one of God's blessed angels?"

"No. Do as I say."

"But I already feel much better," he whispered gallantly.

"Quiet," said Raquel. "And drink."

And when he fell into a sleep deep enough to be only

partly conscious of the pain, Isaac began the delicate process of straightening out the broken bones in his left hand.
Raquel bound them to smooth slivers of wood with soft
cloths. When they had all been set as best they could be,
she fastened the wrist and hand to a small piece of board
and tied it across his chest.

"It is fortunate," said Raquel, "that they did this to his
left hand. For I think from how he wears his sword that he
is right-handed."

"Not fortunate," said Isaac, "deliberate. Destroy the
hand you use least, and threaten to do the same with the
one that is left. It is enough to make some men talk."

"Do you think he did?"

"No. I think they continued until he appeared to be dead
and gave up."

All this time the procession was at a halt, and most of
its members had gathered at some distance from the carts,
suggesting, arguing, and complaining to anyone who would
listen.

"I think he should be left where he was found," said
Ibrahim.

Since these were the first words most of the group had
heard from Ibrahim, they aroused considerable interest.
"Why?" asked one of the grooms.

Ibrahim thought about that. It had occurred to him that
giving the real reason—that the young man was taking his
place on the cart and he would have to walk again, and
perhaps lead his master's wretched mule—might not garner
him much support among the other walkers. "He could be
a cutthroat who was justly beaten and left for dead, and
he'll kill us all in our beds as soon as he wakes up."

"There's something in that," said a stable lad.

The maids from the convent, who had kept themselves
well apart from the common herd, had nonetheless been
listening with great interest. "He doesn't look like a cutthroat," one of them objected. "He looks like a very handsome gentleman, no doubt set upon by cutthroats. And I
wouldn't like to trust myself to your charity!" she said
nastily.

"We couldn't leave him by the road," said a groom. "That would be an evil act for a bishop. But we should leave him at the next inn, and let them care for him until his people come to get him."

"Yes," said the kitchen lad, who had seated himself on a convenient rock and was cutting into a loaf intended for dinner. "He'll be a terrible amount of extra work."

"Here. Give us some of that," said one of his mates.

"There's not enough for all. Get us another loaf or two."

The assistant cook tossed them a loaf, and sent the kitchen lad off to fetch more food from the supply cart.

"There won't be enough food with all these extra people," said a stable lad, who had not been in His Excellency's service long enough to feel confident of his next meal.

"Quiet," said one of the convent maids, nodding at the two entertainers, who were by now general favorites.

"Why should I be quiet?"

And the gentle bickering continued as they all found themselves patches of dry ground and sat down in comfort with hearty pieces of bread to await someone else making a decision about something.

Closer to the carts, the Bishop and the captain of the guard were engaged with Isaac in a similar discussion. "Has it been decided what is to be done with him?" asked the captain.

"It is too early to decide, Captain," said Isaac. "I can scarcely tell what condition he is in at the moment."

"We certainly have space to accommodate him," said the captain.

"If he can bear the jolting of the wagon," said Berenguer.

"Unfortunately we did not bring a litter," said the captain. "But in all humanity we cannot leave him here."

"It is a question of leaving him at the nearest inn," said Isaac, "or with the brothers at Sant Pol. I will be better able to judge his condition after he awakes."

"Then we are agreed? We take him with us and decide

later," said Berenguer. "Now let us move out again."

Yusuf brought Isaac's mule over to him and held her head while his master mounted. Raquel mounted her own mule and reached for the lead rein, but Yusuf was already moving the gentle creature to a place right behind the wagon. Slowly, one by one, everyone repositioned himself for travel, and the procession began its ponderous way southward once more.

But as soon as they were all under way, Isaac's sharp ears caught the sound of a horse galloping up behind them. "Someone on the road is in great haste," he murmured to his daughter.

"Yes, Papa." She turned to look. "Papa—it's a huge black-and-tan horse. I don't think I've seen a bigger one. And the poor beast has no rider," she said.

"Is he saddled?"

"Yes, Papa. The stirrups and the reins are flying about. He's slowing down now he's caught up with us."

By now everyone's attention had been caught, but although a few of the walkers grabbed at the reins as he passed by, no one wanted to move too close to those flying hooves. The horse drew level with Isaac's mule and slowed to a walk. "He's not tan at all," said Raquel. "He's all splashed with dried mud. And he looks quite wild-eyed with fear."

Yusuf reached up and took hold of the loose reins, murmuring something to the frightened beast. He led it along, and as long as he was able to keep close to the physician's mule, the big horse was quiet.

The captain and the sergeant rode over to look. "It is a handsome animal," said the captain.

"I suspect that somewhere nearby there is a rider in need of his mount," said the sergeant. "If you let him go, lad," he added, "he'll return to his stable."

Yusuf tied the reins up loosely so that they wouldn't trip the beast and released his hold. The horse paced alongside the mule, showing no interest at all in leaving.

"He seems to have taken a fancy to Master Isaac's mule. And to his young apprentice," said the sergeant.

"That could be," said the captain, "but he must have an owner." The sergeant nodded in the direction of the wagon.

"That's possible," said the captain. "But until we find out, perhaps we should send someone back along the road to check."

"How far?" asked the sergeant.

"As far as the castle, I would say. Let him inquire there and return."

While the sergeant went off to talk to one of the grooms, the captain fell in step by Raquel.

"Do horses really take fancies to other animals?" asked Raquel.

"They're odd like that," said the captain. "I knew one—" and he took the lead rein to Isaac's mule and whiled away the late-morning hours with tales of horses that had pet animals.

The young man slept soundly until the group halted for a late dinner. While the midday meal—a less elaborate one, after all that delay, than the previous day's—was being prepared by the Bishop's cooks, and Naomi was worrying about the dual problems of preparing a proper dinner and looking after her latest acquisition, he awakened again. She left him to her master and scuttled off to her cooking pots.

"How are you?" asked Isaac.

"Thirsty," said the young man.

Raquel propped him up and held a cup to his lips. He drank greedily and sank back on his pillows.

"But I am grateful—no, truly, I am astonished to have fallen among such charitable rescuers. Are you the magician who set my arm and my hand?" he asked.

"No magician," said Isaac. "A simple physician. How long had the arm been wrenched from its socket?"

"When did you find me?" he asked.

"Halfway through the morning. You appeared to have been out all night in the storm. You were very wet."

"Sometime before sunset yesterday. I did not inquire about the exact hour."

"Then you were like that more than half a day," murmured Isaac, shaking his head.

"How did it happen?" asked Berenguer.

"I was . . ." He stopped and drew breath. "I was riding late, looking for the inn, when I was set on by thieves. I drew my sword to fight them off and marked a few of them, but one gave me a good slash on the thigh." He stopped and Raquel gave him another mouthful to drink. "It weakened me and they were all over me. They yanked me from my horse. That's when I injured myself. I fell very awkwardly."

"Such a terrible injury from a fall?" said Isaac.

"Yes," he said. "They took my purse, my sword, and my horse, and dragged me off the road to postpone pursuit, I suppose. I regret my poor horse the most. We have been through a great deal together."

Berenguer looked thoughtfully at him. "I apologize for your present accommodation," he said. "You cannot be very comfortable on that cart."

"I am more comfortable than I was last night," said the young man. "And I have a most careful attendant."

"Ah—Naomi. She is my cook, and loves nothing better than a sick man to look after. We are a sadly disappointing household for her," said Isaac. "Tell me, Raquel, how does he look?"

"Still very pale, Papa, but his eyes are clear. He is a little feverish."

"It would be odd if he weren't."

"Dear God," said the young man. "You cannot see! You set my arm and my hand and dressed my wound and you cannot see. You are a magician."

"No, my son," said the Bishop. "No magician. Just a very skilled man. Should he be taken to the inn, Master Isaac? It is not far."

"He would be better with the monks, Your Excellency. Their care will make up for the extra distance he has to travel."

"I beg you, Your Excellency, if you are going as far as Barcelona, to take me with you. I think you will find me

able to withstand travel in these luxurious surroundings."
His voice thickened and he coughed to clear his throat.

"Let us wait and see how he is this evening," suggested
Isaac.

"Good," said Berenguer. "We will take you to Sant Pol
and see how you bear the journey."

Naomi raised his shoulders a little and put a cup to his
lips. But instead of drinking he stared at something just past
the Bishop's elbow. Berenguer turned and looked into the
soft eyes of the large black horse.

"You must drink, señor," said Naomi.

"Pardon," he said. "I was struck with admiration at that
lovely horse." He drank and lay back, exhausted.

"And what may we call you, young man?" asked Berenguer. "Since we are to be traveling companions at least
for a while."

"I have been discourteous, Your Excellency, in my concentration on my own small complaints. I am—Gilabert.
You may call me Gilabert."

"Very well, Don Gilabert."

"Simply Gilabert. I come from a respectable and honest,
but modest family."

"And where does this modest family live?"

"Between Barcelona and Tarragona."

"What do you think of young Gilabert, Master Isaac?"
asked Berenguer.

"A liar, but a pleasant young man."

"Indeed," said Berenguer. "Perhaps an experienced
horseman could do that to his arm when being pulled off
an animal who by his account was standing still, but how
did he smash his fingers and break two ribs on the other
side of his body? And bruise his back. Someone did that
to him."

"Oh yes," said Isaac. "Someone did that."

"And not someone he is protecting. Who would protect
that vicious an enemy?"

"No. It could be someone he flees from."

"Or perhaps, someone he pursues? He has exquisite

manners for a man of such humble background, Master Isaac. He interests me greatly.''

The captain came over as they were preparing to leave. ''Your Excellency,'' he said. ''The groom we sent to find the horse's owner has returned. No one reports him gone. And when we saw him first, I would judge that he had not been galloping a long distance.''

''I think,'' said Berenguer, ''that we should bring him along as well.''

# SEVEN

## Sant Pol de Mar

The sun was low in the heavens, catching the tips of the waves that crashed against the rocks and over the sand of the shore, before they arrived at Sant Pol de Mar. This visit to the monastery was neither necessary nor convenient—although there was much to their mutual advantage that the Bishop wished to discuss with the Abbot—but Berenguer clung grimly to his excuse for taking the Barcelona road.

One of the guards had ridden ahead to warn the brothers of their imminent appearance; they were met in the courtyard by the Abbot and the infirmarer. The Abbot looked stunned, the infirmarer appalled. "You have a badly injured young man with you?" repeated the Abbot, as if the words had carried no meaning to him the first time.

"Yes, we do. In the wagon. Does that present a problem? We can give you assistance in caring for him, at least for tonight."

The infirmarer nodded humbly. "We will do our utmost for him, Your Excellency. I fear, however, that there are . . . complications."

"Complications?"

"Amongst the novices. And some of the older brothers. They are very ill with feverish colds, and bad throats. The infirmary is crowded, and my assistants are dizzy with lack of sleep.''

"Have you room to accommodate the rest of us?"

"We have beds enough, and benches at the refectory table, but few to serve and but poor hospitality to offer. What we have you are welcome to. But the sick man—"

"A feverish cold would be no help for the young man," observed Isaac. "Do you have a place away from the sick where he can rest?"

"Certainly," said the Abbot.

"Then if you will offer us a roof," said Berenguer, "we will look after ourselves. We have cooks, food, and servants enough to feed and serve our company and all the brothers well enough to sit at table."

"Brother Johan will show you the way and give you what assistance you need."

Gilabert was carried to a large airy chamber with a comfortable bed. The infirmarer looked at him and shook his head. "He is very ill, Your Excellency. There is little that we can do for him, I fear."

"He looks miraculously recovered since we found him this morning," remarked Berenguer.

"The good brother is right, however," said Isaac diplomatically. "In these cases, after a brief rally, fever often intervenes and carries off the strongest of men."

"Precisely," said the infirmarer. "He is best kept away from any of our sick brothers or those attending on them, I think. I would venture to suggest strong broth. Do you think it advisable?"

"Strong broth and a room away from the sick would be my thoughts as well," said Isaac. "And we have enough people in our party who have some skill in nursing the sick to care for him ourselves. Can your kitchens provide broth? Or should I ask our cooks—"

"Don't trouble His Excellency's cooks," said the infirmarer hastily, imagining the instant chaos and ill will this would create in the kitchens. "We can provide an excellent broth. And perhaps if he can support it, some wine and beaten egg."

"Nothing could be better," said Isaac. And the infirmarer left to give orders, with the dual satisfaction of saving his assistants an impossible night, and doing much good to a very sick guest.

When the Bishop arrived to check on the young victim's progress, the room was already well stocked with visitors. Isaac was bent over, with his ear to the man's chest. Raquel stood by the bed, near a table with a candle on it ready for lighting when the light failed.

"How are you, young Gilabert?" asked the Bishop.

"I am surrounded by excellent attendants and lack for nothing." As the Bishop gave him a professionally reassuring smile and turned to leave, the young man reached out his uninjured hand and grasped his sleeve. "A thousand pardons, Your Excellency, but may I speak?"

"Certainly, if it doesn't tire you too much." Berenguer sat on the chair that was placed near the patient's head and leaned closer to him.

Gilabert released his grip and spoke in a lowered voice. "Your Excellency, only now have I realized that you and your companions are traveling to Tarragona. I beg you not to leave me here in the monastery—as kind as the monks are—but to take me with you."

"It will be a terrible journey for a man in your condition."

"No, not at all. I am very strong. I assure you, I have survived worse. And if I don't survive, then I will be in the hands of God and much happier than I have been in the hands of men. No," he said, "please don't stop me until I have said what I need to say to you. My father lives on a tiny *finca,* very poor, but his own, and word reached me where I have been recently that he was very ill, and wished above all to see me before he died." He stopped, panting for breath. "Your Excellency, we had spoken harsh words before I left him, and I could not bear to see him go to his grave not knowing how much I regretted every one of those words, not knowing that I love and revere him more than any man else on this earth. If I die in the attempt to get to him, so be it. I will have tried. But I pray—Your Excellency, you have truly been sent by God. To be discovered at the point of death by a holy bishop, and with him a skilled physician—that cannot have been chance. Who else could bring me safely home so well?''

''You plead your cause most eloquently, young man,'' said Berenguer. ''I shall talk this over with the physician, and if it is possible, we shall do as you request.''

''Is he fit to travel?'' asked Berenguer.

Isaac shook his head. ''The question should be whether he is fit to stay in a house where those who have the skill to care for him are tainted with infection. We cannot leave him here. We must take him with us.''

''And then?''

''In Barcelona, with Your Excellency's permission, he will come with me. We will stay at the house of Mordecai ben Issach, a physician of my acquaintance. There he will receive all possible care. After that we shall see. I have a strong feeling that he is not marked for death as yet, although experience and common sense tell me his hold on life is precarious at the moment.''

''I would like to convey him to his father's house,'' said the Bishop.

''If it is possible, Your Excellency, you shall. But his condition is worsening. His fever mounts. He will need very careful attendance during the night.''

It was a very long night at the monastery of Sant Pol de Mar. Once supper was over, Naomi was sent to bed, very firmly, by Isaac. ''Who will look after him in the morning,'' he asked, ''if you are asleep on your feet?'' And grudgingly, she allowed herself to be sent away.

He turned to his daughter. ''And I, too, shall sleep, at least for a while. If I am needed, I can be sent for. They have given me a chamber close by.''

''Yusuf has walked for two days, Papa. He can scarcely hold his eyes open.''

''Then he, too, should be allowed to rest.''

"I will stay up with the young man," said Raquel firmly "It will not be the first time."

"And I, too, will look after him, Isaac," said another, familiar voice. "Raquel and I will share the task."

"Judith, my dear," said the physician. "Are you not weary from travel?"

"That is a question you should ask the mule who carried me," she said tartly. "How could I be tired? I will sit with him first. Raquel needs to sleep for a few hours. She has been yawning this last hour or two."

"May we be of assistance as well?" The light, pleasant voice from the doorway made Raquel jump. "It is Andreu," he said modestly. "If you can recall to mind the poor entertainer of last night. Master Isaac. Mistress Judith. Mistress Raquel. I apologize if we alarmed you." He bowed with a flourish. "I have some experience in caring for the sick."

"As have I," said Felip, materializing from behind him. "We can lift a sick man if needed, and we can fetch and carry, and we delight in being sent on errands. We are also more trustworthy than we sometimes look with our instruments in our hands and wearing our outlandish traveling clothes."

"Excellent," said Judith, who had been observing them shrewdly as they chattered on and judged them to be decidedly competent. "That would make four of us. You would be of great assistance. Raquel and I will alternate, as can the two of you, unless he worsens. But the others should rest close by. Are there more chambers near this one?"

"My first task will be to discover that," said Andreu.

"Good," said Felip. "And mine will be the fire. There is a cold wind rising off the sea tonight, and the fire is dying. I shall fetch some wood and repair it. We will return in no time at all."

While the others were still considering what was best to be done, the two entertainers returned with a large bundle of firewood and a substantial black kettle filled with broth. Felip mended the fire, and Andreu set the kettle of soup on the hob. Then he reached into his hood and drew out a large loaf. "With the prayers and good wishes of the kitchen for our companion's recovery," he said. "The brothers remarked that those who were looking after the sick during a long night needed to be sustained as well. I will return in a moment with more. And I have secured two chambers close by for our use. This epidemic of feverish colds has done some good; their usual inhabitants are in the infirmary."

He was as good as his word. He came back with a large jug of wine, a bowl with dried fruit and nuts, and another, stacked on top of it, with olives from the monastery's own groves. "Those who elected to sleep during this night are missing the best of everything."

"You have a very persuasive way with the inhabitants of the kitchen, it seems," said Judith.

"I promised to return soon and amuse them with some songs while they work. Between the arrival of so many of us on such short notice and the illness among the monks, the lay brothers are working night and day."

Judith dismissed him to entertain the kitchen workers and snatch a little sleep, Raquel retired gratefully to the chamber next door, and the night sank back into peace. Judith bathed the young man's forehead and coaxed him into drinking. A little broth, a mouthful of watered wine, a spoonful of mint *tisane*, a taste of a soothing infusion of ginger and aromatic spices. Sometimes she let him sleep, listening to his muttering and occasional cries and wondering what horrors he saw in his dreams.

Just before Raquel arrived to relieve her mother, Gilabert's fever began to mount. "I must sleep for a little while," murmured Judith. "I will return soon. Give him more to drink. Moisten his lips, and keep him cool. If he worsens, call me and your father."

Raquel gave her mother a kiss and sat down by the bed, wringing out a cloth and mopping up the sweat from his forehead. At one point he opened his eyes and said, "Am

I dead yet?'' Raquel silenced him with a little broth, and he closed them again.

Judith returned not long after. ''I slept for a while,'' she said. ''I will rest here, lest you need me.''

Andreu and Felip continued to supply them with fresh cool water and clean cloths. They built up the fire and offered mother and daughter bread and olives and fruit.

Gilabert began to toss restlessly in his bed, straining to move his injured hand, and then pulling at the bandages that held it in place. Raquel placed a firm restraining hand on his arm and was tossed aside. ''Mama, help me,'' she said. ''He is trying to free his hand. And if he keeps moving like this, I am afraid that he will loosen the dressings on his leg as well,'' she added. ''They are not so tightly tied. He is very strong. I cannot hold him still.''

''We must get your father,'' said Judith.

Andreu, who had been hovering at Raquel's elbow, anxious to help and loath to interfere, turned and left the room without a word.

Isaac listened intently to his patient's heart and labored breathing as best he could, pressing him down to keep him still enough to examine. ''We must calm him and lower the fever,'' said Isaac, straightening up. ''I had hoped that his own strong constitution could throw off the worst effects of his experience, but it was perhaps too much to ask.''

''Why are you so hesitant, Papa?'' asked Raquel.

''Because he requires rest and quiet, and soon we must force him to move from here. And in every drug there is good and evil, my child. You know that. This is not an auspicious way to use these compounds. But measure it out, and moisten his lips with it. Andreu will hold his shoulders firm to the bed for you.''

Felip had joined his companion while Isaac was bending over the sick man. ''I will do it,'' he said. ''My arms are longer than my friend's.''

''How goes the night?'' asked Isaac.

"The first hint of dawn troubles the night sky," said Andreu. "And the wind has dropped."

Raquel brushed the young man's lips with the potent compound, and gradually his shoulders relaxed, his unbandaged arm fell by his side, and he appeared to sleep. "He is quiet, Papa. Shall I—"

"Give him no more. Moisten his lips with water and let him sleep."

Isaac returned to his chamber, leaving his wife and daughter to sit with the patient. As the light strengthened outside, it crept in through the cracks in the shutters, turning the candlelight deathly pale. Raquel took a close look at the young man. "Are we winning, Mama?" she asked.

"We're not losing. Go and wash and ready yourself. You'll feel better."

But out in the corridor, Raquel heard the stirring of the monastery coming awake. Andreu appeared bearing a basket covered with a napkin and a jug. "The brothers are up," he said. "They are about to wake the others."

"Must we leave soon?" asked Raquel. "He has only just begun to sleep."

"That I cannot say," he said. "But I have brought some cold chicken and other delicacies from the kitchen. With your permission, mistress, we shall break our fast in the sickroom with you, and then pack our few things and return to help move our poor young lord into the cart."

"Young lord?"

"Only an affectation of speech, Mistress Raquel," he said. "With all these attendants, he must be at least a lord."

She laughed and returned to her mother, where they fell on the contents of the basket with a will. And not once during that long and wakeful night had Raquel had a moment to mull over her own private fears.

Berenguer entered the chapel well before prime, followed by a sleepy-eyed Bernat and Francesc, who had been dragged from their beds only minutes before. The Bishop knelt to his prayers, effectively preventing any questions, much less complaints, and stayed that way until the choir and the brothers filed in. It was not until the service ended that he spoke.

"Put your things together and come to the refectory," he said. "We will break our fast with a mouthful of bread while they are saddling my horse. The monastery kitchen has packed us something to sustain us on the road."

"We're leaving?"

"We are. As soon as possible. We shall be in Barcelona in time for our dinners. The grooms are awake; they will start to load the wagons soon. But we shall not wait for them. I intend to set out before you can say a paternoster." All the time he was speaking he was walking quickly toward the refectory. "The young man survived the night," he added. "We had only to wait for that news."

"But Your Excellency's knee!" said Francesc.

"Looking at that young man yesterday made me realize that my knee was of very little importance to anyone but me. And perhaps my physician. If you are quick, my friends, you will not have to travel fasting."

Before the wagons had been loaded—before the grooms had broken their fast—Berenguer and his two priests, escorted by two of the guards, were quietly bidding farewell to the monks of Sant Pol and leaving for Barcelona at an easy canter.

More than an hour later a small group waited in the courtyard, ready to leave. The baggage train had already set out, leaving the rest to catch up as best they could. All the servants, except for one of the grooms, were gone, along with both carts. The sergeant walked briskly away from the stables and noticed Yusuf.

"Well, young Yusuf," he said, looking appraisingly at him. "I had thought you had gone ahead with the rest. But you are not heavy. You may ride behind me until we catch up, if the thought doesn't frighten you."

"Not at all, Sergeant," said Yusuf politely.

"Sergeant? What do we do with the black horse?" called the groom. "Leave it here? It should have gone ahead with the lads."

"I will ride him," said Yusuf confidently.

"You?" said the sergeant. "What do you know of riding and horsemanship?" he asked. "That's not a little donkey over there."

"I believe he knows a great deal," said Isaac. "Don't you, Yusuf?"

"Yes, lord. I have ridden all my life, until—"

"He rode all the way from Granada to Valencia," said Isaac. "You might let him try."

"Saddle him," called the sergeant.

When the black was led out of the stable, he had been brushed clean of mud, his coat was glossy with rubbing, and he looked to be an entirely different creature. Yusuf took him from the groom, set a foot in the stirrup, and jumped up into the saddle as if he were climbing a high wall. As they watched, he leaned over, shortened the stirrups, and urged the restless creature into a trot around the group in the courtyard. He swung its head around and rode back to where the sergeant was standing. Doing his best to hide his satisfaction behind a mask of composure, he said casually, "He has an excellent gait, but he is larger than the horses I am accustomed to. I am sure to be stiff and sore tomorrow."

"You are a scamp," said the sergeant. "Where did you learn to ride?"

"At home," he said uneasily. "I always rode, everywhere, as far back as I can remember.

"Well—it will save one of the lads from having to lead it," said the sergeant. "And as far as we can tell, his owner won't mind."

The black was startled by the guffaw of laughter that resulted, and danced nervously away from the crowd. The groom ran to catch the horse's bridle, when he was interrupted by a voice from behind him.

"Wait. Let the lad show us what he can do." The sergeant watched carefully as Yusuf steadied the horse and returned it to a walk close to his master's mule. "The lad spoke true. Shall we move on, sirs? We have a long day ahead of us." Almost before he had finished speaking, his own mount was moving out of the gates toward the road south to Barcelona.

Because the road ahead of them was well traveled and it seemed unlikely that they would run into trouble, only two guards remained as their escort, one of whom was entirely concerned with Sor Agnete. Two had ridden with the Bishop, and the captain had taken the remaining two to protect the baggage train.

"We shall catch up soon to the rest of them, Master Isaac," said the amiable voice of the sergeant. "Do you find your mule to your liking?"

"She is a good beast," said Isaac. "I have ridden worse, many, many times."

"You are accustomed to their gaits?"

"Indeed, Sergeant. As a boy and a young man, I traveled many miles, on horse and on mule, on beasts of all descriptions, the stubborn, lazy, ill-tempered, and unpredictable ones, as well as the good-natured. His Excellency's mules are superior creatures."

"She is a patient and obedient beast. The captain chose her himself for your use."

"She must be," said Isaac, "since my daughter, who is not an experienced horsewoman, is able to lead her."

"She shall be relieved of that responsibility, Master Isaac. I will take the lead rein myself." He moved forward and reached out for the rein. "I will take charge of your father's mule, Mistress Raquel," he said. "You have enjoyed the privilege long enough. We might even assay a short gallop," he added, with a laugh. Under his charge, the mule moved forward at a brisker walk than she had lately fallen into, and gradually they all speeded up and began to close the gap ahead of them.

It was a quiet group. Raquel's sleepless night had taken its toll, and her muddled thoughts darted between home and the road, merging into waking dreams in which Daniel lay gravely injured and, when she tried to help him, turned disconcertingly into the young stranger. The nuns rode in silence. Marta attempted to chat with the Abbess, received no response, and gave up. Their shy and unhappy priest, deprived of someone to talk to without Bernat and Francesc, stared restlessly at the road ahead.

"Are we far from Barcelona?" asked Raquel finally. "Is that the mountain that towers above the city?" She pointed at a peak some distance to the west and south.

"We're not that close, Mistress Raquel," said the sergeant. "We'll be hard-pressed to arrive before sundown."

"But we're moving much faster than we did yesterday, Sergeant," said the nuns' priest.

"True," observed the sergeant. "But those up ahead are slower than we are, and will slow down even more. As the heat increases, they will begin to tire."

As soon as he said that, they all became uncomfortably aware that the sun was growing very hot. A breeze, smelling of fish and salt and all the mysterious fragrances of the sea, had been keeping them cool, but whenever the road wound behind the omnipresent hills that sheltered the coast from the onshore winds, the spring morning felt more like a midsummer afternoon. The beasts slowed down and tried to wander off the road and their riders grew hotter and shorter of temper the farther they traveled.

Up ahead, the baggage train had reached a long stretch of sheltered road. Since Gilabert, Naomi, and Judith had taken over one of the carts completely, and the baggage was now all piled on the other, those who had been expected to walk were now forced to do just that, not steal rides on the wagons. Some of them could have walked alongside the sturdiest and most willing mule by sunlight and starlight together without flagging, but the rest grumbled in discontent.

In his coveted place on the wagon, Gilabert moved in and out of consciousness, burning with fever. "We must stop for a while, mistress," said Naomi. "He is worsening. This jolting is surely bad for him."

"Perhaps," said Judith. "Although I think it is the heat of the road that affects him most." She bathed his face and neck, and then his uninjured hand and forearm. When she moved the covering away from his leg, she frowned. "His wound needs to be looked to," she said. "And we must have a fresh supply of cool water."

"How is your patient, Mistress Judith?" asked the captain of the guard, as he had been doing at regular intervals since the journey started.

"Not well. We must stop for water, and to dress his wound again."

"His Excellency bade me make sure that he received the best of care," said the captain, "and I shall do so, early though it is. But this is no place to halt."

"No," said Judith, looking around. "I agree with you, Captain."

"A mile hence the road rises, and we come to a small grove on either side of a river. There is shade and fresh water there for him and for the beasts. Can he wait that long?"

"But we just passed a stream," said Judith sharply. "I wondered that you did not stop and at least allow us to collect cool water."

"That stream is muddy and slow moving, Mistress Judith," said the captain. "I would not water the beasts at it if I could find another. The one ahead is fresh and cool. We will stop there," he said firmly.

And indeed, shortly afterward the road began to climb, and the breezes returned. Behind them, the tail end of their group, with its reassuring extra guards, was gradually catching up. Felip unslung his instrument from his back and began to play. Andreu grabbed a mouthful from a skin of water and then started to sing. Soon half of them were joining in. The mules plodded on, up the slope, until they reached the grove and its clear stream.

Gilabert was carried to a cool, quiet place under an oak, and Raquel quickly began to undo the bandages covering the wound on his thigh. The grooms took the mules down to the river to water them, and everyone else scattered to bathe faces, hands, and in many cases, feet and most of the rest of themselves.

Isaac sent for the captain of the guard. "Things are not well with your patient," said the captain. "I can read it on everyone's face."

"Very true," said Isaac. "His wound has opened. We have cleansed it and bound it up once more with healing herbs, but even an hour of lying still before he must be moved would be of some help." He paused, waiting for a response, and when none was forthcoming, went on. "I realize, Captain, that this is not a good time to halt. The day is warm, and will get warmer before long. It will mean traveling when we should be resting."

"What cannot be helped must be endured," said the captain, cheerfully enough. "I would not have the young man die because I wanted to spare this pack of lazy wretches a warm hour or two. Besides, soon enough the road comes down into the plain, as you know. The sun will be hot, but the walking easy, and there should be a wind off the water. Send me word when you think it safe to move him. I have preparations to make." And the captain strode off in the direction of the wagons, where the cooks sat and gossiped under a tree.

"I fear," said the captain directly, "that we must stop here awhile. The young man has worsened. I would prefer not to make another long stop in two more hours. That way we will never reach Barcelona."

"How long are we here?" asked the head cook.

"An hour or more."

"Good," he said. "We have time to prepare something to be eaten cold later. For we cannot have traveled more than six or seven miles yet."

"I wish it were that much. We are five miles from Sant Pol at best. I had hoped to accomplish twice that before halting."

The change in plan was implemented with disciplined speed. As soon as Naomi saw the Bishop's kitchen lad lay a fire, she screamed for Ibrahim and her dinner was under way. The grooms loosed the beasts to graze, the guards rapidly surveyed the site, and the rest of the party scattered into quiet nooks in the shade.

Everyone settled into comfortable somnolence, except
for the cooks, who were working, and the guards, who cir-
cled the area slowly, identifying possible sources of danger.
Their survey complete, they made their reports and split up
again to keep a watch. The captain looked at the sergeant
and shook his head.

"Are you worried about this place, Captain?" asked the
sergeant.

"Not at all," said the captain. "But we'll have to stop
again. You know that. We can't reach Barcelona this evening no matter how we hurry them," he murmured, nodding in the general direction of the wagons.

"Then we spend the night on the road," said the sergeant
philosophically. "But at least we can have an hour or so
of peace now."

Which made the attack, when it came, all the more startling.
The Bishop's cooks were watching a simple dish of rice
and lentils that bubbled gently on the fire, and gossiping
lazily. The monks had supplied them with fresh bread, cold
meats, and a fine cheese to accompany it, and there was
little to do but let it cool when it was ready. Naomi was
busily preparing a saffron rice in competition, and the scent
of spices mingling with that of the sea and the meadows
was pleasant indeed.

Isaac mixed Gilabert another preparation to ease his pain
and feverish symptoms, and he slept soundly at last. Judith
sat at his side, fanning him, and nodding into sleep from
time to time. Nearby, Raquel stretched out lazily on the
soft ground under the tree and listened to Yusuf talk about
travel, and the monks, and the wonderful black horse, and
any other random idea that crowded into his brain. She
drifted off somewhere between sleeping and wakefulness.

The beasts were gathered some distance away where the
open meadow met the grove, in a grassy spot shaded from
the bright sun. They grazed, or slept, or simply stared into
space according to their fancy, at peace with the world.
They were in the nominal care of three children—for the
stable lads were no more than that—who were sleeping

with the soundness of youth and extreme fatigue. The two grooms were nowhere to be seen.

The nuns were seated together in a small hollow, ranged along a fallen tree like three large black birds on a branch, talking in low voices. Or at least Sor Marta and the Abbess were talking earnestly to Sor Agnete, who merely stirred the ground with her foot and shook her head mutinously. The guard who had been posted to watch Agnete had withdrawn to a rise a little distance away, where he could watch the hollow and the hill behind. He had a feeling that it was more important to be able to scan the horizon than to follow their conversation. He hoped he was right. The nuns' priest sat down beside him.

"It's lonely out here on the road," said the nuns' priest in a very low voice. "I can't very well go down there and join the Abbess. Do you mind if I sit here?"

"Not at all," said the guard, who thought it was a great nuisance. "I would think the Abbess could be difficult," he added, speaking just as quietly.

"Difficult! You wouldn't believe it," he answered. "Especially right now. I don't like travel very much," he added. "Especially on that cursed mule. Coming along was not my idea, but in spite of how impossible the nuns are, it's a good post I have with them, and . . ." Suddenly he seemed to realize that he was being indiscreet. He turned red, mumbled, and rose to his feet with great dignity.

The guard was watching his silent confusion with barely concealed amusement when a loud crack from a dry branch snapping under a heavy foot drew his attention back to his charge. Then, out of the corner of his eye, he saw something that brought him instantly to his feet.

Two hefty men, armed with long daggers, and apparently unaware of his presence, had materialized from the hill to his right, and were heading straight for the nuns.

# EIGHT

## The Shady Grove

A dozen or more men—in the end, no one was ever quite sure of their numbers—had moved quietly down from the hills beyond and were gliding through the wood and around the broken rocks toward the scattered and very somnolent travelers. The captain was standing on a small hill, looking over at the grazing animals and their sleeping keepers, while carrying on a conversation with his sergeant.

Isaac was the first to notice that something was amiss. He was sitting near his injured patient, leaning comfortably against a thick, smooth-barked tree, and thinking. Most of the group had a restless and unhappy air, except for Judith, who would be seeing her sister again and was as pleased as a child with a new toy. And Yusuf, for whom riding that horse seemed to be a pleasure beyond compare. But even so, the boy seemed wary and nervous as he retraced his route south. Isaac knew very little about his long trek north-ward from Valencia, in those years after his father was killed in the rebellion. No doubt he was troubled by un-happy and frightening memories.

All the time he was considering these things, he was also aware of a host of predictable sounds around him. The deep voices of the guards in murmured conversation, the rattle of cooking pots, Yusuf at his feet, and Judith and Raquel to one side, all breathing the deep even breaths of those who sleep. From time to time he even heard the distant, higher-pitched voices of the nuns. Nothing from the animals, as they must have been pastured some distance away, and nothing from the lads, who when they weren't at work were usually playing and shrieking like ordinary children. They, too, must be asleep, poor, tired creatures. Then suddenly a few noisy birds who had been chirping and quarreling in the grove fell silent. Dry branches cracked under someone's footfall, not once, but several times, and from several places, and dry leaves rustled more than could be accounted for by the light breeze that ruffled his hair.

He leaned forward and placed a hand on Yusuf's shoulder. "Yusuf," he murmured. "Are you awake?"

A slight pause. "Yes, lord," mumbled Yusuf.

"Be very quiet. I think there are people in the wood, coming toward us. Tell the captain. Where is my staff?"

"By your left hand, lord," he murmured, and disappeared.

Before Yusuf could find the captain, the slightly nasal tenor voice of the nuns' priest rang out through the wood. "Leave that woman!" he shrieked. At the sound, general chaos broke out.

"Judith! Raquel! Get Gilabert and hide yourselves!" said Isaac.

"See that big log over there, Mama? We'll be well hidden behind it," said Raquel, standing up. She bent to pick up one end of the rough litter that had been fashioned for the injured man. "Help me with him."

"Isaac, you must come with us," said Judith, who had not stirred. "Or I'll not leave you here."

"Nonsense. I will shelter behind this tree. Now go, woman! I order you." He rose to his feet and, staff in hand, interposed the tree between his body and the noise of the attack.

Judith rose to her feet, but made no move to pick up the litter. "Isaac," she said. "You cannot stay there."

"You must carry the sick man to safety, and stay with him. I cannot see to do it. Now go, at once."

Judith and Raquel hoisted up the litter and carried it into a small thicket. They set Gilabert down behind the log and then crouched down beside him.

And suddenly the wood, the distant clearing, everywhere was filled with running men.

Naomi heard the sounds of trouble as she was shaking the rice in its pot. She listened, threw in a pinch more saffron, and gave the mixture a stir. The sounds continued. She stopped, frowning, and snapped at Ibrahim, "They're up to some nonsense up there. If it goes on too long, dinner will be ruined." She picked out a grain of rice from the spoon in her hand and chewed it thoughtfully. With an air of decision, she snatched up a heavy iron ladle. "Kick out the fire, Ibrahim, and lay a cloth on the rice. I will go to see what's happening." She picked up a long chopping knife in case it was real trouble, and stalked off. Never once did it occur to her to send Ibrahim instead.

Naomi collided with Yusuf on the edge of the wood. He put an urgent finger to his lips, grasped her by the wrist, and pulled her, crouching, in the direction of his master and mistress. Isaac was still by the tree, listening intently, and holding his staff at readiness in front of him. Yusuf left Naomi and crossed the narrow open space between himself and his master. Isaac whirled at the soft pad of Yusuf's feet on the forest floor and raised his staff. "It is I, lord," murmured Yusuf. "I told the captain, and on my way back, found Naomi. Where is the mistress?"

"Do you see a log on the forest floor?"

"Yes."

"They are behind it."

"They cannot be seen from here. We have been set upon by brigands, lord. At the moment they are still far from us, and if they stay where they are, you are safe by this tree. But if they come closer, you are a very visible target, lord. Stay with the mistress and the sick man, where you cannot be seen. I beg you, lord. The brigands know the wood and you do not.''

"Who is that?" said Isaac, turning his head sharply.

Yusuf whirled. "It is Andreu. He is approaching."

"Master Isaac," said Andreu in a soft and gentle voice. "If you would allow me the use of your staff, I could be of help to the hard-pressed officers. I have no weapon."

"Please, lord," said Yusuf. "Give it to him. Then hide and be safe."

Silently, Isaac held out his staff, and allowed Yusuf to lead him to safety.

At the same moment that Naomi was marching with her heavy ladle and her knife to settle the quarrel in the wood, the captain and his sergeant had just started running across the meadow toward the noise of fighting. Suddenly the sergeant grasped his captain's sleeve and pulled him down.

"Look, sir," he whispered quickly. "To your left. On the edge of the wood. Sun flashing off steel, Captain."

"How many?" he asked, for the sergeant was sharper-sighted than any other man in the guard.

"Six . . . ten . . . perhaps as many as a dozen."

"Moving in the direction of the baggage wagons," said the captain. "I see them now."

"They're likely to kill anyone they come against," said the sergeant.

"We must do what we can. Where are the others?"

"Still at their positions," said the sergeant. "Since they were not in pairs, I am afraid they have been over-whelmed."

"Then where are the grooms?" murmured the captain. "What's happened to those two fools?"

"I haven't seen them since we stopped, Captain," whispered the sergeant.

"We've no chance without them," said the captain.

"Shall I summon them, sir?" The captain nodded. "It will bring those villains over here," the sergeant warned.

"So be it."

"Jaume! Marc!" roared the sergeant, rising to his feet,

and holding out a hand to his superior officer.

There was no response from the grooms, but the men in the wood turned, saw two men alone, and started across the meadow, six of them.

The two officers drew their swords and looked at each other. The sergeant nodded at a straggler on the left; the captain gestured toward the man in front. Unless the men they were facing were hopelessly incompetent swordsmen, their best hope— and that a fairly slender one—lay in picking off one at a time, very quickly.

They were two highly trained, very good, and experienced warriors facing six disorganized and undisciplined-looking armed men. Even so, no matter how unprepossessing the outward appearance of their opponents, the odds on defeating them were rather poor. The fight was taking place on wide-open ground. Their attackers appeared to have six or eight more men lurking in the wood to take the place of any who fell. The two guards had no hope of reinforcements. The grooms were gone; the other guards were clearly under attack as well; in any case, one of them was under orders not to leave Sor Agnete under any circumstances, even these. Unless the attackers started falling over their own feet, they were well aware that their optimistic plan of disposing of them two at a time didn't have a chance.

The captain lunged at his man as soon as he was within striking distance, getting under his guard and inflicting a glancing blow. The resulting wound —no more than a scratch—might well have daunted a feebler opponent. This one was clearly more accomplished than he looked. The captain attacked again and met a defense worthy of his skill. His opponent, now warned, fought on in desperate earnest; any chance for a quick and easy kill was gone.

The straggler on the left was no match for the sergeant, but when he fell, bleeding profusely, two more were there to replace him. Then a new opponent lunged at the captain from the right as he was parrying an attack from the left. He was lost.

·  ·  ·

Yusuf had left Naomi with his mistress and scrambled up a tree to get a view of what was happening. When he counted up the figures he could see in the wood and the ones in the clearing, he dropped down out of the tree onto a patch of soft dead leaves and ran for the wagons. He had no clear aim in view except that he knew there were weapons stored in the baggage wagon, easy to reach if you knew exactly where they were, and he wanted to be armed.

He unknotted the rope holding down a protective canvas sheet and he tossed it aside. Underneath was a cache of swords; he pulled one out and tried it. It was too long and heavy in his hand. As a seven-year-old he had been adept at wielding the child's-size sword his father had given him, but this was no time to learn how to handle one of these. He put it back and pulled out a long, sturdy lance with a sharp point, tucked the canvas back where it belonged, and ran off.

Among the other noises of battle, the captain was only dimly aware of an approaching horse behind him. But in the instant before the thrust aimed at him hit, his new opponent twisted to one side, stumbled, and fell backward with a curse. The captain realized three things at that moment that came close to destroying his concentration. The head of a lance had penetrated his opponent's shoulder; someone else must be fighting on their side; most dangerous of all, they might have a chance. But in front of him the six had turned into eight or twelve men, and he brushed hope away before it could make him careless. He dealt a disabling blow on the arm to the man directly in front and turned toward three more who were swarming in to overwhelm him.

Behind him, Yusuf, still clutching the lance, was picking himself up off the ground where the force of his blow had pushed him. The black horse had backed away, and stood trembling, waiting for guidance. He yanked the lance head out of the shoulder it was embedded in and moved back.

Then from the left, a long heavy staff wielded with strength, if not much accuracy, tipped the sergeant's opponent off his feet and landed next on the shoulder of the man beside the captain. It was in the hands of Andreu, who had come up behind the brigands, and was laying into anyone, anywhere, as fast as he could. He was followed by Felip, who was grasping a small dagger in a low attacking position. Andreu dropped another man on the ground; Felip ducked in, snatched his sword, planted his own dagger in the stunned man's chest, and backed away from the scrum for a moment.

Over by the fires, the cook and his two assistants, occupied with dinner, were slow to realize what was going on. Certainly no one expected any help from them. Stripped to the waist, and wearing barely enough in the way of breeches and apron to fulfill the sketchiest requirements of modesty, they did not have the air of warriors. The kitchen lad was an undergrown youth of twelve; the assistant cook was a melancholy-looking man, who sang sad songs in a cracked, out-of-tune voice when he had had too much wine; the head cook was big and heavy and short-tempered.

"Fetch my staff, lad," said the cook. "I think I'll have a look at what's going on over there."

"And mine," said his assistant laconically. The boy ran off.

He returned dragging two long, heavy staffs.

"Keep an eye on the fire, and don't let the rice stick."

The two cooks picked up the heavy staffs as if they were pieces of straw and walked toward the edge of the woods as lightly and as silently as a pair of dancers. A close look at them revealed the reason for these two phenomena. Their thighs bulged with muscle; they had arms and shoulders a wrestler would envy. Day in and day out, they wrestled, not men, but heavy iron pots, and sacks of flour, and hogsheads of wine and oil. Either one of them could carry a whole sheep with as much ease as if it were a kitten, or toss a hundredweight of rice like a child's ball. They erupted onto the field of battle noiselessly, looking completely unmoved.

• • •

The two men with the long knives who had made the attempt on the nuns may well have mistaken their orders, for they had swooped down and seized, not the rich and powerful Abbess, or the disputed, and therefore valuable, Sor Agnete, but Sor Marta. Startled by the shriek of the nuns' priest, they had let go of her, turned to fight, and met a whirlwind of opposition. The guard dealt expertly with one of them; he slashed his forearm, disarming him, stepped on his fallen dagger, and shoved him off his feet before turning to dispose of the threat of the other. It wasn't necessary. The second attacker had lost his dagger and was being clubbed with hard, well-placed blows from a thick and heavy chunk of wood wielded by the priest. The last blow landed square on his wrist, and sent him reeling backward.

Then out of the corner of his eye the guard saw Sor Agnete scrambling up the hill toward freedom. By now the second attacker was holding his wrist and screaming in pain. The guard kicked the man on the ground to encourage him to stay where he was, handed the priest his own dagger, and said, "Get that other knife and hold them here."

He raced up the hill after the erring nun. He was a fit young man. She was much hampered by her habit and soon winded. He caught her easily and returned her to the furious Abbess and the indignant Sor Marta.

The bleeding man on the ground had crept away. The guard shrugged, commended the nuns and the man with the broken wrist to the care of the nuns' priest, and headed back—in spite of orders—to help the others.

By the time he arrived two guards, two musicians, a boy, and two enraged cooks, having among them four swords, a lance, and two staffs, had achieved the rout of more than a dozen armed bandits. When the cooks had arrived, the guards, Andreu, and Felip were surrounded. The captain had sustained a wound on the arm that was bleeding freely, and Felip had suffered a cut just above the boot and another near his wrist. Andreu had traded Isaac's staff for one of the attacker's swords, which had snapped in his hand, and was standing, disarmed, trapped in the thick of the fight.

The captain, wounded and breathless, had stumbled and dropped his guard; his attacker lunged with a stroke that could not fail. Yusuf had tried to land another telling blow with his lance; it had missed its target, but caused the attacker to shift his line of sight by a hairsbreadth and lose his sense of where he was. The captain had ducked; his opponent's powerful stroke had penetrated the spring air. Turning in a fury to meet this new threat, he had seen only a boy sprawled on the ground.

At the same time someone had raised his sword and headed for the helpless Andreu.

The cook approached with a bellow, and the first blow of his staff hit the back of the head of a man who was about to run Andreu through. He dropped like a stone to the ground. The second blow hit someone else's arm, and the sound of the bone cracking could be heard above the general tumult.

His assistant, a methodical man, went for legs. His first blow smashed the knee of the man who was heading back to the captain, leaving him on the grass, screaming. His second blow hit him on the head, cutting short his screams. His third hit a shinbone, and another swordsman landed on the ground. The tide had turned, and suddenly the balance was on the side of the travelers. Very soon, there were only four attackers left still fighting. Then, as if they were one, those who could still run scrambled away and fled back up the hills. The third guard loped after them, caught two, and let the others go. The rest of the exhausted defenders turned to their wounded.

Andreu looked around, somewhat dazed, dropped his broken sword, and picked up Isaac's staff. "With all my heart, good sir," he said to the head cook, "I thank you for my life. I would have been loath to lose it to such a bunch of ruffians."

"We would have no more of your merry songs if they had killed you, sir," said the cook. "We couldn't have that happen."

•    •    •

By common consent the defenders moved away from the battlefield and headed for the wagons and the cooking fires, collecting the rest of the party along the way. Behind the log, Isaac's patient, a persuasive witness to the efficacy of his potions, slept on. Willing hands picked up the litter and carried it back to its cool place under the oak.

Raquel and Judith bathed and bandaged the hurts of the wounded. The cook silently broached a cask of the Bishop's best wine, and the entire party erupted with the pent-up elation of victory. For not only were there individual triumphs to recall, but there was an audience—the women, the physician, the boys who had been kept away from the conflict—to hear, again and again, of the valor of the guards, the bravery of Andreu, the unexpected swordsmanship of Felip, the amazing ability of Yusuf, and the massive, wonderful performance of the cooks.

Naomi and Ibrahim carried their cooking pots over, and in spite of the early hour they all discovered that they were famished. They ate together, with a fine disregard for manners, propriety, or anything else. Even though the rice was a little overcooked, never had there been a meal so delicious. Never had triumph tasted so sweet.

Only the guards were absent. They found their two fellows, one stunned, the other wounded in the first rush of attack. As soon as their wounds had been bound up, those who could went back to the battlefield. Five men lay on the ground, alive but helpless; two were firmly tied to trees.

"What do we do with them?" said Enrique, the youngest of the guards, looking at the wounded opponents.

Three of them, who had sustained murderous blows to the head from the cooks' staffs, were unconscious and likely to remain so. Two with broken legs lay cursing or moaning on the ground. The rest of the opposition wounded had crept away during the fighting.

"Those three will die anyway. Hang the rest," said the captain.

"I'm not sure we have that much rope," said the sergeant pragmatically. "Not that we can spare, I mean. We weren't expecting to have to hang four men.''

"Then use your knife. My right arm is not much good at the moment,'' said the captain, "or I wouldn't leave it all to you.''

"Don't bother about that,'' said the sergeant. "The two of us will finish them off.''

"Don't we want to know why they attacked us, sir?'' asked Enrique again.

"It seems pretty clear to me,'' said the captain. "You,'' he said, nudging one of them with his foot. "Why did you attack us?''

"We was told to,'' he said. "Why do you think? Lots of rich stuff in those wagons.''

"That's what I thought,'' said the captain.

"And someone wanted the big nun,'' he added helpfully.

"Which one is the big one?'' asked the sergeant.

They considered this. Tall, thin Elicsenda? Plump Marta? Broad-shouldered Agnete? None of them was small.

"Who wanted her?'' asked the captain.

"Don't know. Not my business. Whoever he was had an agreement with Mario. He got paid, we got what was in the wagons. They never said there'd be an army guarding it.''

"Doesn't matter,'' said the captain. "That's good enough. Hurry up,'' he said to the other two, "before they get too drunk down there to travel the rest of the way.''

"Shall I let that one go?'' asked the sergeant, pointing at the helpful one.

"If you like,'' said the captain. "He won't get very far anyway.''

"Do you want me to search for the grooms, sir?'' asked the sergeant, once he had cleaned and sheathed his dagger.

"Where do you expect to find them?'' countered the captain. He was staring at the meadow, where the mules and horses mingled together in a comradely fashion.

The sergeant shook his head. "I don't. Either they're dead or they were paid off.''

"Of course," said the captain impatiently. "And we have no time to waste."

"I'm curious," said the sergeant. "I'd rather find out they were greedy than careless enough to let their throats be cut," he added. "I trained them. Not that I expect to find their bodies, Captain. Their horses aren't in the field. But I believe His Excellency would want us to take a turn around the meadow before we leave. Just to check."

"I believe he would," said the captain.

"Why would they bribe the grooms, sir?" asked young Enrique.

"They weren't grooms, the treacherous bastards," said the sergeant. "They were guards. Ours. Armed, trained, mounted. His Excellency thought it would be a good idea to have one or two extra men who weren't in colors on an expedition like this. He's a cautious man. And a good tactician. But still—it's not easy to make allowance for treason."

In the end the halt at the grove cost them close to three hours, making it longer than the captain's gloomiest predictions. Between too much wine and a great deal of elation, the process of eating, clearing up, repacking, and getting on their way took a long, long time. The sergeant glanced up at the sky, where a few clouds blew over the bright noonday sun, and shook his head. "I doubt we have a chance, sir," he murmured.

The captain nodded. "We will journey until the sun is just above the hills. If we are not within sight of Barcelona, someone will have to ride ahead to look for accommodation."

The rest of the group started out on a high, triumphal note, and suffered the fate of all things that begin too well. By the time the road had taken them down to the plain, the wine had worn off, and with it, the elation and the numbness it had brought. All of the combatants in the battle except for the cooks bore some traces of it—cuts, some deep, some superficial, scrapes, bruises—and the ferocious encounter had left their bodies aching. Ahead of them there was only a never-ending flat road that wound its way toward Barcelona, crossed at intervals by rivers, punctuated by villages that slept in the noonday heat.

The sun glowered down at them, and their pace slowed. Once more they halted where there was water, and some shade, more out of mercy for the beasts than for the people. The cooks handed out the cold meat and bread and cheese from the monastery kitchens. Gilabert dozed uneasily, and muttered in his sleep, apparently unaware of the heat or the flies or the jolting of the cart. Judith and Naomi took turns in fanning him, and sponging cool water over his brow.

They set out again, grouped in what was gradually becoming their habitual formation. The wagon with the sick man went first, to spare him the dust raised by the rest of the train. Raquel, her father, and Yusuf rode beside it, and the musicians walked next to it on the other side. The cook and his helpers strode along between the wagons, keeping one eye on the supplies and the other on the rest of the servants; all the others moved from position to position, as mood and conditions changed.

The sun began to redden as it moved down toward the looming hills ahead to their right. "How far is it to the city?" asked the kitchen lad apprehensively.

"Long way yet," said the assistant cook.

"We'll never make it tonight," said the nuns' priest. Loneliness and the desire for conversation had led him to attach himself to the kitchen party. He had dismounted from his mule and was leading her, finding it easier to control the stubborn creature from the ground than from the saddle.

"What will we do?" asked the kitchen lad, his voice quivering with alarm.

"Cheer up," said Andreu. "We can sleep in a field. We've done it often, Felip and I, haven't we?"

"Certainly," said Felip gravely. "Very pleasant it is, too, unless it rains. Or the lions come down from the woods."

"Lions?" said the kitchen lad.

"Just small ones," said Felip. "Nothing to worry about."

"There are inns," said the nuns' priest, looking warily from one to the other of the young men.

"Filled with cutthroats," said Andreu. "Unless it rains, I prefer the field and the wild beasts to the inns on this road."

"Don't tease the lad," said Raquel sharply.

The two musicians bowed, grinned, and began to play a lively tune. A plume of dust appeared on the road ahead, and out of it rode the sergeant.

The captain listened to him and called a halt. "If you look ahead," he said, "you will see the top of the mountain. That is Barcelona. We cannot reach it tonight, but there are two inns in the village not two miles farther on that can accommodate us all. We shall be in Barcelona in time for our dinners tomorrow. Let us proceed," he added, "with all possible haste." He sounded desperately weary.

He moved his horse over to the wagon with the wounded man. "Physician, how is your patient?"

"He is no worse," said Isaac. "And that speaks well for his recovery. I am more concerned about you, Captain. You should be in this wagon as well, resting."

"I will have time to rest tomorrow," he replied, and continued on his round of the company.

# PART TWO

# ONE

### Barcelona

Berenguer de Cruilles and his two priests arrived at the Bishop's palace early in the afternoon, hot from the sun and their exertions, and dirty from travel. They were ushered into the study of Francesc Ruffach, canon vicar of Barcelona. As always, the Bishop, Miquel de Riçoma, was in Avignon on permanent leave of absence from his diocese.

Ruffach came to meet them. "Your Excellency. This is a most unexpected pleasure. I am delighted," he said with more politeness than truth. "Are you on your way to Tarragona with a retinue? We must—"

"My dear Ruffach, don't be disconcerted," said Berenguer. "We are traveling to the council, but there is no great retinue waiting out in the street. Not yet. We three rode ahead, leaving the others to arrive when they will. I do not expect to see them before nightfall."

Ruffach rang a small bell on his desk. "As soon as you have had a chance to wash away the dust of travel, Your Excellency, and repose yourselves, we would be delighted to have you join us for a simple dinner."

"First Bernat must pen a brief letter to His Majesty,"

said Berenguer, "and then we will make ourselves fit to dine."

"Your Excellency?" asked Bernat.

"Inform His Majesty of our arrival, and beg leave on my part to wait upon him tomorrow."

"Why wait until tomorrow, Your Excellency?" asked Francesc Monterranes. "Time is very short. He might have a few moments for you this evening."

"Because when I have an audience with His Majesty, I want to be able to assure him that Sor Agnete is safely stowed away at Sant Pere de les Puelles."

Don Pedro of Aragon, Count of Barcelona and King, listened to Berenguer's request and nodded to his secretary. "Tell His Excellency we will see him tomorrow—no. Let him wait. Saturday at midday. And have him bring our ward, the boy Yusuf, if he travels with him."

"The Bishop of Girona is a wise and loyal friend," remarked Doña Eleanor, his queen, after the doors had closed behind the secretary. "And subject."

"Who can be slow to obey when the mood takes him," said Don Pedro. "It is almost a year since we ordered him to deliver that nun from the convent of Sant Daniel. It has taken him until now. If she is with him. That is not how a loyal subject behaves."

"My poor papa, who did not have your skill in such matters," said Doña Eleanor, "often said that only a fool trusts a man with a long history of wrongdoing, but a wise man also mistrusts a man who is too virtuous. The first betrays you for profit, and the second to prove his righteousness. Take Don Vidal de Blanes. Such an admirable man," she added quickly. "And trustworthy. He will always insist—against the entire world, if need be—that the right thing be done, no matter what the consequences."

"He is a man of unquestioned virtue and high principles," said Don Pedro, somewhat sardonically.

"I have observed that Berenguer prefers to seek compromise to maintain peace in his diocese, and that is often in Your Majesty's best interests. Don Vidal would create a lasting peace between two quarreling neighbors by hanging both of them.''

"Where did that political wisdom come from?'' said Don Pedro, laughing.

"My papa's court in Palermo was an excellent school, Your Majesty. As filled with plots and intrigues as anyone could wish for. I learned early how to tell the difference between the vulture and the songbird.''

"Don Vidal was a sop to throw to His Holiness the Pope,'' said the King. "As well as a reminder to Don Berenguer to mend his manners.''

"And His Holiness is no easier to deal with for all the sops he has been thrown.''

"But Don Vidal's unbending virtue will also refuse to bow to Avignon, especially in political matters. And we trust that we will not be out of the country long enough for it to come to harm.''

"As long as I am with Your Majesty, it matters not how long we are at sea,'' murmured the Queen, glancing at him from under downcast eyes.

He smiled indulgently at her bowed head. "But you are right about Berenguer de Cruilles,'' he continued, in a more expansive mood. "We shall exert a little pressure on the Archbishop of Tarragona, and rescue the good Bishop of Girona from his present uncomfortable position.''

"Don Sancho is a reasonable man, is he not, Your Majesty?''

"For an archbishop.''

Bernat brought His Majesty's response to Berenguer. "Well, man,'' said the Bishop impatiently. "Will he see me? Or was this whole diversion a great waste of time and effort?''

"Surely not a waste,'' said Francesc Monterranes. "We may have saved a young man's life.''

"Possibly,'' said Berenguer. "But what does His Majesty say?''

"That he will be pleased to receive you at midday on Saturday.''

"Saturday," said Berenguer. "I had hoped for tomorrow, and feared Sunday evening. He wishes merely to give me time to think, rather than to inconvenience me entirely."

"Surely His Majesty did not concern himself with such small details as our travel plans . . ." said Bernat.

"His Majesty always concerns himself with details, Bernat. That is why he has been a successful—indeed—a great sovereign lord."

Well before the sun reached its height the next day, the rest of the travelers, dirty, disheveled, and ill-tempered, straggled into Barcelona. They had spent the previous night in rooms that were small, filthy, and crowded; their conversation on the road into the city never strayed beyond the question of which inn was worse, and which group had slept the least. The captain and his officers, who had not slept at all, rode in weary aching silence.

The nuns left first. They were greeted with cordiality and swept inside the gates of Sant Pere de les Puelles, in the relative peace and calm of the suburbs. The rest of the party wearily retraced its steps to the highway and headed for the city.

Once inside the gates of Barcelona, Felip and Andreu murmured good-bye to the captain and melted into the crowd. Isaac, his family, and servants, along with the sick man, were brought to the east gate of the *Call,* where two grooms were assigned to bear Gilabert to the house of Mordecai and his wife. The captain then turned his depleted troop and led them up the road toward the cathedral.

The house of Mordecai ben Issach was commodious, and his larder and wine cellar were well stocked. He and his cheerful wife were hospitable and generous, and viewed the arrival of five unexpected guests—including one who appeared to be near death—with servants, as an unexpected pleasure. Even so, the visit did not have the air of starting well. The house was large but crowded. Judith was flustered; Yusuf morose; Raquel was ill-tempered and worried.

"Papa," she said, as soon as she could get his attention without appearing rude, "do you find Gilabert much worse?"

"No, my child, I do not. Do you?"

"No, Papa," she said, in a puzzled voice. "But I could not help but hear when you told that priest you had no great hopes that he would survive this coming night." For although she had not noticed a change, she always deferred to her father's extraordinary ability to detect improvement or deterioration in a patient.

"I am not surprised you heard. I spoke very loudly. It is sometimes better to warn friends to expect the worst; then, when the patient recovers, they are that much happier," said her father.

"I would not have thought the priest cared a fig for Gilabert's chances of recovering," said his daughter.

"Probably not. But I do, and I feel that he may be safer if the word spreads abroad that he is beyond help."

"You mean if whoever tried to kill him believes that, Papa." She paused to consider his words in this new light. "I will go and see what I can do to make him comfortable. Mama is too tired."

"Yes. Let your mother enjoy the company of another woman for a while," said her father. "And I will wash the dust of travel from me. Where is Yusuf?"

"Here, lord," he said, in a subdued voice.

"It is time you washed and ate something," said the physician. "Then we will have work to do."

Mordecai's house was on the principal street of the Jewish Quarter, an avenue wide enough for the very largest carts to pass with ease. Yusuf opened the door and stepped into a crowd of housewives examining fish and poultry, prodding vegetables, and scolding unruly children. Servants and poorer women with no one to help them were fighting through the throng carrying heavy jugs of water from the nearby fountain. Everyone was out, for whether you were rich or poor, it was Friday, and there was a great deal to do before sundown brought the start of the Sabbath. He edged his way through them all, turned into a quieter street, then onto a busier one, and found the west gate of the *Call*.

The street outside the *Call* was lined with tall houses and thriving businesses, and was almost as noisy and crowded as the streets inside. It was also, he realized suddenly, completely unfamiliar. Before leaving the house, he had assured his master that his travels had taken him through Barcelona, and he knew it well; but he recognized nothing here. The city must be larger than he thought, and the section he had stayed in two years before, as a homeless waif, just a small portion of it.

You have a tongue in your head, he told himself. Anyone around here will know where the Bishop's palace is. He crossed the street and headed for a respectable-looking olive merchant who was dragging barrels and baskets into his shop in anticipation of the dinner hour. "Excuse me, sir," he said. "Can you tell me where the palace of the Bishop is?"

"Over there," said the preoccupied merchant, with a wave of his hand. Then he looked up from his wares for the first time and seemed to be struck by something. "What would you want a bishop for?" he asked speculatively. "Or did you just come into town that you can't find the cathedral?" And suddenly his hand snaked out and he grabbed him by the arm.

"Let me go!" Yusuf cried.

"I could use a boy like you," he said. "Masterless, are you? Or runaway?"

He shook himself desperately, pushing against the olive merchant. "Let me go!" he repeated.

"You jest, lad," said the merchant.

"Here, now, Esteve," said a voice from the next shop. "What are you doing with that lad? He's not yours."

"Yes, he is," said the merchant. "I just bought him."

"Now? While you were dragging your olives in?"

His attention diverted by the flank attack, the olive merchant's grip slackened. Yusuf didn't wait for the outcome of the discussion. He ducked and broke away, running for the street ahead, where the huge mass of the cathedral loomed.

Panting for breath, more from fright than exertion, this time he asked a young woman dragging two small, crying children home to their dinners.

She looked at him as if he were mad. "Right there, boy," she said. "Where else would it be?" She gave the larger, noisier child a shake, and plowed grimly on.

It was also the dinner hour at the episcopal palace. The Bishop could not be disturbed. Yusuf insisted. The porter narrowed his eyes stubbornly.

"I bear a very important message to His Excellency from His Excellency's personal physician, porter. His Excellency will be annoyed when he discovers that a porter who knows nothing of His Excellency's concerns has prevented him from receiving the message."

Whether it was his elaborate speech, or the call of the porter's own dinner that led the man to back down, is not recorded, but when Berenguer walked slowly by in company with Francesc Ruffach, the canon vicar of Barcelona, on their way to the great hall to dine, Yusuf was permitted to seek the Bishop and deliver his message.

"I am delighted to see you, young Yusuf," said the Bishop. "Have you dined?"

"Not exactly, Your Excellency," said Yusuf.

"Then you may join us, may he not, Ruffach? And you may deliver your message then. Unless it is a great crisis that requires my immediate attention."

"Oh no, Your Excellency," said Yusuf, and soon found himself seated at the Bishop's side in the spacious hall.

Eighteen men were gathered in the great hall of the Bishop's palace in Barcelona for dinner the afternoon of the travelers' arrival. Most of them—priests attached in one capacity or another to the cathedral—would have been there anyway. In addition to Yusuf and the four clerics from the party from Girona—the Bishop, his secretary, his confessor, and the nuns' priest—there were three laymen: an affable landowner named Gonsalvo de Marca and two shrewd merchants who were part of the city's Council of a Hundred.

"Why are they here?" asked Bernat in a low voice.

"According to Father Bonanat," murmured Francesc Monterranes, nodding at the priest who sat across the board from them, "the councilors have urgent affairs to discuss with the canon vicar. I know nothing about that gentleman, not even why left his cows and pigs to visit the city," he added, indicating Gonsalvo de Marca. "Only that he is rich, and that his long-dead great-uncle was a lord of some importance."

It was a curiously muted meal. Most of the travelers were weary, and their tempers were wearing thin. The countryman, Don Gonsalvo, had launched into a long and rambling explanation of the causes of discontent amongst the peasantry that would have lulled his most ardent supporter into sleep. At last he drained his cup, attempted to find his way back into his argument, and failed. After a moment of embarrassed silence, Francesc Monterranes, in an effort to revive the lagging conversation, turned to the Bishop. "Has Your Excellency heard further news of our unfortunate young Gilabert? He was in a perilous state when we left yesterday morning, I believe." He spoke loud enough to drown out any further attempts at conversation from Don Gonsalvo.

"Has another misfortune befallen your retinue on the journey?" asked the canon vicar hastily. "In addition to the attack?"

"Not to one of us," said Berenguer. "But we came across a young gentleman by the side of the road. He had been attacked by thieves, it seems, and left for dead. I have heard nothing new of him since yesterday. Is he better than he was, Yusuf?"

His guest shook his head, and said quietly that there had been no noticeable improvement in his condition.

There was a murmur of sympathy, mingled with confused looks from those who had no idea what anyone was talking about. Then one of the cathedral canons turned his attention from a dish of braised mutton in front of him. "They are everywhere. It seems unfortunate that the roads into the city are so badly patrolled that bandits from the hills feel free to attack honest Christian folk."

"Travel is always hazardous. You, sir," said Gonsalvo to Berenguer, "will have traveled much, and are aware of that. When I left my *finca,* I took care to bring three stout lads with me, along with my servants."

"You would not expect a group as large as ours to be set upon by armed ruffians," said Francesc defensively.

"I am happy to say," said Berenguer, "that those in my retinue, from this lad here to the guards—and that includes my cook—defended themselves bravely and skillfully. And what was *your* purpose in making this hazardous journey, sir?" asked the Bishop, turning to Gonsalvo without the faintest glimmer of a smile.

"The law, Your Excellency," he said, beaming with pleased assurance. "When one is in pursuit of justice, one cannot relax one's vigilance for a moment. Have you not found that to be so, sir?" he said, to one of the merchants, who had been deeply engaged in a quiet conversation with the canon vicar.

The merchant gave him a startled look. "Indeed, sir," he said politely, and returned to his discussion, having no idea to what he had agreed.

"You have a case in law before the courts?" asked Bernat.

Gonsalvo paused before answering. "In a manner of speaking," he said. "A small case, of little consequence, that touches upon me."

"I wonder you troubled to come so far to pursue it, then," said the Bishop.

"It was convenient for other reasons," said Gonsalvo with a wink at Bernat. "One has family, and friends, and connections," he added in confidential tones. "In my case, a daughter who is reaching marriageable age." He nodded in the direction of the canon vicar. "I took the opportunity to seek an audience with the canon vicar to hear if any news had arrived concerning my case."

"Ah," said Berenguer. "Then this is an episcopal court your case is being heard in?"

"I speak carelessly, Your Excellency. It is not my case," said Gonsalvo. "It involves a neighbor whose land is within the diocese of Barcelona. A small portion of my land watered by a certain stream might be affected in the dispute."

"And is the neighbor here to support his cause?" asked Bernat.

"Not that I have heard," said Gonsalvo. "But the case was not being heard in Barcelona. It has been taken to the papal court."

"I am afraid," said Francesc Ruffach, the canon vicar for Barcelona, "that we have received no word from Avignon on that case. Not as yet." He spoke coldly, as if he had had enough of Don Gonsalvo's requests. Or perhaps of Don Gonsalvo.

"Do not concern yourself, Father," said Gonsalvo. "Word has spread that the papers are on their way; a wise man always prepares himself for judgment, especially if he thinks it might be an adverse one."

Berenguer rose. "My dear Ruffach," he said to the canon vicar, "as pleasant as this has been, I must beg you to excuse me. I will take His Majesty's ward for a stroll through your orchard since we have news to exchange. Then if you can give me a half hour alone, there are many issues that concern us both on which I would like your thoughts." Francesc Ruffach rose and escorted the Bishop of Girona and Yusuf from the hall.

"But what do I tell His Majesty if he asks me to stay at court?" asked Yusuf in a troubled voice. "I have thought of little else since we left Girona, Your Excellency, and it causes me great grief. My master is blind and helpless. I cannot leave him. And he has much to teach me."

"You are important to your master, Yusuf, but he is not as helpless as you may think. Should you decide not to leave him, however, you will find that His Majesty understands affection and loyalty as well as any common man," said Berenguer. "He may think you foolish, but he will not be offended. Certainly Her Majesty will not be offended, and she has more power over his thoughts in these days than any of his counselors do."

"Thank you, Your Excellency."

"I see Ruffach heading directly for me," said Berenguer. "Can you wait awhile? After I discuss a few matters with the canon vicar, I will know what message to return to my good master Isaac."

"Certainly, Your Excellency. I shall await your return near the door."

Moving as quietly as always, Yusuf went back to the great dining hall. He found himself a perch in a deep window embrasure, where the pieces of glass filling in the window were so expertly made and carefully fitted together that not only did they prevent the wind from entering, but they allowed light to pour in. He could see the garden outside almost as clearly as if there were nothing there. Yusuf was impressed. Even Master Mordecai—who was wealthy enough to have glass beakers and wine jugs—had only one glass window, and this hall was filled with them.

Two men lingered over the board in the hall, with their backs to him, deep in conversation. Bored, the boy gave them some of his wandering attention. The servants were gradually clearing the long table and tidying away the remains of the sumptuous meal. As they finished their tasks and drifted away, the voices of the two men became clearer and harder to ignore. He listened, heard a few words, and looked curiously to see who they were. They were not priests. One was Don Gonsalvo, for no one else at dinner had worn a tunic cut in that particular manner; the other was younger and more fashionable looking. He had not dined at the palace, but he looked vaguely familiar in a way that Yusuf could not place.

Then the word "Gilabert" jumped out at him; he began to listen in earnest. "But that is all I know about his condition," said Gonsalvo.

The other man's reply was too faint for Yusuf to hear.

"And what happened to the money I paid Norbert?" asked Gonsalvo.

The younger man stood up. "I know nothing of that," he said. "I'm sorry." He smiled, patted Gonsalvo's shoulder consolingly, and bent over to murmur something further in his ear.

Gonsalvo shook his head. As he watched the younger man leave, he seemed to be staring straight at Yusuf in his window seat, but with eyes as blank and unseeing as a statue's. He rose, stood where he was for a few moments, and then walked quickly from the room.

"His Excellency asked me to tell you that he never felt better. His Majesty has consented to see him tomorrow, and has asked him to bring me."

Since this was obviously a question, Isaac answered it. "Of course, you may go. You must go, since His Majesty wishes it. What else?"

"He does not need you as a physician, but he would like to have some conversation with you if you can see him tomorrow morning."

"Then we shall go. You found the Bishop's palace without difficulty?"

"Yes, lord," said Yusuf in a low voice.

"What happened?" he asked, his ear quick to notice a hesitation.

"I was caught by an olive merchant. He took me for a Muslim slave," he said, with great bitterness. "Although I am of better birth than he is."

"I think while we are here, it would be best if you did not leave Mordecai's house alone," said Isaac.

"I have been living in safety for so long that I thought I was too old to be the prey of greedy merchants," he replied. "I am ashamed."

"Forget your shame, Yusuf, but be wary of too much confidence," said Isaac. "We are not as safe here where we are not known."

# TWO

## The Sabbath

The long and ceremonious Sabbath meal seemed to last forever. Raquel, feeling weary and isolated, sat between competing conversations. Her mother and Mordecai's young wife were entirely absorbed in the couple's children, two boys and a girl, who alternately giggled and pushed each other, and then retreated, solemn-eyed with shyness, when the strangers at the table noticed them. Isaac chatted quietly with his fellow physician for the entire evening on medicine, and politics, and the grim situation for Jews in Paris and other Frankish-speaking cities.

As soon as she could, Raquel went up the stairs to the airy chamber where Mordecai's wife had placed Gilabert. "How is he, Naomi?" she asked.

"Sleeping," whispered Naomi. "He drank some broth, and ate a morsel of bread, and then fell asleep. His fever is not as great now, I think."

Raquel laid her hand on his brow and nodded.

Gilabert opened his eyes. "Hola, angel," he said. "What is this place?"

"A chamber in the house of Mordecai the physician," said Raquel.

"You do not leave me here, do you? When you travel to Tarragona?"

"I don't think so," said Raquel doubtfully. "But I will ask Papa."

"I am sure they have no angels in the house of Mordecai," he said, and fell asleep again.

Isaac ran his fingers over the Bishop's knee without eliciting a single complaint. "The heat and swelling in the joint have gone at last, Your Excellency," said his physician. "Now we must see how to keep them from returning."

"All in good time, Master Isaac. Let us speak of pleasanter things. His Majesty wishes to see his ward today."

"His Majesty is always gracious," said Isaac. "Yusuf is waiting on the steps. I shall tell him to stay and accompany you to the palace."

"But he is needed to go home with you, Master Isaac. He can join me at the royal palace when he is able."

"I am reluctant to send him out into the city alone," said Isaac. "He is proving to be a temptation to those who trade in slaves."

"Then you must wait for us here. Come with me to the orchard," said Berenguer. "It is a pleasant spot to pass the time. I will send Francesc and Bernat down to amuse you with tales of my transgressions."

"Your Excellency is most gracious," said Isaac.

"Come, Master Isaac, let us walk down together. I have written a letter to my friend concerning Friar Norbert. I trust he will have information for us."

"When do you expect a reply?"

"Not until we return to Girona. If he is quick."

"And then, I trust, Your Excellency will sleep soundly."

The orchard was cool and pleasant in spite of the heat of the morning. Someone brought him a cool drink of mint and lemon, and he waited in the dappled shade with light breezes playing about his face. Travel and the unfamiliar noises in Mordecai's household had disoriented him. They confused his hearing and, with it, his other senses. He hoped the good Fathers would not hurry. He wanted time to reflect and to enjoy the peace.

Then he heard footfalls on the steps from the palace. He was to be interrupted sooner than he had expected, and sighed with resignation. "Let us go out here and conduct our business in peace," said a voice he did not know. "You travel to Tarragona?" It was not an unpleasant voice, but it made the physician shiver involuntarily.

"I do, señor," said another. "I have a full dispatch bag to take to the Archbishop before the conference starts."

"This will not weigh heavily on your horse's back," said the first man. "Can you carry a message for me? I would be very grateful."

"What sort of message, señor?"

"At the tavern on the street of the Scriveners, ask for my friends Benvenist and Miró. Tell them that they are to make the agreed-upon preparations for my return. If you can remember that, I have here half your fee; the other half will come from my friends."

"I can remember that, señor. I know the tavern. I am to ask for Miró and Benvenist, and tell them to make the agreed-upon preparations for your return. Do they need your name, señor?"

"You remember well. You may tell them it is a message from their young master."

"It is my office to remember, señor."

Isaac heard the clinking of a purse that contained a substantial number of coins, and the footsteps of the two men disappeared into the palace. He shook his head. It was too elaborate and expensive a manner in which to warn servants that a master was returning. That young man with the menacing voice—and he sounded young—had poisoned the spring air.

"Master Isaac, we apologize for the delay," said the familiar voice of the Bishop's secretary. "I hope time has not been passing too slowly."

"Not at all, Father Bernat. I have been most interested out here. The orchard has many birds singing strange songs in it."

• • •

Berenguer followed a lackey up the staircase leading to His Majesty's private apartments. Don Pedro, Count of Barcelona and King of Aragon, had spent the morning with his secretary and his treasurer, Bernat d'Olzinelles. The men were hard at work at a table covered with documents, attended only by a pair of guards. Berenguer glanced rapidly at his monarch's face, trying to assess exactly how annoyed with him Don Pedro was.

"Your Majesty," he said, bowing. "I am most grateful to have been granted this audience."

"We are always pleased to see you, Don Berenguer," said Don Pedro. A slight wave of his hand indicated that the Bishop should sit. Someone glided in and unobtrusively supplied him with wine and water, and small bowls of almonds and spiced olives.

"You are in Barcelona to deliver us a letter, Don Berenguer?" added the King in tones of mild curiosity. "A strange errand for a bishop."

"It is, Your Majesty," said Berenguer. "But the letter came into my possession under such singular circumstances that I could not decide whether it was of great consequence or not. Since to see Your Majesty is always a source of comfort and pleasure, I seized upon the excuse to bring it myself."

"And what were these singular circumstances?"

"The letter was discovered by a small child on the body of a murdered Franciscan. One whom no one knows," he said. "That, in my diocese, is singular enough."

"We would see this missive."

"Certainly, Your Majesty."

Don Pedro's secretary stepped forward, took the letter from the Bishop, and placed it in front of the King.

Don Pedro turned it over and looked up. "It speaks most eloquently of its recent history."

"It does, Your Majesty," said Berenguer.

"Read it to us," he said to the secretary, closing his eyes and leaning back in his chair.

"The writer has a fine rhetorical style," said Berenguer,
after the secretary had finished. "But I found the letter un-
informative."

"What is the decision you have long awaited, Don Berenguer?" asked the King, his eyes still shut, as if closing
out the world.

"I cannot think what it might be, Your Majesty."

"And Rodrigue de Lancia?" asked Don Pedro.

"A kinsman of Huguet de Lancia Talatarn, Your Majesty," said the secretary. "He was in Avignon to keep an
eye on the protest from Ancona to the Pope. Shipping."

"Yes, indeed. Piracy. And so that decision has gone
astray as well."

"There was no friar by the name of Norbert connected
with that case," murmured the secretary.

"And you do not know this Norbert?" said Olzinelles,
the treasurer.

"I don't believe so," said Berenguer to Olzinelles. "Nor
do I know what he has done, although it would seem that
he has killed a man."

"He must be hot-tempered for a friar, Don Berenguer,"
observed the treasurer. "It is a pity that he does not make
clear in what way Your Majesty's document could affect
the preparations for war."

"But we know that decision, do we not?"

"Not in its final form, Your Majesty," said Olzinelles.
"Where are the documents he speaks of? Not with the
child, one would hope."

"With those who shed his blood," said Berenguer. "Or
so it would seem."

Don Pedro opened his eyes again and looked sharply
over at the Bishop. "We will consider this letter further,"
he said briskly. "We have a council meeting that we must
attend, my noble friend," he added. "We seek your opinion
on a matter to be discussed."

"I am ever at Your Majesty's disposition."

"How is our young ward, the Moorish boy, Yusuf?"
asked Don Pedro as they walked slowly toward the small
council chamber.

"He is very well, Your Majesty, growing in wisdom and learning, as well as in body. He is waiting below for Your Majesty."

"Send for him," he murmured, and one of the retainers who were everywhere and yet not noticeable disappeared to do his bidding.

Five or six councillors sat at the large table, also waiting for the arrival of Don Pedro.

"Don Berenguer will join us for part of the meeting," said His Majesty. "We spoke earlier of a fresh pair of ears and eyes in Tarragona. Don Berenguer will be there in a few days. Show him the latest report."

And Olzinelles, the treasurer, sat down, looked through the documents in front of him, and pushed a single page across the table.

It described in the plainest language the beating of a certain Jewish merchant, and the burning of his premises, which were located on the farthest edge of the Jewish Quarter of Tarragona. The merchant died, as did two of his assistants, a slave, and a small child. Berenguer looked up when he had finished.

"This is the latest report from Tarragona," said Olzinelles. "It is possible that the loss of life was not intentional. The merchant's apprentice was unpacking a new shipment of goods at the time. The shop was littered with dry straw."

"But that does not excuse the attack," said Berenguer.

"You will comprehend, Your Excellency," said Olzinelles, "how disastrous an outbreak like this can be while we are preparing for war."

Berenguer nodded his head. All humanitarian considerations aside, it came at a very bad time. Burned-out premises and dead merchants yielded no rent and paid no taxes. And the Jewish community paid its taxes directly to its liege-lord, the King.

"Precisely," said Don Pedro. "We wish to confirm the reports. And, if they are true, to know who lies behind them, and whether they are the result of treachery, mis-

guided religious zeal, or greed. Is the Archbishop aware of
the trouble? And if he is, does he condone it?"

"Does Your Majesty have reason not to trust those who
sent these reports?" asked Berenguer.

"We have great faith in the loyalty and honesty of the
young man we sent to look into these matters. But it is
possible that he has been deceived. Many men have reasons
to foment trouble between the Crown and its subjects."

"One hears," said Olzinelles, "that the papal nuncio is
in Tarragona."

Berenguer looked at the three men in front of him and
paused. "Could he not be there for the General Council,
and no other reason?" he asked.

"If so, we would be overjoyed to know it," said Don
Pedro. "We received a report—one only, not substanti-
ated—that the nuncio has been involved in fomenting riot
and dissent; we would not like to think that it is true. Because if it is, he is acting in direct contravention of the law.
Any attack upon the King's Jews is an encroachment on
royal rights, and could be considered an attempt to support
Sardinia in our just war upon her. We will not stand for
that," said Don Pedro, in tones of cold fury. "Nor will we
submit to our archbishop intriguing with the papal nuncio,
should we obtain evidence of that."

"I am Your Majesty's loyal servant," said Berenguer.
"I shall do whatever I can to assist Your Majesty."

"Where is our ward, Yusuf?"

"At the door, Your Majesty," said a flunky.

"Bring him in." Don Pedro rose. "We can, in all likelihood, smooth out the difficulties between Girona and Tarragona regarding these foolish accusations, Don
Berenguer," said the King as he strode out of the room.
On the way, he took Yusuf by the arm and swept him off
into his private world.

"I am most grateful . . ." began Berenguer, but he was
speaking to a closed door.

"This is a great relief to His Majesty," said Olzinelles.
"The Jews of Tarragona—like those of Valencia and Girona, and here in Barcelona—have been generous in sup-

port of this war, and he is angry at these attacks. His Majesty's information," he added delicately, "comes from Pons de Santa Pau. He is a nephew of the great admiral who died in the recent conflict, and I believe—or hope— is absolutely to be trusted. He is, however, young, and perhaps not as experienced in the ways of deception as he might be. Your Excellency is to observe discreetly what is going on and, when you have some sense of it, to report back to His Majesty. I have here a letter from His Majesty for the Archbishop, written on your behalf."

"Convey my profound gratitude to His Majesty," said Berenguer.

Olzinelles nodded and pushed the letter across the table. "The Church is ever a thorn in His Majesty's side."

Berenguer paused on his way to the door. "Does His Majesty know that bandits attempted to abduct the nun we were escorting to Tarragona?"

"He does," said Olzinelles. "His Majesty takes great care to stay informed."

"I thought he might," said Berenguer with a bow.

At dinner hour that afternoon, the courtyard of Mordecai ben Issach's house was warm and filled with Sabbath quiet. The long trestle table had been set out under the lemon trees, with an abundant but simple meal on it for those who were hungry. Raquel regarded the food in front of her without any appetite. She helped herself to a little, nibbled at it, and then slipped away from the table. Taking some creamy flan with her to tempt Gilabert's appetite, she went up to his chamber.

Naomi was seated by the bed, fanning him gently. "Go and have some dinner, Naomi," said Raquel. "I will stay with him."

"I don't know what's wrong," said Naomi crossly. "It's as hot as June here. You can't even catch your breath in these heathen places. And they say it will be worse in Tarragona. We should have stayed at home."

"It's pleasantly cool in the courtyard," said Raquel. "Go, have something cold to drink, and something to eat."

Still grumbling, Naomi left the room and Raquel surveyed the patient. He looked pale, but he was awake.

"It is my angel from heaven," he said. "I have been wondering where you were."

Raquel laid her hand on his forehead and found it cool. "You are improving," she said.

"How is your patient, Raquel?" said a familiar voice.

"Papa. You startled me. His fever is even lower today."

"Good," said Master Isaac. "You may go and rest. I wish to speak to him." Raquel picked up her work and left. "How is your hand?"

"Painful, I confess."

"Sharp pains or dull, aching pains?"

"Sometimes one, sometimes the other. I try not think of it. If I do, it troubles me. I must bear it and I do."

"Have you eaten anything today?"

"Some soup," he said. "Earlier. Your excellent daughter has brought me some flan, but—"

"Can you eat it now? It is important."

"I cannot," he said impatiently. "I am helpless, lying here, and I have too much to think about. I cannot eat."

"You have nothing to think about except recovering your health and strength," said Isaac firmly.

"Master Isaac, I am a dead man. I do not even know whether I am condemned to remain dead forever, or may suddenly come alive again. In my delirium I thought that you had been appointed to carry me off to heaven. Or perhaps to watch over me here." He tossed his head restlessly. "You have a quality, Master Isaac, that is not of this earth."

"That was your fever speaking to you, my friend," said Isaac gently. "I, too, am made of clay, not spirit."

"Did you think I meant being a dead man to be taken at the very letter of the word?"

"No," said Isaac. "I only wondered what brought you to such a pass."

"It is simple," he said, his voice growing tired and discouraged. "I have an enemy."

"Who is he?" asked Isaac.

He shook his head and closed his eyes. "I do not know. A neighbor. A friend. A kinsman. Someone near to me wishes to destroy me."

"What has he done?"

"Nothing," he said. "Destroyed me."

"Explain it to me," said Isaac quietly. "Take as much time as you wish, but I think for various reasons it would be better to tell me."

"Much of this is known to the world," said Gilabert. "But I would prefer if you did not speak of it yet."

"If that is your wish, I will not."

"My father's lands were extensive and well watered. On the hillsides are olive trees that bear more than can be picked and vines whose choicest wine fills a thousand cellars, with a good deal of ordinary wine left over. And we have flocks and herds as well."

"An enviable position," said Isaac.

"There are many others who enjoy the same bounty from God," he said, "but seem not to be satisfied. Then my father died during my fifteenth year. Within a few months rumors began to spread about my licentious and disgusting practices. There was little I could do to curb them, but since they had no foundation in fact I didn't believe they could do me serious harm. I was wrong. By the time I was sixteen I was forced to flee my lands. I hid—never mind where— and my friends began the long and difficult task of clearing my name."

"Who looked after your property?"

"My uncle. My mother's brother. Throughout all this he has dealt with nothing but trouble and has remained steadfast. But he expected it. An heir to rich lands who is a minor is always surrounded by vultures. Three neighboring landowners all have their greedy eyes on it."

"Do you have other kin who feel they have a claim to your lands?"

He shook his head.

"What of your uncle?" asked Isaac.

"I suspect all men, Master Isaac, but I cannot suspect him. My uncle is my greatest friend. He has impoverished himself fighting my enemies." He paused and closed his eyes for a moment or two. "I think we may have won at last. It may be for that reason that in desperation they try violence against my person."

"Desperation?"

"They must be desperate. Else why would they try to kill me?"

"But, Don Gilabert, they did not try to kill you. Clearly they hoped to keep you alive until you gave them information they needed. Badly."

As Isaac spoke, Gilabert closed his eyes. He opened them again for a moment. "I am very weary, Master Isaac. I beg you again to say nothing of this, even to the Bishop, until I have seen my uncle."

Later that same day a messenger arrived from Avignon, carrying a leather pouch, firmly sealed and stamped with the arms of the Bishop of Barcelona, absent on permanent duty at the papal palace. The messenger handed over the bag for delivery to the canon vicar, Francesc Ruffach, and retreated to the abundant comforts of the palace kitchens.

There was nothing particularly startling amongst the contents. The pouch contained three weighty documents, two in parchment, the other on paper, that the canon vicar had sent to Avignon for the Bishop's approval, signature, and seal, all of which had been duly returned. There were two others originating in Avignon for the canon vicar to take action upon. There was also a letter from the Bishop addressed to Ruffach personally.

It was neat, elegantly written, and completely predictable, laying out a number of explanatory points having to do with the documents that had accompanied it. It wasn't until the final paragraph that the absent Bishop touched on anything puzzling.

> You will have received by now the documents sent four days ago, all being well. Because of a passing illness, and the press of other duties, I neglected to

contact the Bishop of Girona concerning them. There are issues that arise from the decisions in them that I wished brought forward at the council. I trust that the Archbishop has received the list I prepared, even if Girona has not, although I had, of course, counted on his most valuable support. I would esteem it a favor if you were to have the list copied and sent to the Bishop at the Archbishop's palace.

Should an opportunity arise for you to speak to him about these issues on our behalf, it would no doubt be wise to do so.

"Did we receive a dispatch from His Excellency earlier this week?" he asked his secretary.

"A dispatch? Certainly not, Father," he said. "I would have given it to you at once."

"Then it is lost. That is most unfortunate. His Excellency will not be pleased."

In Girona that pleasant afternoon, the canon vicar, Don Arnau, had finished initialing a thin sheaf of documents that contained permissions, routine judgments, and the rota for services for the month ahead. It was not an onerous task; in each case someone else had made the decisions, worked out the arrangements, or weighed the merits of every case. Even so, he dropped his pen and closed his eyes wearily. Five days of the routine bustle of cathedral business had pushed his strength beyond its limits, and to the great relief of the other canons he no longer sought to participate in every crisis, no matter how minor, or every arrangement.

So that when Marc, the uncle of the little girl from Sant Feliu, appeared at the palace, dragging his niece behind him, and demanding to see the canon vicar, he met with a chilly reception.

"His Excellency—His substitute Excellency, that is—" said Marc, "told me—on pain of terrible punishments and such—that if I knew anything else I was to come and see him. Him. Not a pack of priests."

"Anything else about what?" asked a canon who had been absent the day the friar's body was found.

"The dead Franciscan," said Galceran de Monteterno, yawning. "Take him to Don Arnau," he added, "even if it means interrupting his meeting."

"Who's he meeting with?" asked the first canon.

"Morpheus," said Galceran. "By now he should be lying flat across his table, with the god of sleep himself comforting him with dreams of His Excellency's return."

"Playing bishop is not a task for someone who feels the need to scrutinize every detail, from the butcher's account to the number of wax candles Monteterno here burns beyond his allowance," said Ramon de Orta.

"The man is a fool," said Monteterno.

"You judge him wrong. He is no fool," said Orta. "Watch yourself."

Don Arnau woke with a start, passed a silk handkerchief across his lips, and told his secretary to bring in the man and his niece.

"They didn't want to let me in, Your Excellency," said Marc, "but I remembered what you said, and when the little one here saw the man at the market, and said he was the one, like, I thought I'd better come, and bring her, because I know you'd like to hear her say it."

The canon vicar blinked. He thought for a moment and then turned to the girl, as the one more likely to make sense of the two of them. "You were in the market today with your uncle?"

"Yes, Your Excellency," she said. "Mama said I might go."

"And you saw something you thought I should know about." He smiled encouragingly, his tight, unwilling smile.

She accepted it for what it was, an offer of goodwill, and went on. "I didn't see, Your Excellency," she said firmly. "I heard this man talk and it was like the friar. Not like it was the friar, but it made me think of him."

"As if they came from the same place that was not near Girona?"

"I don't know, Your Excellency. I never was in such a place. I just thought they spoke the same way, almost."

"Would you recognize him again, my child?"

"Oh, yes," she said confidently.

"Would you like to go back to the market again to find him? My secretary here will take you, with two of my guards to keep you safe. And I have here a penny that I will give to my secretary. He has leave to buy you something pleasant while you're there." And as good as his word, Don Arnau opened his purse strings, took out a penny, and handed it with due ceremony to that young man.

To her great disappointment, the man she had so confidently spoken of had disappeared. But Don Arnau's secretary bought her some sweetmeats with the penny, and a little cake to go with them, with a farthing from his own pocket, and she went home comforted.

# THREE

## The Departure

Early Sunday morning, Berenguer and the canon vicar of Barcelona strolled through the Bishop's orchard. "It is a fine day," said Ruffach. "I trust Your Excellency will have a good journey."

"If my little army does not hurry, the sun will be unpleasantly hot by the time we leave," said Berenguer. A breeze flapped the skirts of their garments. "Let us hope for a good east wind to cool our tempers and speed us on our way."

"I wish you a speedy and peaceful journey for the rest of the way, Your Excellency."

"Thank you, my friend."

"And I am sorry that I cannot give you His Excellency's list."

"What list, Ruffach?" asked Berenguer.

"A list of matters he wished raised at the General Council. I cannot even tell you what's on it," said Ruffach. "Because I do not know. He sent it, but it was neither in this dispatch, nor in the previous one. I fear one of our messengers has been lost."

"Perhaps it was destined for the Archbishop, and sent directly to him."

"That would be odd, Your Excellency. He asked me to send you a copy."

"Odd indeed," said Berenguer.

All the Bishop's impatience to set out could not hasten the departure of his retinue by more than a few moments. He stood on the palace steps and watched the wagons being loaded. Then the physician and his party arrived, with Gilabert on a litter. Group by group, the party reconstituted itself for the slow move from the bishop's palace to the Via Augusta in the direction of Tarragona. When it was almost complete, Berenguer sent a passing servant to fetch Yusuf.

"Did you speak to His Majesty on the matter we were discussing?" he asked discreetly.

"About staying?" asked Yusuf.

"Yes."

The boy smiled. "He told me I had learned much, and would learn more, but that someday—perhaps when I am fifteen—I must come to court and learn other things that I should know. He was very kind and pleasant to me. He gave me a gold buckle and promised me a sword."

"Excellent. And you have told Master Isaac?"

"Yes, Your Excellency."

"Now return to your master in case you are needed," said Berenguer.

Yusuf ran back to where the bearers had left Gilabert on the litter. The injured man had pushed himself to a sitting position.

"I'm happy to see you. Now, if you would be gracious enough to lend me your arm," he said, "I can stand." Yusuf gave him a doubtful look, grasped him by the hand, and pulled with all his strength. Gilabert rose to his feet and brushed off his mismatched clothing—the remains of his own garb and a long hooded tunic, cut on the small side, provided by Mordecai. "It is pleasant to be away from a bed," he said. "Very pleasant. If I had a horse, I would ride, but since I do not, I will make my way toward that accursed wagon again."

"Are you fit to ride, señor?"

"If I am fit to live, I can ride," said Gilabert grimly.

Yusuf paused. "Can you manage a horse with one hand, señor?"

"I have always been able to, young Yusuf," he said.

"There is the big black we found on the road. I have been riding him," he said, "but I am happy to walk. He is nervous and difficult at times, though."

"If I cannot manage him, I will dismount and let you have him back," he said, with a conspiratorial wink. "We will share the noble beast. But I assure you, I am as comfortable on a horse as I am in a bed. And much more comfortable than in a wagon."

Yusuf brought the horse over to where Gilabert was waiting. "Stand where you are," said Gilabert to Yusuf. "And you," he said to the nearest groom, "help me raise this leg over his back."

"Let me fetch the steps we use for the ladies," said the groom.

"No." And with a further wrench of Yusuf's shoulder, he put his weight on his bad leg in order to set his foot in the stirrup; then he thrust himself up on his good leg far enough to swing the wounded one stiffly over the beast's flanks and settled himself in the saddle. "The stirrups," he said, in the tones of one used to having the stable yard filled with servants whenever he chose to ride. The groom adjusted the stirrup leathers to accommodate his legs. Gilabert handed Yusuf his purse—a discreet replacement from the Bishop of the one that had been stolen from him. "A coin for the groom," he said. "Please. I cannot manage the purse strings with one hand."

"Are you truly fit to ride, señor?" asked Yusuf with a worried frown, belatedly taking the horse's head.

"I most devoutly hope so," said Gilabert. "Indeed, riding will not be the problem. It will be ceasing to ride. I fear that I can only dismount by falling off. I thank you for your help," he added graciously. "If you will give me the reins, I will see if I can manage this ferocious beast." White of face, and still grimacing with pain, he smiled at Yusuf.

And throughout it all, Berenguer remained on the palace steps, watching the horse, quiet and patient as an ox, hold himself still until his new rider was prepared to move out.

By the time the party from the convent had joined them the sun was growing hot, and the shade offered by the surrounding buildings was growing smaller and smaller. The captain checked the list in his careful memory, had a word with the Bishop, and the wagons moved out toward the gate.

Seated on a stone bench close to the broad city gate were Andreu and Felip. "Would Your Excellency object if we joined you again?" asked Andreu.

"The city of Tarragona will be an excellent place for two like us to learn while earning our bread with harmless amusements for the crowds," added Felip.

"You are most welcome," said Berenguer. "Although I am puzzled to discover how you knew we would be passing by at this moment."

"Your Excellency's movements are the admiration of the town," said Andreu, with a bow.

The road ran straight and flat across the plain of the Llobregat River. On either side of it lay flourishing gardens, fields, and groves, green and inviting. Here and there, substantial houses as well as small farmers' cottages dotted the countryside. The landscape shimmered in the heat of the sun, but for the moment there were breezes, and trees that offered travelers intermittent shade.

"It's hot," said the kitchen lad, "but it's easier walking than the road to Barcelona. We could do twice the distance each day if it weren't for some of those," he added, nodding contemptuously at the rest of the party. "And spend more time in the city."

"You'll spend enough time there," said the head cook. This was not the first time he had traveled this road, and he had no illusions about it. "And it will cool down when we hit those," he added, pointing at the dark shapes that hung on the horizon over the shimmering plain. "Won't it, Sergeant?"

"It will," he said.

"Those clouds?" said the kitchen lad.

"Clouds," said the sergeant, laughing. "Those things are mountains, lad, just like the ones at home, only bigger. It wouldn't be very far to Tarragona at all if those weren't in the way."

And indeed, the procession had not been on the road quite two hours before everyone's legs were telling them that the gentle rise of the road over the plain had given way to a sharp ascent. The sun was high above them, and what shade there had been shrank to a negligible amount. Raquel loosened her veil and chatted easily with her father on a host of inconsequential matters. His mule was now so accustomed to being led that she fell into step with Raquel's mount and they moved side by side like a pair of draft animals.

Out of the corner of her eye, she caught a glimpse of Gilabert swaying slightly and then righting himself with a hand on his horse's neck. The color began to drain from his face. She called for Ibrahim to lead her father's mule, and then, rather nervously, kicked her heels tentatively into her beast's sides. Nothing happened. She did it again, firmly, and rode up beside him at a trot. "You are in pain," she said. It was not a question.

"Not very much," he answered. "I am much better than I was."

"I'm sure that's true," said Raquel. "When we found you, you were almost dead."

He tried to smile. "Very well," he said. "I am in pain."

"Then we must get you down from that horse and onto the wagon to rest." She looked around until she caught the sergeant's eye and waved discreetly. "Here is the man who can help us."

In a moment he was beside her. "Mistress Raquel," he said cheerfully. "What may I do?"

"My patient," she said, "has talked his way onto a

horse, and is now ready to dismount. And that is the problem."

"Not at all," said the sergeant. "I will return presently."

And the two ambled on quietly for a few moments. "I'm not complaining, and I don't wish to sound foolish," said Raquel, "but how do you make an animal move when you want it to, and go where you want it to?" she asked. "The way yours does. This is a gentle enough creature I'm riding, but she—"

"She's a mule," said the young man, "and she will only cooperate if she knows you and likes you. Then she can be the best mount in the world. It is better to start with a strange horse than a mule that doesn't know you, Mistress Raquel. But the horse must have been trained expertly and you must handle it with determination. You have not ridden before?"

"Only once before," Raquel admitted.

"Then you are doing very well. I almost wish . . ."

"Wish what, señor?"

But the baggage wagons halted, and the sergeant returned on foot with another stout guard. He caught the black horse's reins and held him still. "Señor, if you will be good enough to lean over toward me, and put your hand on my shoulder, we will catch you. Can you hold his horse, boy?" he said to Yusuf, handing him the reins.

And it was done. Gilabert was in the litter, and Raquel, after settling him, was back on her mule, arranging her skirt modestly over her rather exposed legs. Yusuf mounted and the horse moved to its accustomed place behind the wagon.

They were by no means the only travelers that day. As their straight road began to wind, searching its way through the steep hills, looking for the river valley, they were overtaken by several riders. To judge by their speed, all of them, alone or in company, seemed to be on more urgent missions than theirs. And theirs appeared to be growing less and less urgent. The draft mules had slowed considerably, and all the other animals had slackened pace to match. "What's going on?" asked the captain.

"I'd like to look at the lead mule's near foreleg," said the head groom. "She seems to be the problem."

"Pull up there," said the captain, pointing to a flat stretch where another traveler was resting while his horse grazed. "By that stream."

And while the grooms were fussing over the lead mule, removing a sharp pebble from her hoof and finding a soothing ointment to rub on the broken, irritated flesh, the others scattered. Raquel found her father a flat-topped rock to sit on near the stream, promised to return with a jug of cool water, and promptly disappeared. "You have been abandoned, I see," said Felip. "May we join you?"

"Certainly," said Isaac. "I suspect my daughter and her mother both find our invalid more fascinating right now than someone they have known most of their lives. And where is your fellow musician?"

"He has talked the head cook out of a jug of something, and is approaching us at this moment. It is one of his skills—talking things out of people. But I see we share this comfortable place with a stranger," he added. "Excuse me, sir," he called. "Will you join us?"

"Gladly," said the other traveler, who was lying on the far side of the stream. "For a few moments, at least."

Isaac turned his head in sudden interest. "What brings you out on the road this warm afternoon?" he asked.

"I am a messenger, señor. It is my livelihood."

"An honest one, but not easy, I would judge," said the physician.

"Those are true words, señor. And now that my horse is somewhat rested, I must soon be on my way again. I am not paid to enjoy the fellowship of the road, unfortunately."

"Do you travel far?" he asked.

"To Tarragona," said the messenger, taking the cup of wine and water proffered by Andreu.

"Today?" asked Isaac.

"No, señor. Tonight I hope to sleep in a village near Martorell where I have kin. Not a long journey for one day, but my horse and I have both had a hard week of it."

"You have come from Barcelona?"

"Yes," he said. "Leaving on less than a day's rest." He passed the cup back and stood. "We must be on our way. A good journey to you, señores. I thank you for the refreshment." He whistled to his horse, who trotted obediently over. With a bow to the company, he mounted, and was off.

"A talkative fellow," said Andreu.

"Only because I wanted to listen to him," said Isaac serenely.

"And why was that?" asked Felip, in a puzzled voice.

"I wanted to be sure he was the same man I heard yesterday in the Bishop's Orchard. Although the man who hired him interested me more."

"And why was that?" asked Andreu, suppressing a yawn.

"This fellow sounds like a sober, honest sort, but the one who hired him to take a spoken message to Tarragona was not to be trusted. It was to go to a tavern in the street of the Scriveners. For this, our messenger was paid with a purse much too heavy for the value of the task."

"How can you can tell the weight of a purse?" asked Felip.

"One learns to judge these things by their sound. The weight of the coins made it jangle with a dull tone. In addition, the two men who are to receive the message will pay him the same amount again. All this for a message that is of no importance at all."

"What was it?" asked Andreu, with an amused glance at his companion.

"Miró and Benvenist are to make the agreed-upon preparations for their young master's return."

"That does seem to be a slender message for a weighty purse," said Andreu. "Was that why you assumed the man was not to be trusted?"

"Certainly not," said Isaac. "That would only suggest that he spends his money foolishly. That young man brought evil with him into the Bishop's Orchard," he added thoughtfully. "But I doubt that we will ever know why he paid so much for those words to be delivered."

"Evil?" said Andreu, startled. "How can you tell?"

Isaac raised his hands in a helpless gesture and smiled.

"I wonder if the messenger knows anything of it?" asked Felip.

"I think not," said Isaac. "He is not paid to be curious."

The mule was looked after and the group was back on the winding road once more when a shout and a loud scream halted them again. A group of six horsemen had come around a sharp curve and barely missed riding down those walking at the end of the Bishop's retinue.

"Look who rides up behind us," said Berenguer to Francesc Monterranes, pointing to a master in costly apparel, on a horse with silver-decked trappings jangling and gleaming in the sun, and his five servants.

"It is that country fool we dined with in the palace," said his confessor. "Is anyone hurt?"

"I think not," said Bernat. "No thanks to them."

"I wonder if we are to be graced with his company for long."

"I trust we may be spared that punishment," muttered the Bishop uncharitably.

Don Gonsalvo de Marca swerved to avoid another group, raising a good deal of dust in the process, and pulled up as he approached the passenger wagon. He stared at Gilabert, who lay quietly with his eyes closed, and shook his head. "Poor fellow," he said. "Good day, Your Excellency."

"Good day, Don Gonsalvo," said Berenguer. "We had not expected to see you on the road. This is indeed good fortune."

"It is, Your Excellency," said the landowner, beaming with apparent pleasure. "I hope you are having a pleasant journey."

"Most uneventful," said Berenguer, "until your arrival, of course."

"The best journeys are uneventful, are they not?" He lowered his voice slightly. "I see that the unfortunate you happened upon on the Girona road is still with you. Unless those are his remains you carry back to his family," he said, in a worried voice.

"Oh, no," said Berenguer. "He is still alive. In fact, he rode by my side across the plain. Unfortunately, the exercise exhausted his strength and our physician insisted that he rest."

"He rode? Then he is not on his deathbed," said Gonsalvo, with an odd look on his face. "Excellent."

"But in these matters," said Berenguer, "we are in the hands of God, are we not? Usually."

And on that enigmatic remark, Berenguer nodded magisterially. Gonsalvo took a hasty leave and clapped spurs to his horse.

The road climbed and dipped, climbed and dipped, through deepening forests, twisting and bending north and west endlessly ahead of them. "But Tarragona is south of us," complained the kitchen lad. "We have taken the wrong road. The sun is at our backs. We are lost."

"Quiet," said the assistant cook. "We are not lost."

"Would you prefer to swim the river and scramble straight up over the mountain?" said the head cook. "Because the rest of us would rather go 'round by the road, and take bridges."

"Yes, sir," muttered the lad, cowed but still mutinously convinced they were lost.

As they approached Sabadell, their usual patterns began to shift. Francesc Monterranes took pity on the nuns' priest and rode beside him, patiently listening to an account of his difficulties with the nuns. Raquel joined her mother near the passenger wagon, and Bernat found himself leading the physician's mule; Bishop, secretary, and physician fell into easy conversation to while away the time.

At Sabadell they joined the road from Girona. "All these days of walking," said Naomi to her mistress. "And here we are back where we were supposed to be days ago. Just so a bishop could go visiting." Then she recollected where they had picked up her patient, and looked ashamed, for she was enjoying herself thoroughly.

"You have done almost no walking, Naomi," said Judith. "I wonder your limbs are not too stiff to move."

It had been agreed among those on foot that when they reached the town, they would stop, rest themselves, eat a hearty meal, drink deep, and move on later—much later—refreshed. They came in, passing by taverns and inns, listening to the cheerful laughter and boisterous conversation of those lucky enough to enjoy their delights, and trudged on. Berenguer was grim-faced and adamant. They could afford to lose no more time.

A gloom settled over the party. Once the Bishop called for a song, and Felip halfheartedly pulled out his rebec and bow and began to tune it up. Andreu started to sing, and then excused himself, saying the dust had caught in his throat. He took out his little flute and played a mournful air or two. As if by common consent, the music was put away.

"What is wrong with everyone?" asked Berenguer impatiently.

"They are tired, and hungry, and they know that we have several days more travel in front of us," observed Bernat.

"We cannot stop," said Berenguer. "Not yet."

The breeze that had been caressing their faces was turning into a stiff wind. The clouds that had gathered on the horizon suddenly raced across the sky, blotting out the sun. A few drops of rain suddenly turned into a deluge. The wind howled down the valley, driving it into their faces, slowing man and beast almost to a standstill. "Your Excellency," said the captain, "there is no point in attempting to go on. Those trees ahead will afford us some shelter and we can use the time to eat."

Berenguer gave in to the combined forces of the tempest and his men.

Fires were next to impossible. The cooks passed around cheese, fruit, and bread, but everyone was too cold, wet, and tired to appreciate food that was equally damp and cold. The guards, reinforced by three from Barcelona, were posted around the perimeter, sitting as high up as they could get, lashed by the wind and the rain, except for the one who was watching Sor Agnete. With the memory of the last attack sharp in his mind, the captain permitted no one to be alone. They all huddled together, friends, enemies, servants, masters, old and young.

The storm raged until the road became a river; it pelted down on the unprotected mules and horses, who clung unhappily to each other for protection. When it finally blew itself away, the captain's first concern was for the animals; everyone who could grabbed fistfuls of dry straw from the wagons to rub them down. Then the travelers wrung out their clothes as best they could and started off again, westward.

It was a miserable and sodden group that arrived late that afternoon at the comfortably elegant guest quarters of the Carthusian monastery in Terrassa. The monks looked at the rain-soaked Bishop of Girona in horror. They were devastated. They might be able to accommodate His Excellency, but there was not enough room left anywhere in the monastery for even two or three of his attendants. "If Your Excellency's retinue were to go to the priory of Santa Maria de Terrassa on the other side of the river," said the Abbott, "I am sure the prior will do what he can for them."

"We shall all go, and I thank you for your help," said Berenguer.

"Do what he can?" said Bernat. "That sounds rather ominous."

At Santa Maria, after a meager meal, the supper bowls and plates had been cleared away. Gilabert, protesting, had been taken to a separate chamber, where he was being fussed over by Naomi and Raquel; the Bishop and his secretary were closeted with the prior. The rest of the group, warmed and cheered a little by the hot soup and cup of wine provided by the brothers, lingered in idle conversation.

"I was surprised to see Don Gonsalvo pass us by," said Bernat. "I understood him to say that he was spending some time in Barcelona."

"Who is this Don Gonsalvo?" asked Judith boldly. Until now she had sat by her husband at the supper board, saying nothing except in a whisper directed only to him. But nature had not framed her to stay silent in the middle of interesting conversation. To her husband's great amusement, she was beginning to treat priests as if they were in some senses honorary women, safe and comfortable to gossip with.

"He is a landowner from somewhere to the south or west of here, I believe, Mistress Judith," said Bernat.

"So I had concluded," said Judith tartly.

Bernat bowed with a somewhat apologetic air. "Very true, Mistress Judith. Since he is traveling on our road. I can tell you nothing else about him, but that we dined together at the Bishop's palace in Barcelona. I confess, Mistress Judith, I don't enjoy his company at the table. He speaks endlessly, about nothing, in a loud and unpleasant voice."

"We were privileged to learn his opinions on all subjects from marrying daughters to prosecuting lawsuits," added Francesc dryly. "It was a most enlightening meal."

"In fact, it was a lawsuit that kept him in Barcelona, was it not?" asked Bernat.

"No," said the nuns' priest flatly. "You are wrong, Father. He made it very clear that the lawsuit was in another court."

"But it was because of the lawsuit that he stayed," said Bernat.

"I was listening very carefully to him," said the nuns' priest. "And he gave no reason—"

"And it was mere chance we saw him again," said Felip, before already tried tempers could flare. "Chance is a strange thing, do you not agree? That one unpleasant landowner whom no one knows should have dined one day and not another at the palace, and then chosen that particular moment to leave the city unexpectedly can only be chance."

"Indeed," said Andreu. "The winds of chance carry us where they will." He smiled. "And today they blew us together on the road. It is odd how often that happens. I once entered an unspeakable tavern in a miserable village high up in the mountains. It was a full ten days hard travel from my birthplace, and inhabited by eight surly families and five times that many goats. I sat down at the first empty place, and right beside me was a man who had been a schoolfellow.''

"Indeed," said the nuns' priest. "I, too . . ."

And the conversation trailed on with endless accounts of coincidence.

The nuns' priest, who seemed to have lived a life up until that point composed entirely of coincidental meetings with people he had known before, had just finished his third anecdote when Yusuf looked up. "I wonder, señores," he said, "if it is all chance. For Don Gonsalvo pretended as he passed by us not to know Gilabert, and yet in Barcelona he spoke of him to a friend as though he had known him a long time."

"Perhaps it was another man named Gilabert," said Isaac. "There must be many with that name."

"True, lord," said Yusuf, "I had not thought of that."

"Otherwise," said Felip, "it is a most curious thing, I agree. But the hour grows late. Shall we see if Gilabert needs anything?" he asked, turning to Andreu. "And then I shall seek my bed. I wish you all a good night."

And in general agreement, the travelers rose and sought their rest.

"And how is Your Excellency's knee?" asked Isaac. "I would not want pain to keep you from your rest."

"It does not trouble me at all," said Berenguer. "Had you heard Yusuf's account before?" he added.

"No, Your Excellency," said Isaac. "Yusuf?"

"Yes, lord?" said the boy in a small voice. "I should not have spoken like that, I know. But I had forgotten that conversation until this moment, and it just came out."

"Don't concern yourself. No harm was done," said Berenguer.

"There was something else as well, lord."

"What was that?" asked Isaac.

"Don Gonsalvo asked what had happened to the money

he had given to Norbert. Or paid him. I can't remember which."

"That is most interesting," said Berenguer. "This Gonsalvo bears watching."

# FOUR

## The Mountains

The clangor of the rising bell awakened the travelers before prime the next morning. One by one, they rose wearily from their thin mattresses to face the day. Banks of clouds, threatening more rain and wind, hung heavily over the priory; there was no temptation to linger in the frigid air of the crowded dormitory or the sparsely furnished chambers. Once up, they were soon moving.

Breakfast was slow in coming. When it arrived, it was a cold and spartan meal. As soon as they finished, Berenguer took his farewells, and his retinue hastened from the chill comforts offered by the monks to what seemed by comparison the warm fellowship of the road. "I would not be a monk," said the nuns' priest, who had a gift for saying what others were too tactful to express. "The sisters do not live in a lavish manner, but on a cold morning their refectory is warm, and the food is abundant and good."

Berenguer frowned. "We stretched their resources to the utmost," he said. "And they offered what they had. They have been much depleted in wealth and numbers in late years."

"I did not mean to seem uncharitable, Your Excellency, but . . ."

"I am glad of that," said Berenguer. "I am sure you pity them their current distress."

"Indeed, Your Excellency," murmured the nuns' priest.

Their elation at leaving Terrassa soon dissipated. The road ahead was discouragingly like the road behind; their clothing was still wet from yesterday's rain, and Andreu was sneezing.

"How far do you think we can travel today?" asked Berenguer.

"Castellvi is well within our reach," said the captain.

"It is a great distance from Tarragona."

"We did not travel as far as we had hoped yesterday, Your Excellency," said the captain. "There was the storm, and—"

"Yes, Captain, I understand all that. Well, if we can go no farther, a kinsman of mine near Castellvi will take us in. But it will be difficult for him to offer hospitality to so many. It would be much better to go on to Lloselles, where we can be accommodated at the castle. That way we might reach El Vendrell tomorrow. Also they have more room at the castle, and are not so poor as my unfortunate cousin."

"If we can reach Lloselles tonight."

"We must try," said the Bishop. "In Castellvi, I suppose all of us could sleep in the hall. It would be cleaner and quieter than an inn."

"We will need a room for the women, and one for Sor Agnete."

"I am sure my cousin can arrange that." Since without a doubt the Bishop would be sleeping in the best chamber, wherever they stopped, and his host and hostess in some drafty corner in the servants' quarters, Berenguer could afford to be philosophical about the crowding.

"I will do my best, Your Excellency," said the captain. "But the road is not easy, and the distance through the mountains is considerable."

The sun broke through the clouds. The wind, which had been tormenting them with chills, was gradually drying out their clothing. But the farther they traveled from Terrassa,

the more heavily the mountains seemed to loom above
them. They were dark with thickly growing pines; their
ridges rose sharply, close together, like the teeth of a comb.
Even the slowest of walkers hurried, as if this were enemy
territory, to be crossed as quickly as possible. The world
did not open out around them until they began to descend
again, heading once more into the valley of the Llobregat.
"We cannot halt yet," said the captain, looking at his unhappy troop. "But since many are hungry, we will stop
long enough to hand out some bread and cheese."

"Don't sit down," said the assistant cook as he passed
among the servants from the convent, carrying a large basket of chunks of bread and good-sized slices of cheese.
"We eat as we walk."

"The bread is stale," muttered one of the grooms.

"Account yourself fortunate it is not green with mold,"
snapped the sergeant. "The monastery gave us what bread
they could."

"We will stop to rest when we have crossed the river,"
said Berenguer, with a black look at the complainers.

The pines gave way to leafy trees and shrubs, the rock
of the mountains to more hospitable land. One of the guards
had been sent ahead on a mission known only to the captain
and his sergeant, but the rumor spread that he was looking
for a place to halt for the night. Spirits soared.

"Surely we are not to stop here for the night?" asked
Raquel as they drew within sight of the river. "We've hardly started."

"I would not think so," said Gilabert, who was back in
the wagon, sitting up with his wounded leg stretched out
in front of him. Yusuf rode the black horse. "We have a
considerable distance to travel before we get through the
mountains."

"But we just came through the mountains," said Raquel.

"There are more," said Gilabert, smiling. "But surely
they cannot frighten you, Mistress Raquel. You must be
accustomed to mountains."

"I am," she said. "But not these mountains."

• • •

The town sat on the far side of the bridge, downstream from the point where the Anoia flows into the Llobregat. Enrique, the young guard who had been sent ahead, was waiting for them at the bridge, bearing a sack filled with fresh bread and local cheese to supplement their dwindling supplies. They stopped on the bank of the Anoia, in a meadow on the far side of the town, for a hasty meal of cold meats, bread, and cheese.

The river meadow was warm and richly green. A path meandered down to the water for those who wished to bathe, and the sun drove the last memory of the cold morning from their bones, leaving them with a pleasant sense of lassitude. But just as everyone settled in to doze away a quarter hour or so, the captain was calling on them to pack up and move on.

"I am sure we could walk much farther if we had time to rest," said the kitchen lad.

"Listen to the boy who wanted to walk twice the distance every day," said the head cook. "Be glad His Excellency didn't hear you, or he'd make us all try it. He's in a mortal hurry to get where he's going."

"Do we follow the river all the way?" asked the kitchen lad, who was beginning to develop some respect for the cook's knowledge of the road.

"You might say so," said his master, choking down a laugh. "We're a little above it most of the time. But it's down there, somewhere."

"What do you mean?"

"You'll see," said the assistant cook.

Ahead of them the mountains towered, dark and high. The road began to rise sharply, and the sergeant called a halt.

"What is this for?" asked the kitchen lad.

"Work," said the head cook. "We have to move some heavy pieces to the other wagon to even up the weight. There are steepish hills ahead."

"We should have done it earlier," said his assistant, tossing the remark over his shoulder as he walked to the passenger wagon. "And you, señor," he said to Gilabert.

"Will you be able to shift over? We could put a barrel or two in beside you if you would. And those two," he added, looking at Naomi and Ibrahim, "will have to walk, along with the rest."

"Better than that. I will ride," said Gilabert. "Yusuf can take my place on the wagon. He weighs less than I do."

"I can walk, señor," said the boy.

"Yusuf will ride my mule," said Berenguer.

They shifted some of the heaviest cargo over to the passenger wagon to even the loads and Yusuf sprang up on the Bishop's mule.

The road began to climb again.

It climbed through thick forest, thicker than any Raquel had ever seen before. Oaks and poplars grew like weeds in the spring rain, clinging to the steep slope. They spread their branches over the road, cutting off the sun and enshrouding it in perpetual dusk. Higher up, evergreens loomed darkly behind them. A mist that seemed to ooze out of the red, rocky soil clung damply to their skins.

"It is almost like night in here," said Raquel uneasily.

"It is nothing like night," said Gilabert, whose horse had fallen into step beside Raquel's mule. "You don't want to be caught in the forest at night."

"Are there no people here?"

"Certainly," he said. "Villages, and monasteries, and some solitary miserable huts. Although many of the little villages were devastated in the plague, and now lie almost empty of inhabitants. But most of the people live farther away from the road, where they feel safe."

"How do they live? You cannot grow things here, can you?"

"There are many ways to earn a living in the forest," said Gilabert. "Some of them are even honest," he added. "There's forage for pigs. Farther up there in the meadows they keep sheep and goats, and mountain cattle."

Raquel shivered. "I don't think I could ever get used to living here, without the sun."

Every set of legs in the entire train was well accustomed to climbing the steep streets of Girona every day. There were those who were fond of complaining, but in truth, hills had no terrors for them. Even so, their pace began to slacken. They had already walked close to twenty miles, and the young stable lads were weary-eyed and stumbling with fatigue.

Finally the captain called a halt in a relatively level spot next to a milestone. "We will take five minutes to rest," he said.

"How far to the castle at Lloselles?" asked Berenguer.

"At least ten miles, Your Excellency. Of this. They are doing their best, but they are not conditioned soldiers. We will have to let them rest every two or three miles. It will take us four hours, and there's a risk we will be caught by the fall of dark. Tomorrow will be another day of the same, only downhill, which is harder on tired legs."

"And to Castellvi?"

"A little over five. We can do that in two hours, tired as they are."

"Then we will halt at Castellvi. Not far beyond the castle lies the small keep belonging to my mother's kinsman. My cousin will take us in."

"I know the one you mean. Should they not be warned?"

"Indeed. Send Enrique ahead."

And at the keep in the forest beyond Castellvi de Rosanes, the castellan's wife curtsied to the noble Bishop. "You are most welcome, Your Excellency," she said. "We can offer you but poor harborage, I fear, but we will gladly share with you what we have."

And indeed, her humble disclaimer was no more than the truth. Her hastily donned gown and surcoat, no doubt her best, were much the worse for wear, as were the furnishings of the hall. But a bright fire burned on the generous hearth, and the hall felt dry and warm, even though the castle was heavily shaded, and still had something of the winter's chill about it.

The Bishop was well aware of the sacrifice required to entertain such a company, and at that moment the grooms were staggering into the kitchens carrying two fine dried hams, a cask of wine, two large and heavy cheeses, a sack of flour, and a basket of sundry other things—rice, and spices, and choice dried fruits.

"Why are they giving away all our food?" asked a stable lad in an agony of apprehension over the prospect of starvation ahead.

"Why do you think we brought it?" said the assistant cook. "Did you think the Bishop was going to eat it all himself? You cannot pay a penniless knight for lodging, as if this were an inn, nor can you make him a grand donation of gold, as you would at a monastery. So you bring him choice things from your native city."

"But—"

"Don't worry. We will replace what is needed in Vilafranca. There is an abundance of excellent food there."

In their relief at being inside the stout walls of the small castle, the members of the party forgot their fatigue and aching limbs. They sat down cheerfully to a supper of stewed salted venison with onions and garlic, and a roasted lamb, all of which they ate with gusto. The castellan talked hunting with Gilabert, who spoke knowledgeably and with due deference to his host, and ate but little.

"Are you well, señor?" asked the castellan, pressing another cup on wine on him. "You seem pale, and weary. And I cannot help but notice that you, and one of your fellows over there, are both deprived of the use of one arm."

"I am very well," said Gilabert, white-faced but with a smile. "Not many days ago I despaired of life because of wounds. To be alive and sitting at table is to be very well. His Excellency's physician and his most skilled daughter rescued me from almost certain death."

"You were set upon on the road?" asked the castellan.

"We were," said the captain truthfully, while skillfully avoiding the question of the attack on Gilabert. "I'm pleased to say that our attackers suffered greater losses than we did, but we have our cuts and bruises."

"Are such attacks common on this stretch of the road?" asked Bernat.

"Not common," said the castellan. "But they do occur. The prudent traveler goes in company, and stays on guard. Some of the mountain dwellers are wild men, and very poor."

"And some grow fat on the pickings from unwary passersby," said his lady suddenly, and with vehemence. "Like vultures." Those around her looked up in surprise, for until that moment, she had been very subdued.

When the board was cleared away, the hall was transformed into a dormitory. In a quiet corner, Isaac, with Raquel's assistance, was unbinding the bandages on Gilabert's leg. "It is almost healed, Papa," said Raquel.

"Good," said Isaac. "Bind it once more, but not so heavily."

"Are you the physician?" said a soft voice. "Master Isaac?"

"I am," said Isaac.

"My mistress begs you to come to her, Master Isaac."

"For what reason?"

"She will tell you."

"Come, Raquel," said her father, and they followed the maid up a steep flight of winding stairs and into a chamber where a fire crackled cheerfully on the hearth. Isaac stopped in the doorway, listening. The maid grasped his hand and tugged to bring him inside.

"Master Isaac," said a voice, the same one that had sounded so bitter over the supper table, "I am Emilia, wife of the castellan," she said humbly. "And I beg you to look at my son. He has been ill for four days, and I despair now of his recovery. Nothing from my own poor stock of remedies in the still room seems to help him. But I heard the young man speak of you, and your miracles—"

"I am a physician, Lady Emilia," said Isaac. "I do what man can do to help. No more. No miracles, but my best. How old is he?"

"He was born this time last year."

"And has he been sickly in that time?"

"No. He has grown well, and learned to walk, and to run a few steps. He has four teeth, and can say Mama . . ." Here she dissolved in tears, and Isaac left her in the care of her little maid.

The child lay in his cot, whimpering and twitching restlessly. "He is very pale, Papa," said Raquel, "and his eyes are glazed and sunken."

"Do you have the cask, Raquel?"

"No, Papa. I will fetch it."

"No. Send the maid for Yusuf. He will fetch it. I need you here. Is there a kettle of water on the hob?"

"Yes, master," said the maid, and ran off to fetch Yusuf and the cask.

Isaac felt the child's body, gently but with great thoroughness, from neck to feet. He felt the sharp little teeth, placed his ear on its chest and listened intently, and then softly massaged its belly. "Tell me, Lady Emilia, does he have a nurse?"

"Yes, Master Isaac, but he has been refusing the breast. At first he spewed up the milk he drank, and now he refuses to try. The nurse looks ill herself from worry and lack of sleep. There was no use in keeping her here, so I have sent her to my maid's bed to rest."

"I would speak with her, Lady Emilia. It is important."

When the maid returned, she was sent off again to fetch the nurse and then to the kitchens for broth.

"Lady Emilia," said Isaac, when Yusuf arrived with the cask, "your own wisdom has already told you your son is very ill. He is in great pain, and his body craves sleep, water, and food. The pain keeps him from eating or drinking, and the great danger now is that he will die of hunger and thirst. But if we ease the pain, he will sleep, and then hunger and thirst will surely kill him. You see how gray his face is and how sunken his eyes? And his skin feels very strange. He needs water first, and then food."

"I see that," his mother, "but how do you?"

"I feel it, and my daughter sees it. We will give him a tiny amount of something to ease the pain so the cramping of his gut does not prevent digestion, and then you and I and my daughter must stay with him all night and keep him awake, and try to give him water. It will seem cruel, but otherwise he will die. Are you willing?''

''I will do anything.''

''We would not trouble you, for I doubt that you have slept since he fell ill, but it must be his mother who holds him, or he will be even more distressed.''

Raquel brushed a cloth soaked in bitter drops diluted with wine and water against his lips until he had swallowed some; they let him sleep a few minutes, and then jogged him awake, with songs, and noises, and tickling his feet and anything else they could do without hurting him, and moistened his lips with water.

The nurse arrived, a solid-looking young countrywoman, making a great show of brushing sleep from her eyes. ''You asked for me, my lady?'' she said rather sullenly.

''Yes, Lluisa. The physician would like to ask you about the baby.''

''Yes, my lady.''

''Ah, Lluisa,'' said Isaac. ''Tell me. What have you taken to stop the boy from nursing?''

''Nothing, señor,'' she said in a panic-stricken voice.

''I know you took something,'' he said. ''If I knew what it was, and how much you took, it might help to save his life.''

''It weren't anything bad,'' she said, her voice rising. ''My cousin gave it me. All it does is make the milk taste strange, and he was chewing on my teats so bad they bled sometimes. It always works, my cousin said.''

''What was it, woman?''

''I don't know. She gets it from a witch woman, and she gave me a cup. I was to take three drops, but that didn't help, so I took the whole thing, and it made me sick, I tell you. But she said it couldn't hurt the baby. She promised. I never would have hurt him.'' And she broke into howls of weeping until she was sent from the room to consider her probable fate for the rest of the night.

"Since he has lived this long," said Isaac, "he must be very strong. That is our greatest hope."

"She poisoned him?" said Lady Emilia. "Lluisa poisoned him? If he dies," she whispered in a voice that made Raquel shiver, "I will kill her."

"Then we must try to keep him from dying, if only to save you from the terrible sin of murder."

As they worked, the castle keep settled down for the night; in the ensuing quiet, the sounds of the forest filled the room: the hooting of owls, the snap of a dead branch under the foot of a nocturnal animal hunting, or being hunted, until it seemed that the dense woods behind were filled with a vast silent army gathering around the castle, watching.

By the middle of the night, when the moon rose and her light filtered in through the shutters, he drank a spoonful of water. "Let him sleep a little longer," said Isaac. "For he needs rest almost as desperately as he needs that water."

They let him sleep near an hour, and then he drank thirstily, and whimpered. "Give him more to ease the pain, Raquel. One drop."

She did, and they let him sleep another hour. Raquel woke him gently and gave him some warm broth. "He drank it, Papa," she said, "and they are both falling asleep."

His mother protested that she was awake.

"Is there a bed in here?"

"The nursemaid's."

"Let them lie down together, then," said Isaac. "I will sit awhile to make sure that all is well. Go and rest, daughter."

And mother and baby slept until the morning sun coming in through the shutters woke them both.

# FIVE

## The Mountains

They breakfasted well on rice, hot and spicy, and an abundance of excellent bread just out of the ovens, with one of the Bishop's hams and a good quarter of one of the cheeses on the table. Before they said their farewells, Berenguer sent his secretary to fetch a parcel wrapped in fine linen, which he presented to Lady Emilia. "You have welcomed us with such grace, cousin, even when your house was filled with trouble. We would not have disturbed you had we known."

"If you had not," said the castellan's lady, "my son would have been dead by now. Your arrival was an answer to all our prayers."

"Not my arrival, my lady," said Berenguer. "My physician's. I brought him on this journey for my own selfish reasons, but I am overjoyed that for your sake alone, it has been worthwhile."

Lady Emilia carried the parcel over to the window embrasure, where the light was better, and opened it up. Inside lay a pile of heavy silk, carefully folded, enough to make the richest gown with the widest, longest sleeves she could imagine, and have enough left over for her daughter, when she grew to be a young woman. "Your Excellency," she said, "your generosity knows no limits. If ever we can be of service to you—"

"Madam," he said gallantly, "you may regret those words. We shall be returning by this same road."

"You will be most welcome," she replied.

The castellan accompanied them to the courtyard, and repeated his advice that they be on their guard while in the forest.

"Have you heard of attacks upon travelers in this district?" asked the captain.

"No," said the castellan. "But my wife's maid—the daughter of my best woodcutter—told Emilia that our guests had best be wary. I think she heard something from her father. But he is a gloomy fellow by nature, and always foresees the worst. As well, last night I heard what sounded like poachers in the forest, but they are more likely to attack my deer than my guests. I do not know of any particular reason why you should be concerned. But I would be on my guard, Captain."

"Can you handle a sword?" asked the captain bluntly.

"I can," said Gilabert. "Not as handily as when I had use of both hands, but well enough. Can you supply me with one?"

"Yes. That makes us ten armed men," he said half to himself. "His Excellency will wear his sword, as will his priests. They are well able to protect themselves. We should be adequately prepared. And there's the cook and his assistant, and the head groom will bear a lance. You ride today?"

"Yes, indeed, Captain. I ride."

"You may have difficulty dismounting if we are attacked."

"I can fight from the saddle; the horse will do as I say."

"Are you sure? He seemed unpredictable to me." The captain gave him an odd glance, and sent someone to fetch him a sword.

•   •   •

They moved up the road, quiet, tense, and wary, expecting at any moment a rush of men—on foot or on surefooted mountain ponies—to fall upon them. The nuns, the rest of the women, and the lads too young to wield a staff or pike were huddled in the middle of the procession, between the two wagons; everyone else had been posted on the edges of the group. The road climbed, and twisted; nothing happened. They began to relax.

Then the sergeant and two of the guards rounded a sharp curve with the first wagon right behind them, and stopped in their tracks. The road in front of them was filled, not with ferocious-looking bandits, but with a crowd of women, accompanied by a few old men and children. They were mostly barefoot and clad in coarse gowns, kilted up out of the way to reveal a good length of sturdy leg. Some were armed. In front stood two determined-looking women brandishing kitchen knives. "Where is the blind man?" asked the bolder of the two. "And his daughter?"

"What do you want of him?" asked the sergeant. "Stand back, woman, and let us pass."

"Not until you give us the blind man," repeated the woman.

Then another woman, with wild hair flying about her head, wearing a torn and dirty gown, broke out from the crowd, carrying a child of two or three. "It is for me she asks for the blind man," she said. "She is my sister. She means no harm, I swear. My baby is dying, and I heard what the blind man did for the baby at the castle. He must help me. Last winter I lost all my children but him. He is all I have left."

"That's true," said a voice from behind her. "Crazy Marta is no liar."

Berenguer rode up to the front and looked down at the poor creature. "Master Isaac?" he said.

"I will examine the child," said Isaac, "but if it is an infection that has carried off all the rest of your children, it may be beyond my poor ability to help."

"They died in a fire," said the sister with the kitchen knife. "This one has a fever, and a swelling. And not a plague sore, I swear. I have seen those, and I know. May I die in agony and burn forever in hell if it is a plague sore, sir.''

"Let me see it," said the sergeant. "Stand off and let me see it.''

The mother raised the child's foot and showed it to the sergeant.

"It is a pustulant infection," said Raquel. "I can tell from here. Bring the boy over.''

They laid out a covering on the road and set the child on it. Then Raquel gave him a small draft for the pain, washed the infected foot well, cut into it, and let the putrid matter escape. She swabbed and cleansed it with wine, bound it up with herbs, and returned the sobbing child to his mother. "Go to the castle, and ask the good lady there for broth, and fresh eggs, and other delicate food for him for a few days. And don't let him walk on that foot for—'' Raquel paused.

"Five days," said her father, magisterially.

"Thank you, sir," said the woman. "Thank you. He will be well?''

"If you are careful.''

The women looked uneasily at each other. "We must tell them," said the mother of the child. "It isn't right not to. After all, they stopped and helped us. And Lady Emilia.''

"Tell us what?''

"The road isn't safe ahead," said the mother. "You mustn't go on.''

"There's a bridge down, that's what there is. You could fall and be killed." The voice came from the middle of the crowd, and murmur rose from those around, whether of agreement or dissent was hard to tell.

"You can get around it up this track and then down the other side of the ridge," said the sister. "Be sure to bring the sick man with you.''

Now, as soon as the procession had halted, Yusuf, not considering that he might be needed, had climbed up the mountainside to their left to see what else might lurk up there. He found a pine that looked easy to climb and scrambled up as high as the tree would allow. From his vantage point he could see the road ahead curve and curve again, before it disappeared from his view, and what he saw startled him. He slid down, scrambled over the mountainside to the road, and whispered in the captain's ear.

"I think we should accept the good woman's advice," said the captain.

"Are you sure?" asked Berenguer.

"Very sure. They seem to be honest souls," said captain solemnly. "Can our wagons travel up your road, mistress?"

"Ours can. Don't see why yours can't. You'll have to give 'em a push now and them."

They emerged at the other end of the road muddy and exhausted. In the end, everyone had dismounted and helped. Going up, they had pushed the wagons through the soft and muddy soil, and coming down, they had held them back with ropes to keep the mules from being bowled over.

When they had straightened themselves out and were on their way again, Berenguer turned to the captain. "What was that about? I was sure it was a trap."

"It was, Your Excellency," said the captain. "There were thirty armed men waiting for us at the bridge. Yusuf climbed a tree to look around. Out of simple curiosity, I think," he added. "And that was what he saw."

"But the women did not want to confess that there was a trap waiting on the road."

"It was a trap made up of their sons and husbands, I would guess. Odd that they should mention a sick man."

"They were after young Gilabert," said the Bishop. "Clearly. And that means that someone hired them to attack us. No ragtag group of mountain men could possibly have any interest in him."

It was a long, hard walk along the mountainside. They stopped every hour or so, when the road was flat enough to justify it, and rested briefly. There was food in abundance, but soon enough most were too tired to eat it.

"When do we get to the top?" asked the kitchen lad.

"We never get to the top," said assistant cook. "Do you want to? It's a long way up. But we start coming down again soon."

"That'll be easier," said the lad, incurably optimistic.

"In some ways."

It was. Easier on the lungs, but hard on tired legs. It was well into the afternoon when, with aching calves, they ended their slow descent at the bridge over the river. The captain called a halt.

"Papa," said Raquel, "it's beautiful."

"What is, my dear?" said her father, whose mind was filled with other things.

"Olive groves, Papa, and vineyards. They look so green and well tended. There are hills ahead of us, but not a single mountain."

The sun was low on the horizon before they entered Vil-afranca de Penedès, heading for the royal palace. It was the twenty-ninth of April; Tarragona was thirty miles away. The conference would begin in thirty-six hours. While the cooks and their helpers were revictualing the wagons, and the stable lads were cleaning the mud and dirt from the horses and mules, Berenguer sat in council with Bernat, Francesc, and the captain.

"We will leave at sunrise," said Berenguer. "Before the others. I must reach Tarragona tomorrow, and I'd like to avoid the heat of the day."

"Do you wish me to accompany you, Your Excellency?" asked the captain.

"No, Captain. I need you to stay and look after the rest of them."

While the others were dealing with mud on boots and tunics and gowns, Gilabert looked at his torn hose, his stained and muddy riding boots and ill-fitting physician's tunic, wondering whether it was possible to wear them to dine in the royal palace, even if there were no royal presence in the great hall. "It is one thing," he explained to Yusuf, who had been sent to see how he was after his day's exertions, "to be dressed like a travel-stained and muddy gentleman. That is excusable. It is another to look as if one robbed corpses for their garb," he said ruefully.

"If I knew where to find you something else to put on, señor," said Yusuf, "I would do so at once. My master has an extra tunic that would fit you better, but it would reach to your ankles."

"Then I would look even more like a physician. I cannot carry off the pretense, I fear," said Gilabert. "I shall brush the mud off these, and clean my boots, and present myself as I am."

"I will find someone to clean your boots," said Yusuf.

When Yusuf returned with the boots, Gilabert was lying on his bed, staring up at the dark ceiling of his chamber. "You are a welcome sight, Yusuf," he said, sitting up. "Let us go down to the courtyard and enjoy the evening. My thoughts make poor companions at the moment."

Slowly, but more easily than before, Gilabert descended the elaborate stone stairs into the courtyard. He walked over to a bench near the fountain and sat down gratefully. "You are interested in horsemanship, are you not, Yusuf? You ride well—almost as well as I did at your age."

"I have had little opportunity to practice, señor," said Yusuf.

"Very true. And one can see it in some of your movements. But your abilities impressed me."

"His Majesty said that if I were to come to court, I would have my own horse from the royal stable, and my own mule for traveling," said Yusuf, in wistful tones.

"And will you?"

"How can I leave my master? He clothed me and fed me when I was in rags and starving. He saved my life, he has hired masters to teach me to read and to write in your manner, and he has already taught me much about healing the sick. Also he is blind, and if his daughter marries, who will assist him?"

"She is very beautiful," said Gilabert. "And very skilled."

"Yes. So she will marry. When she is in the city, my mistress makes her wrap up like a parcel to keep staring eyes away from her."

"She is wise. The eyes of every man here—including the priests'—are fixed on her. I watch them sometimes to while away the time."

"You are a wonderfully skilled rider," said Yusuf. "I never saw a man so wounded mount a horse like that, or control it so well."

"You flatter me, young Yusuf. I ride tolerably well, but in the last few years I have done a great deal of it, for one reason or another. It has been a restless life, the one I have led." He fell silent. "Could you ask His Excellency if I might have a word with him, young Yusuf?" he said at last. "I would go myself, but these days I am not so swift as you are."

"I will go and ask him," said Yusuf, and slipped away.

"I am sorry to disturb Your Excellency," said Gilabert.

"It is nothing," said Berenguer. "It is a pleasant evening, and the courtyard is most inviting. Do you object to the presence of my physician?"

"Not at all. Everything I have to say he is most welcome to hear."

"Then you have all my attention," said Isaac gravely.

"An hour from here, off the Tarragona road," said Gilabert, "is my father's modest *finca*. With your permission and gracious help, Your Excellency, I will leave your party tomorrow for there. When I recover my health and strength, I will follow to Tarragona. In a few days, I hope."

"You wish us to take you to your father's house?"

"No. That is too much to ask. I only request the use of a mule to take me to the *finca* when we part, and a man to bring the mule back to you. Once I arrive, my uncle will give me a horse."

"Your uncle?"

"A very generous man. Or my father, of course," he added. "It is not a difficulty. I have business in Tarragona, and expect to see you there, Your Excellency, before the General Council ends.''

''And what does my physician think of that?''

''It is possible,'' said Isaac. ''But if Your Excellency does not object, I would like to accompany him, and to take my daughter with me. I think he will find the exercise more difficult than he imagines, and I wish to examine his wound after he arrives. And rebandage his hand before he disappears from my care.''

''Is that acceptable?''

''It is,'' said Gilabert.

''Good. The captain will arrange it. I wish you a joyous reunion with your father, and I pray that you are not come too late to see him.''

''To see him? Oh, of course. I try not to count on that. But my uncle will be there, even if my father is not.''

''And certainly you may have a mule and an escort to take you to your family. For now, I bid you farewell. At daybreak I leave for Tarragona; Francesc and Bernat go with me. And, young Gilabert, no matter who you are, with all my heart I wish you more happiness than you have had.''

''And who do you suspect I am, Your Excellency?''

''I do not know,'' said Berenguer. ''But God be with you tomorrow and always. Shall we go up to dine?''

And the three men, followed by Yusuf, went back up the staircase and along the gallery into the great dining hall, where the company was gathering for supper.

# SIX

**Wednesday, April 30**

The hall at the palace was almost empty the next morning when the captain entered. "Hola, señor," he said. "I am glad to see you up and at table. Does this mean that you can ride?"

"I can ride," said Gilabert, who was sitting at his breakfast.

"Good. His Excellency and the private left at sunrise. You are to ride His Excellency's mule. She is a tractable beast—or as tractable as one can expect from a mule. And I am to have the honor of escorting you."

"I am most grateful. Have you seen the physician? Is he also ready?"

"He is, indeed, Captain," said a voice from the broad doorway.

"You are most punctual to your hour, Master Isaac," said the captain, turning to answer the physician and his daughter. "If we leave now, we will be able to rejoin the rest of the procession without delaying them. Today's journey is somewhat long."

"Then let us go at once," said Isaac.

"His Excellency told me that your father's *finca* is an hour away at a moderate pace. Is that so?"

"It is. Even at walking pace it cannot be much more."

The rest of the party should have set out less than an hour later but, at the time decided upon, only a handful of people were in the courtyard waiting. The sergeant and His Excellency's cook were still busying themselves with the purchase of bread and sundry other supplies to restock the wagons. "We are ready to leave, I think, Sergeant," said the cook. "Once we have checked the supplies and the loading of the wagons."

But the wagons were not loaded.

The sergeant looked coldly about him, counting up his troops. "Where is everyone?" he asked, in tones of barely controlled rage.

"In the stable," said the kitchen lad, when no one else spoke.

"What are they doing in the stable?" asked the sergeant.

"They had to rise before dawn, and do their morning's work, and then saddle up the animals for those who left early, and now they are too weary to go on, they told me," said the kitchen lad, and scurried off to the supply wagon to give the appearance of being busy.

"I'll give them weary," said the sergeant, and headed for the stable.

The sergeant's roars lifted them onto their feet, but still the work was done with slow and awkward fingers, and took twice the time it usually did. The sun was shining clear in the sky above the trees before the mules were saddled and the wagons were ready to leave.

Gilabert and the captain, followed by Isaac and Raquel, rode sedately for somewhat longer than the young man had promised. "I apologize, Captain," said Gilabert. "I am not used to taking this road at such a relaxed pace. The small track that leads to our lands is just over that rise, and soon I can promise refreshment for man and beast."

"If we are ahead of the others, I am content," said the captain. "It is a pleasant morning."

Although the road kept to the level plain, the landscape on either side was hilly and wooded; to their left, distant mountains formed a barrier between them and the sea. The riders crested the small rise, crossed a fast-flowing stream, and stopped. "Is that the road?" asked the captain.

"It is," said Gilabert.

The captain hung a scrap of black cloth on a branch overhanging the brook. "The sergeant will know from this banner that he has reached the road," he said. "He will wait for us here."

A hard-packed track ran straight across the plain. "It is not far now," said Gilabert. "A mile or so."

The road to the *finca* branched off two miles farther on and wound through a dark, still grove on the banks of the river Foix.

"It is quiet," said Gilabert uneasily. "Everyone must be sleeping."

"Then your father's household is not a very industrious one," said the captain. "Unless the silence is because of . . ."

"My father's death? Probably not," said Gilabert. "Come now, my gallant mule, let us find out where everyone is. They are likely in the fields, all of them, out of earshot."

"Your father's property must be extensive," said Isaac. "I hear only distant birds and . . . a horse, I think. Far off. It may be at some other property."

Made cautious by the silence around them, they moved ahead quietly. At the next turn in the road the house came in view and they stopped. Two low wings on either side of a blocklike center section enclosed a courtyard protected by stout wooden gates. The gates were half-opened, as if the porter had been interrupted in the middle of his task and had forgotten to return and complete it. Smoke rose from one of the chimneys.

The captain pointed to the ground ahead of them. A pool of blood had soaked into the earth, and was darkening in the sun. He dismounted in silence, drew his sword, and bent over to touch the spot. "It is still not quite dry," he murmured. "I wonder whose blood it is."

"There should be a porter," said Gilabert uneasily. "And a dog."

"I am going to the house to look. Stay mounted and come no closer."

"No, Captain," said Gilabert quietly. "Help me dismount."

"What do you see?" asked Isaac softly; while Gilabert was being helped from the mule, Raquel sketched the scene for him.

"Listen," said Isaac. In the ensuing hush, even the birds were silent. "I still hear nothing. The house may be empty."

A scrabbling sound in the brush near the gate made the captain whirl, sword at the ready. Then they heard a whimper, and a huge mastiff plunged out of the bushes and fell on the ground. "Cesar," said Gilabert, and swore in fury under his breath.

"What is it?" said Isaac.

"I would guess that someone tried to break into the house while the men were in the fields," said the captain. "He injured the guard dog."

"Stay back," said Gilabert softly. He called again, and the dog struggled to his feet. Congealing blood covered the side of his broad head, and he shook it gently, as if to clear it. He took a step, lurched, and almost fell again. Then he lowered his head unhappily and stood where he was.

"Poor little fellow," murmured Gilabert. The mastiff raised his head and wagged his tail; this time he managed to walk, wobbling somewhat, over to Gilabert. "Poor thing," he went on, stroking him gently. "They've hit you on the head and you're dizzy, aren't you?"

"Is he badly injured?" asked Isaac.

"There's a cut on his head, but the bleeding seems to be stopping."

"If the dried blood on the ground is his," said Isaac, "his attacker has had time to leave before we rode up."

"Unless he lies in ambush for us," said the captain, and started across the courtyard.

Gilabert snatched up a pole from behind the gate to use as a staff, and went after the captain. The big dog leaned against him, and they limped together to the door. "You were just a puppy when I left, weren't you?" he said. "Now let us go in and see what else has been done," he added grimly.

The mastiff stopped, stiff-legged and with his hackles raised, as soon as they walked into the house. Then, growling and tense in every muscle, he stalked toward the room closest to the entrance and pushed open the door. Gilabert put a hand on his neck, ordering him to stay where he was; the two of them blocked the doorway, staring inside. The captain, unable to see what they were looking at, pushed his way past.

In the pleasant, well-furnished room two men, seated at a table at an angle to each other, lay with their heads almost touching, as if they were engaged in negotiations of greatest secrecy. But the table was drenched in blood, as was the cloth of their soberly cut tunics.

"Is one of these men your father?" asked the captain. "There are two of them, Master Isaac," he added in a low voice. "They have been stabbed, over and over, with long daggers, I would guess."

"Dead?" asked Isaac.

"There is no question of that," said the captain. "No man could live and bear that many thrusting wounds into his body."

"Not my father," said Gilabert. "My uncle, Fernan—my mother's brother—and my steward, Ramon. They were watching over the estate in my absence."

"Come out of this room," said the captain, and led Gilabert into a small sitting room, where he collapsed on a carved wooden bench, deathly pale. The others followed. "Where would your father be?" he asked.

"Where he has been these last six years—in his tomb," said Gilabert. "Where he lies beside my mother, and they gaze on one another there as they did in life." He shook his head. "This was such a senseless act. What good could they imagine this would do them? He was not an heir. He had no interest in the estate. But I will avenge it," he said, with a chilling lack of emphasis. "Even if it costs me my life, I will avenge it."

"Do you know who did this?"

He looked up. "I think I know, Captain," he said. "I doubt that I could prove it against him before the law, but I think I know who he is."

"I will look through the house," said the captain briskly. "They may still be here. Keep the dog with you and bolt the door until I return."

"I will see to my patient," said Isaac.

The sound of the captain's spurs clattering on the floor echoed through the empty house. Gilabert sat, his hand on the mastiff's neck still, listening to his protector walk from room to room as he searched the building. Raquel found a jug of wine, and one of water, and mixed him something to drink. She held it to his lips. He shook his head vaguely and continued to listen. After an eternity the footsteps returned, and the captain called out, "Don Gilabert, pray open the door. It is the captain."

"How do we know that?" said Gilabert, assailed by sudden horrible doubts.

"You rode at a snail's pace beside me on His Excellency's mule from Vilafranca to here. I placed a scrap of black cloth on an oak tree over a stream. Is that enough? Ask the physician. He knows my voice."

"If that is not our captain," said Isaac, "I shall cease the practice of medicine."

Gilabert pulled back the heavy bolts and opened the door. The captain stepped inside, dragging after him two trembling, weeping women whose hands were as red and chapped as their noses. "I like a cautious soldier," he said. "He lives longer, and therefore does not waste his training."

"I am not well equipped to fend off enemies at the moment," said Gilabert. He looked at the two women, who in better times would have been plumply pleasant looking, and nodded. "I am glad someone is still here."

"Don Gilabert!" said the taller of the two, turning white-faced with shock. "You are still alive. Heaven be praised."

"What happened?"

"There was a crowd—" she said.

"A horde—" interrupted the shorter one.

"Indeed, a horde of men came riding up, and when Josep opened the gate to them, they killed him and threw his body into the ditch in the meadow. The new chambermaid saw it from the window, and we went and looked, too, and then she turned and ran as fast as she could out of the house by the back way, calling to cook and the maids to run."

"And did they?" asked the captain.

"I think so. But then we hid in the clothespress," said the short one. "They didn't find us. We heard people screaming, didn't we?"

"We did, and we stayed where we were."

"Then someone screamed that the master was murdered. After that it was quiet. We stayed in the press a long time but we had to come out—"

"I couldn't breathe," said the tall one.

"And just after that we heard this gentleman in the hall-way."

"They were trying to scramble back into the clothespress when I caught them. They said that you would know who they were."

"I do indeed. Did you recognize the men who did this?"

"No," said the short one.

"Not really," said the other, doubtfully. "I only saw their backs from the window."

"Where are the rest of our men?"

"Out in the far fields. Pau should be back very soon—the master wanted to see him this morning." At that, she burst into tears once more, covered her face in her apron, and rocked back and forth.

"Can we wait until he comes?" asked Gilabert, turning to his companion. "I would like to give him some instructions. But then I must go to Tarragona."

"Of course, Don Gilabert," said the captain.

Gilabert turned to the two maids. "Only you and Pau may know I am alive. Otherwise I will be pursued, slaughtered like my uncle, and you will be sent away to earn what you can or starve. Do you understand? Not a word. Pau will see that my uncle, and Ramon, and Josep are buried; you will not breathe my name. If you stay silent, I will return, and you will be well rewarded, more generously than if the assassins buy your disloyalty."

"Yes, Don Gilabert," they said together.

"Good." He pulled out his purse and handed it to Raquel. "Please, Mistress Raquel, take two coins and give one to each woman. There are many things it is difficult to do with only one hand."

"Certainly, Don Gilabert," said Raquel.

"There will be more—much more—for you when I return," continued the young man. "If you have been true."

"We will, Don Gilabert," said the short one, her voice quavering.

"Now, bring me Pau when he returns, and say nothing. Right now I need you to get me some clothes."

It was not long before the four riders were returning along the winding narrow road to the highway. Gilabert was now dressed in a sober suit of clothes befitting a gentleman and mounted on a horse. The captain was leading the Bishop's mule.

The main party noted the fast-flowing stream, the narrow road, and the little black banner, and stopped. "We might as well wait and water the animals," said one of the guards. "They must still be here."

"I agree," said the sergeant casually. "I believe I will ride up that road to greet the captain."

"I'll come along with you," said the guard.

"What if we're attacked again?" asked the nuns' priest nervously.

"Cry out for help," said the sergeant. "We won't be that far away."

They came across the captain around the first bend in

the road, riding in their direction, leading the mule. By his side was Gilabert, on a glossy bay mare, looking as if he were about to fall off her back, and closely followed by Raquel and her father. Before they could say anything, the captain gestured forcefully for silence. He pointed them back to the road, and the little party returned without a word to the highway.

"Get Don Gilabert off the mare and onto the wagon," said the captain quietly. "Before he swoons away. We will wait until the physician has time to look after him, and then move the wagons out as soon as possible." The sergeant nodded, noting with interest that his captain had used the servants' jesting honorific for the young man in sober earnest. The captain removed his signal from its branch, and as soon as Don Gilabert was settled, the group was on its way.

They had not traveled far when Felip fell into pace with Isaac's mule. He smiled at Raquel and took the lead rein from her. "How is the young lord?" he asked. "We have heard terrible rumors."

"You take a great interest in him, do you not?" asked Isaac.

"We sat with him that first night, when his life was despaired of," said Felip. "Perhaps our modest assistance helped him."

"I understand that," said Isaac. "His uncle was savagely butchered. Along with his steward and the porter. He is shaken."

"Why would someone have done that?" asked Felip.

"He might have believed the uncle would claim Don Gilabert's estate."

"Surely, Master Isaac, you cannot believe that young man ordered his uncle's death."

"Not at all," said Isaac. "As long as Don Gilabert lived, the uncle had no claim to the property. It was only if he died that it would be useful to dispose of his uncle."

"Then why kill the uncle first?" said Felip. "That is taking the long road to your destination."

• • •

The rest of the day passed excruciatingly slowly. At each milestone, the captain checked the position of the sun and urged his weary group to a livelier pace. The shadows shortened and then lengthened again. "We are not making up for the time lost this morning," he said to his sergeant.

"With all respect, Captain," replied the sergeant, "we cannot reach the city tonight. Not with this group."

"Send Enrique ahead to find a respectable inn, Sergeant. If there is one that can house and feed so many at once."

"We have our own food. We will eat by the wayside. Any inn will have drink and somewhere we can sleep, even if only in a stable loft on straw."

# SEVEN

## The Inn

The road had been following a relatively straight course to the southwest, pursuing the sea, when it began to curve into the westering sun. "We are nearing the sea," said the head cook to the kitchen lad. "Not so very far now."

"What's that thing in the middle of the road?"

"That's the arch," said the cook.

"What's it doing there?"

"Who knows? But the city lies ten miles from this point."

"Ten miles more?" said the kitchen lad, and his heart sank.

"Don't worry," said the cook. "We'll be stopping soon."

The inn was like most of its kind. Crowded, noisy, and not very clean, offering cheap wine and worse food. But in spite of the quality of its food and drink, and the tawdriness of its surroundings, the establishment was evidently popular. Its benches were almost full, and the landlord had trouble keeping up with the calls for more wine.

The women looked at the crowd and, without a word, withdrew to a small, ramshackle porchlike shelter that had been constructed over the entrance at one time. They sat, jammed together on a narrow bench and perched on empty wine barrels, without regard to anything except their common dignity and safety—mistress and maid, Christian and Jew—and waited until arrangements were made for them to withdraw.

The men looked for places in the tavern. Isaac followed Yusuf, his hand resting on the boy's shoulder; Don Gilabert came after them, assisted by the young guard, Enrique, and the sergeant. Yusuf picked out the quietest corner, and headed straight for it. The rest of the Bishop's entourage followed.

One man was seated on the bench nearest them. On the other side of the table, against the wall, two men were deep in an incoherent dispute over the likelihood of a change in the weather overnight.

"Excuse me, gentlemen," said Yusuf boldly, "but my master, who is blind, and this great lord, who has been wounded while on service for His Majesty, must sit. If you will move just a little." And he began settling his two charges down. With each reorganization of their persons and belongings, he commandeered more space, which the Bishop's retainers filled, until the disputants, edged off the end of the bench, wandered away to carry on their quarrel by observing the night sky.

The sergeant, who was holding a purse from the Bishop for just this emergency, went off to order jugs of wine enough to wash the dust of the road from everyone's throat, and to make sure that there would be beds for all, in one form or another.

"Sergeant," called the cook as the officer was leaving. "Don't concern yourself over a bed for us. We will sleep in the supply wagons. It would be best, I think."

"Take two of the lads," said the sergeant, after assessing the varied crowd in the room.

"They're out there already," he said. "Stealing His Excellency's wine, no doubt," he muttered into the assistant cook's ear.

And the assistant cook withdrew his lanky frame from

the bench and padded silently out to have a look at the
wagons. The cook waited for his cup of wine, drained it,
and followed.

Judith looked at the beds in the chamber they had been
given and sent Ibrahim and Naomi to fetch their box. From
it she withdrew clean bedclothes to spread over the dubious
ones left by the innkeeper. The four narrow beds that had
been pushed into the room had stretched the inn's resources; most of the men had to make do with straw pallets
on the floor downstairs in the common dining room. At two
to a bed, the room would barely accommodate all the
women.

"Oh, Mama," whispered Raquel, looking around in dis-
may at the crowd of tired women. "I think I would rather
sit downstairs for the night."

"Nonsense," said Judith firmly. "You are much safer
up here."

And Raquel and her mother took off their surcoats, loosened their gowns, and composed themselves. Raquel
watched from under her half-closed eyes as the nuns removed their veils and wimples and did the same. The servants, who had walked all or most of the way, were too
tired for anything but a few complaints. Of Sor Agnete, as
usual, there was no sign. She was somewhere safe, Raquel
supposed, with her guard. Then, weary, aching, longing for
space and privacy, she gave herself up to brooding thoughts
and soon slept, from pure exhaustion.

It was early when a noise from somewhere awakened Isaac.
He knew it was light. The birds were noisily busy, and the
air had a tang that disappeared after dark. Someone was
moving about, no doubt in the kitchen, but his weary chamber mates slept on, undeterred by the noise or the discomfort of their beds. "Yusuf?" he called softly, and waited.
There was no reply. The lad was still sleeping. He reached
down, found his staff, and rose to his feet.

Making his way cautiously across the room, he headed
out the door and around to the well. He stripped off his

outer garments and his shirt, pulled up a bucket of water, and washed vigorously, as thoroughly as he could. Shivering in the cool of dawn, he combed his fingers through his wet hair and beard, shook out his shirt and tunic, and put them on before saying his morning prayers. As he finished, he heard a giggle behind him. He was not the only soul to be awake at the inn this morning, he knew; he guessed that whoever had been working in the kitchens, lighting the fires, was now sharing the inn yard with him.

"I wish you good morning," said Isaac.

"Good morning, sir," said a child's voice. "What were you doing out here?"

"First I washed," he said, "and then I said my prayers. Now I am ready for the day to begin. You are also an early riser, are you not?"

"I must start the fires before my master wakes," he said, and paused for a while. "But someone in your party was awake before you, sir. He came to ask me if the injured man was still with you. I said I didn't know who who he was talking about, because there were two men with bandages on their arms. I saw them last night when I crept in to see all the gentry."

"Are you sure he said he was with our party?"

"That's what he said, for all that he didn't come with you. He was the fat one who fell behind on the road."

"Where is he now, lad?"

"He was here at first light this morning. I think he's gone on ahead. And sir, if you come into the kitchen with me," he said in a conspirator's voice, "I know where the bread is hidden. I will share some with you. They won't even know it's gone."

"That is very kind of you," said Isaac, "but I must go back to my friends." He reached into his purse and took out a penny. "Here," he said. "This is for you, for beginning my day with an offer of kindness."

"Pardon?" said the boy.

Isaac flipped the coin in the direction of the voice and strode confidently back the way he came. As he rounded

tho corner, he felt a whisper of warmth strike his cold
cheek; the sun was rising.

There was no temptation to linger at the inn any later than
was absolutely necessary. The others were on their feet by
the time Isaac returned, readying themselves for travel as
quickly as they could. The scent of their destination was
on them, and they all stepped out with a livelier tread.

The sun was low in the sky but bright. A cool breeze off
the sea swept across their faces. Andreu and Felip started
to sing, and were joined by the two cooks, and then a couple of stable lads, and finally most of the rest of the party.
At the top of every hill they caught a glimpse of the sea
dancing off to their left. Finally at the top of a steepish rise
Raquel saw a tall spire floating in the air ahead of them.
"Look," she said. "What's that?"

"The cathedral, Mistress Raquel," said the captain. "It
has a fine tower, has it not?"

"And that thing, down there?" she asked, pointing to a
solid structure of weathered stone that stood beside the
road.

"They say the Romans left that, when they were here,"
said the captain. "That was a long time ago."

And well before the sun was high in the sky they rode
through the gates of Tarragona.

# PART THREE

# ONE

### The Archbishop's Palace

Berenguer de Cruilles arrived at the archiepiscopal palace and requested the honor of an immediate audience with Don Sancho Lopez de Ayerbe. The Archbishop's reply was swift. His Excellency was desolate, but he was resting. Berenguer rid himself of the dust and mud of travel, changed his clothing, and dined. The Archbishop did not appear. When he had eaten, Berenguer sent another message to His Excellency. Don Sancho regretted inconveniencing the Bishop of Girona, but he was engaged in preparations for the council.

"May I suggest that Your Excellency take some air?" said Bernat. "The view from the ramparts is very pleasant."

"No, Bernat. You may not suggest. And you sound exactly like Don Sancho when you say that. I shall stay in the palace until I see the Archbishop," said Berenguer, whose face was white with suppressed anger. "Then you may suggest whatever you like."

"Certainly, Your Excellency. This might be a good time to go over the papers we brought—"

"The only thing I could bear to do right now is play

chess with my physician, who does not irritate me with suggestions,'' said the Bishop.

"Unfortunately the rest of the party has not arrived,'' observed Francesc.

"Are you sure?''

"The captain would have reported at once,'' he said with calm certainty. "It is quite possible that they will not reach the city until tomorrow,'' he added.

Berenguer left his comfortable apartments long enough to eat a hasty supper. Once more the Archbishop failed to appear at his own board. Berenguer had just started to pace restlessly back and forth when a discreet knock on the door drew him from his unproductive train of thought.

"His Excellency would esteem it an honor if Your Excellency would see him in his chambers,'' said the little servant.

"Now?'' asked Berenguer.

"Yes, Your Excellency,'' he said. "If Your Excellency would follow me . . .''

Berenguer murmured a silent prayer for God to grant him patience and newfound humility and tried to compose himself. He followed the child through the corridors as meekly as he could, and waited, betraying no sign of his inner rage, for the summons to enter.

The Archbishop was seated on the far side of a heavy, intricately carved dark oak table, facing the door. With cold politeness he indicated that his guest should sit; he waited in silence while the little page brought the Bishop a cup of wine. "I trust you had an uneventful journey, Don Berenguer,'' he said.

"Quite uneventful, Your Excellency,'' said Berenguer amiably.

And with a look that indicated storm clouds ahead, the Archbishop leaned forward and paused significantly. "Is Agnete, the nun about whom I have written you, also with you?''

"In my haste to join Your Excellency, I left my retainers a little behind me this morning. She is with the rest of my

party, Your Excellency. I trust they, too, have had an uneventful journey. I have not heard otherwise."

"You left her behind you on the road?"

"She is with a considerable retinue, protected by my
personal guards, Your Excellency. I had no wish to miss
the beginning of the council and rode ahead with my confessor and my secretary."

"Word has reached me that one attempt has already been
made to secure her person—"

"An unsuccessful attempt."

"Do we know who made this attempt?"

"Bandits, under the command of one Mario. It is believed that they were acting for her family."

Don Sancho frowned, catching his lower lip between his
fingers and compressing it. It was a habit he had when
thinking, a very annoying habit, in Berenguer's opinion.
"Perhaps if you had arranged for her transfer here as soon
as the unhappy matter of the kidnapping of Doña Isabel
had been resolved, her family would not have had time to
make elaborate plans for her release."

"I have no doubt Your Excellency is correct," said Berenguer.

"If you had done so, Don Berenguer, the convent of Sant
Daniel, and indeed, the Abbess Elicsenda herself would not
have been drawn into the general scandal that attended the
affair. The delay has not shielded them from the consequences of the event. As you must be aware, it has had the
opposite effect."

"I am only too aware of that, Your Excellency. At the
time I urged the Abbess to send Sor Agnete here to the
Mother House immediately."

"But you did no more than urge, Don Berenguer."

"To my sorrow," said the Bishop, biting back the justifications that sprang to his lips. His silence, he admitted
ruefully to himself, sprang only from a well-developed political sense that this was no time to be defending himself.
Humility was still not one of his strengths.

"I do not suggest, as some have," continued Don Sancho, "that one of our bishops would have attempted to

conceal—for his own purposes—the involvement of the convent of Sant Daniel in treachery." It was clear from his faint smirk that he would have enjoyed suggesting it, but that the suggestion was too outrageous to entertain seriously. "Nevertheless His Majesty is angry that Sor Agnete has not yet been brought to a court—ecclesiastical or royal—for judgment."

"Does His Majesty challenge Your Excellency's right to try Sor Agnete in an episcopal court?" asked Berenguer. "I doubt that he could find any justification for such a challenge, even at this late date."

"No," said Don Sancho. "He admits our right to jurisdiction, but is not happy that nothing has been done so far." The Archbishop paused. "Or nothing that he—or anyone in the diocese—has been able to discern."

"Ah," said Berenguer. "In the diocese. Perhaps His Majesty's procurator, Don Vidal, has mentioned something of it to him."

"I believe he has touched upon the issue with His Majesty," said Don Sancho.

"Many issues become more complex when Church and State are mingled, as in the appointment of Vidal of Blanes," said Berenguer blandly. "It must be difficult for Don Vidal."

Sancho Lopez de Ayerbe looked sharply at the Bishop of Girona. "I suspect it is," he murmured.

"One hears that the papal nuncio will be in Tarragona for the conference," said Berenguer, with the air of a man who has not changed the subject.

"The papal nuncio has graced us with his presence," said the Archbishop.

"May one ask if some particular business brings him here?" asked Berenguer.

Don Sancho shook his head absentmindedly. "It has to do with a jurisdictional dispute," he said. "Quite a different one. He has been sent down to settle it."

"A jurisdictional dispute?"

"Between the archdiocese, the diocese of Barcelona, and the Inquisitor."

"The Inquisitor?" said Berenguer in surprise.

"Hmm," said Don Sancho. "But since the supposed heretic is nowhere to be found, and is thought by his neighbors to have died or perhaps left for France or England, I see no reason why the archdiocese or His Holiness's nuncio should waste time on the case. And it is a great waste of time."

"Might His Majesty have some interest in the case as well?" asked Berenguer.

Don Sancho gave him a long, speculative glance. "It is always a possibility," he said. "I wonder if you could be correct. You say you spoke to His Majesty in Barcelona, Don Berenguer?"

"Yes, Your Excellency, I spoke to His Majesty. Over another matter," said Berenguer. Court gossip traveled fast.

Don Sancho rose with a cordial smile. "I have kept you too long from your bed, Don Berenguer. You must be weary from your journey. But this little talk has been very fruitful, do you not agree? And I am sure the matter of Sor Agnete can be quickly resolved."

"I certainly hope so, Your Excellency. I most humbly take my leave, and wish you good night."

But on his way back to his own chamber, Berenguer wondered exactly what he had said that had pleased the Archbishop.

Another page was waiting for him in his chamber. "Your Excellency," he said, "my master wishes to see you. Will you come with me?"

"And who is your master, lad?" asked the Bishop.

"Pons de Santa Pau," whispered the boy, "servant to His Majesty."

"And where does he wish me to go? It has been a long day . . ."

"To the house of Raimundo. I have a cloak for Your Excellency. The evening is somewhat cool."

"I can withstand a somewhat cool May evening, lad," said Berenguer.

"My master feels it would be best if Your Excellency wore a cloak."

"I bow to his superior knowledge."

The page assisted the Bishop into a cloak of cheap, coarse stuff, and then donned a brown, lightweight one, of the sort worn by every apprentice and student in the city.

The boy led him in the opposite direction from the Archbishop's rooms, toward the smaller rooms and offices. They had just passed through a small but heavy side door when the page stopped and turned to the Bishop. "The way is somewhat confusing, Your Excellency. If you will lay your hand on my shoulder and follow, we will be there in a moment."

"The Inquisitor?" said Pons de Santa Pau. "Yes. There has been some attempt to institute a round of inquiries in the archdiocese. It has been more than twenty years since the last panic died down—"

"Surely you do not remember it," said Berenguer.

"No," said the young man. "I was in my cradle at the time, not at all concerned with such issues. But there are others who remember—and the sweep moved rapidly from fear of heresy to the city's Jews."

"We heard of an attack on a Jewish merchant that resulted in death and destruction of property. It angered His Majesty. Is that report true?"

"It is." And with great precision and economy, he filled in the background of the attack.

"That is most interesting," said Berenguer. "I shall pursue some issues you have touched upon."

"Good," said Santa Pau. "When my next report is completed, Your Excellency, you may include yours with it if you wish. I apologize for bringing you out here, but we can trust Raimundo, who owns this house. He was once part of my father's household; he is loyal and well paid."

"Most convenient."

Santa Pau rose and bowed. "I will send word as soon as my report is ready. It will be soon. The city is becoming agitated."

# TWO

## The Jewish Quarter and The Convent

On the morning of the first of May, the deep-voiced bell of the cathedral rang out in measured strokes, calling the bishops of the province of Tarragona to meet. Not that the summons was necessary. They were already waiting under the arches, dressed in the full splendor of their regalia, gossiping idly, waiting for the Archbishop. That morning, for the opening of the General Council, he would celebrate the Mass of the Holy Spirit, in the precise manner laid down when the first General Council was held, many years before.

The mass was impressive. Even though he had taken part many times in such ceremonies, Berenguer was moved by its beauty. The embroidered silk and fine linen glowed within the dark majesty of the cathedral; the well schooled choir sang the "Veni Sancte Spiritus" with one voice that reverberated under the high-arched roof; the Gospel of the day, "Ego sum pastor bonus," was sung with ethereal clarity by a deacon who possessed a tenor voice of rare quality.

Don Sancho rose to give his first sermon of the council, and Berenguer braced himself for a stinging attack on insubordination. *"Avaritia causa omnium malorum,"* he said. "Avarice is the cause of all evil," and delivered a sermon that was as brief as it was elegantly constructed. It was accounted by all to be a masterpiece of its type, even if the Bishop of Vic, who sat next to Berenguer and doubtless felt that it could not apply to him, fell asleep as soon as it started. He slumbered peacefully in his chair until the reading of the roll began.

Those who were present declared themselves. Those who had been unable to attend were accounted for by their representatives. For many of those sitting in the elaborately carved chairs around him, thought Berenguer somewhat cynically, the major business of the day was concluded. They had turned up; their presence had been noted. They would now feel free to sleep through the afternoon sessions, when particular business was being ironed out informally.

His knee, which had not troubled him since Sant Pol de Mar, began to ache.

It was not until later that morning that Joshua and Dinah's long-awaited guests finally arrived. Judith embraced her sister; Raquel curtsied dutifully to her aunt and uncle and stepped back from the fray just as Gilabert limped in through the gates. "My dear Joshua," said her father, "we bring with us one of my patients. Let me explain . . ."

Idly, Raquel watched Joshua accept Isaac's brief explanations and step forward graciously to greet his unexpected guest. But when his eye fell on the stranger he stiffened, like a man who rounds a corner and finds himself face-to-face with a bitter enemy. She looked at her aunt, who was smiling placidly, and at Joshua, who appeared once more to be the soul of courtesy. Shaken, she decided it had been a trick of her eyes, or of her mind.

"My husband's nephew was most anxious to be here to meet you," said Dinah, looking with satisfaction at her niece. "But he is at the warehouse and could not be spared."

"We are all just as anxious to meet him as he is to meet us," said Raquel, earning a powerful glare from her mother.

Gilabert was settled in a cool, airy room, and the rest of

the party gratefully dispersed to wash away the dirt and
dust of travel and change into clean garments.

The Lady Elicsenda was given no such chance. As hot and
dusty and thirsty as she felt walking into the Mother House
in Tarragona, she was swept at once into the Mother Superior's study.

"My dear Elicsenda, you have done the one thing that I
would never have thought possible of you." The sharp-
eyed and venerable-looking woman studied the kneeling
Abbess and shook her head.

"Yes, Domina," said the Abbess of Sant Daniel. "I have
done great wrong."

"No. That would not have surprised me. We are all capable of wrong. But, Elicsenda, that you—the cleverest of
all my nuns—should have behaved so stupidly, that astonished me. Wickedness can be atoned for, you know. People
understand it. But the effects of rank stupidity need to be
righted. And that can be hard work."

"I am prepared to do whatever must be done, Domina."

"It is somewhat late for that," she said waspishly, and
began walking up and down the room. "I wish that you
had arranged to send Agnete down here right away, instead
of waiting until now. You must understand that it now
looks to the world as if you would never have delivered
her if you had not been forced to do so."

"I see that now, Domina. I wanted to have enough time
to examine the charges against her," said Elicsenda. "Even
with her own words against her, I could not believe that
she had been involved in treachery."

"His Majesty did that, and was satisfied. Was that not
enough?"

"And then I feared that if she were sent to Tarragona
with any less than the strongest of escorts, that she would
be freed by her family. They are numerous, and have powerful friends."

"It would have been better for the order and for the
convent," said the Mother Superior, "to have her escape
while you were following the orders of your king and your

bishop. Instead you have angered Don Vidal, who has stirred up His Majesty's rage. Don Pedro is a generous and forgiving monarch, but he has a long memory for insults to his person and to his family, as everyone knows. He is capable of terrible vengeance.''

''I thought that I was saving everyone a great deal of trouble, Domina,'' said Elicsenda slowly. ''Including myself. Much of what I failed to do was from sloth. I see that now. I have been disobedient, and slothful, and stupid. I am not worthy to be abbess, Domina.''

''That is a thought that should be kept to yourself, Elicsenda. Wallowing in self-pity is a very dangerous form of pride. Rise, daughter,'' she said, holding out her hand. ''Come and sit here beside me, and help me devise a strategy for soothing the Archbishop.''

''And Agnete?''

''Agnete is beyond the help of any but God at the moment,'' said the Mother Superior. ''She is certainly beyond mine or yours, as you well know.''

''Yes, Domina. I have always known that.''

''Then why, if you knew it . . . But let us not indulge in fruitless recriminations. We will accept what is done as done, see what we can do to lessen the harm your actions have caused—yours and Agnete's.''

''Yes, Domina.''

''At the moment Don Sancho wishes to have you transferred here, where you will live in a modified form of perpetual penance.''

The color drained from her face. ''Modified?'' she repeated. And realized how unprepared she was to hear the expected sentence spoken aloud.

''As he sees your behavior, you have been disobedient, but not obdurate in sin. You might find it difficult, though, Elicsenda, to live such a life.''

''I am ready to embrace whatever life His Excellency deems suitable to my fault, Domina,'' she said in a low voice.

''Are you? I wonder. I think it would be more useful to have you return to Girona. The convent needs someone like you, Elicsenda. I have an abundance of repentant nuns, but not very many with your skills. Therefore I would prefer to see you at its head. Now we must see what can be done to set things right again. We cannot hope to see His Excellency right away, but he has agreed to hear us on Saturday after mass.''

Judith had taken a careful look at Don Gilabert and decreed that he should spend the rest of the afternoon and evening in his comfortable chamber. Once a late and elaborate dinner had been laid on the table in the courtyard, and eaten with varying degrees of enjoyment by all the household and guests present, Raquel slipped away once more to sit with him, bringing with her some fruit on a plate.

He lay staring at the wall, a picture of misery and despair.

''Oh, Don Gilabert,'' she said, kneeling on the floor by his bed, ''you must not allow yourself to give way to sorrow. You must recover your strength.''

''What do you know of these things, my angel from heaven?'' he asked, sounding amused.

''I have seen much of people's sorrow, helping my father,'' she said. ''And much of tribulation.''

''And yet you look as if nothing has ever troubled that perfect countenance,'' he said. ''I feel that if I touched it with my tortured fingers they might heal.''

''I doubt that,'' said Raquel, looking alarmed and rising to her feet. ''You are more likely to heal if you eat something. I saw that plate that Naomi brought downstairs. There was as much on it coming down the steps as there had been going up.''

''I cannot be nagged into eating food that could only be enjoyed after a long day's ride through snowy mountains in pursuit of game.''

''She does nag,'' said Raquel, sitting down. ''And Aunt Dinah's dinner was rather . . . substantial,'' she added, after a brief search for the best word to describe her aunt's kitchen. She took an apricot, cut it, and presented half to him.

He nibbled on it. "Food from your hand tastes like food for the gods, Mistress Raquel," he murmured.

"You must not talk like that," she said. "It is wrong . . . and impossible."

"What is impossible? For me to fall in love with a beautiful, skillful, and sweet-tempered woman who comes to me in my despair and makes me want to live again? How is that impossible?"

"I can never tell whether you are serious or not, Don Gilabert, and to listen to you speak like that and not mean it distresses me. It is unkind."

"Why does it distress you? If you do not believe me to be serious, then laugh at me, as you usually do."

"I cannot laugh at you," she said in a low voice.

"Then believe that I love you," he replied.

"You can't," she said, rose, and began to walk around the room.

"Why not?"

"Because we are different. Because I could never become your—I am the daughter of a family of standing in my community. I cannot disgrace them, or myself."

"Dear God, Mistress Raquel, you can't believe that I am suggesting adding you to a *harim* of beauties that I maintain at my *finca*." In his agitation he swung his legs down onto the floor and sat up. "I am proposing honorable marriage, with settlements, and agreements, and all the panoply of the law. Now that for some blessed reason we have been left alone, and I can speak."

Tears began to form in her eyes. "Don Gilabert, I cannot."

"What can't you do, my dearest, most beautiful Raquel?"

"Turn my back on my family and my religion. Not after my sister. It would destroy my mother. And sorely upset my father."

"But not you?"

"It would tear me apart," she said, looking stricken.

"What happened to your sister?"

"She married a Christian," said Raquel.

"Damnation!" said Gilabert. "Why did she do that? And if she hadn't—don't answer me that question. I could not bear to hear your reply, no matter what it was."

"I cannot answer," said Raquel, "whether you wish it or not." And she turned from him to hide her tears.

"Raquel?" called her mother's sharply familiar voice. "I need you. Come down from your room."

"I must go," she said.

"First you must tell me you love me. Say it is true, Gilabert, I love you. And I will live on that for now." He grasped her hand with his good hand. "Say it, or I will not let you go."

"It is true, Gilabert," she whispered, "I do love you, to my infinite pain and sorrow." And she fled.

While Raquel was talking to Gilabert, Judith settled into a shaded corner of the courtyard with her sister Dinah to have a serious talk on the subject uppermost in their thoughts.

"Your Raquel is a beauty," said Dinah approvingly. "She was not a pretty child when I last saw her, but that often happens, doesn't it? The pretty ones grow up ugly. Impossible to marry off without huge dowries."

"She was only five when you left home," said Judith. "But she is much admired, I will admit."

"We always were a handsome family," said Dinah with a laugh. "Even my girls, whose father is no beauty—"

"Hush, Dinah," said her sister, shocked. "You mustn't tempt the Lord by praising your children—"

"You don't change, sister. Still telling me what to do."

"Nor do you. You never did have respect for—well— the people and things you should have respect for. I haven't forgotten when—"

"Now, Judith," said Dinah, raising her hand to stop the flow of words. "Let us see what we can do about this marriage. We can spend the next week fighting old quarrels. What does her father think of it?"

"Isaac? He refuses to interfere, as he calls it. As if a father should not concern himself with his daughter's marriage. But if we arrange it and Raquel is happy, he'll consent. And settle a reasonable amount on her. Of course, she does not need to buy a husband—''

''She has other suitors?''

''Oh, yes. The nephew and heir of Ephraim the glove maker wants her.''

''And what does she think?''

''She does not dislike him. I have been watching her most carefully, and I would say she is not in love with anyone at the moment,'' said Judith firmly. ''Now tell me about Joshua's nephew.''

''We have only the two girls,'' said Dinah. ''As you know. And Joshua is not a young man. I am not likely to have another child.'' She said this defiantly, as if challenging her sister to mock or pity her.

''Your daughters are delightful children, and their father dotes on them,'' said Judith tactfully.

''Yes,'' said Dinah. ''And they will have handsome dowries. But I have raised Ruben since he was nine, when his parents died, and he is almost like a son to me. And to Joshua. He is a good boy, and clever—a little shy, but charming when you get to know him. He will inherit the business and this house. And that is not a small thing, Judith,'' she said.

''I can see that,'' said her sister, looking around her.

''We haven't much family left, you and I,'' said Dinah. ''What will happen to my daughters when Joshua dies? Ruben might marry a girl who thinks her husband shouldn't help his cousins, or his aunt by marriage. A girl who doesn't like me and wants me to leave. This is my house, Judith.''

''You think Ruben would listen to his wife?''

''Yes. He would. He's too sweet and easygoing. He needs a wife who understands the importance of family.''

''Our family.''

''Yes.''

''Raquel can be difficult sometimes, but she never forgets her duty to her parents,'' said Judith. ''And that is the truth. Which is more than I could ever say for her sister.''

''Then we must get them together. Not tonight, I think.

Raquel looks tired from the journey, and Ruben is—well—nervous. Tomorrow, but they must sit as far apart as we can put them, as if we had no interest in a match."

"An excellent plan," said Judith with a nod. "You always were a good schemer. Let me call her. I'd like you to get to know her." She looked up toward Raquel's chamber and called. "Raquel? I need you. Come down from your room." She smiled at her sister. "But not a word about Ruben."

When the heat of the day began to ease, and the city stirred itself from its afternoon somnolence, Andreu and Felip headed for the cathedral, instruments in hand, looking like men ready to explore the riches available from the crowds brought in by the council.

"I think," said Andreu, "that a cup of wine would not go amiss."

"But where?" asked Felip.

"This is the street of the Scriveners," said Andreu. "There is a tavern here, close to the cathedral."

"How very convenient," said Felip, and in they went.

"I wonder if those two men still come by—what were their names?"

"Miró and Benvenist," said Felip just as the landlord set their wine cups on the table.

"Those two scoundrels?" said the landlord. "Are they friends of yours?"

"Only the slightest of acquaintances," said Andreu. "They recommended your wine most heartily to us."

"I haven't seen them in two days," said the landlord. "They used to be here every day. Then this little fellow came in and said he had a message for them, but he couldn't wait. So he gave me the message, and a couple of pence for my trouble. When I told them what it was, they ran out of here, leaving my reckoning unpaid, and hers, too," he said, pointing down the street, "the widow they lived with. No one's seen them since."

"What did they say when they heard it?"

" 'By Christ Jesu,' or some blasphemy like that, 'that's

it.' Or 'that must be it.' Then the big one laughed and slapped the other. They knocked over a bench, and they left.''

"How much did they owe you?" asked Felip.

The landlord gave them a calculating look. "Ten pence," he said. "Enough for a poor man like me."

"You should be more careful with your credit," said Andreu, putting money down on the table for their wine. "They're a scurrilous pair. But if we see them, we'll mention the debt."

"They could have ridden from here to there early Wednesday morning," said Felip as they walked up the steps toward the front of the cathedral.

"Easily," said Andreu. "But I would guess they took advantage of the moon and rode by night a good part of the way."

"I wonder what else the landlord knows about them?"

"And the widow who gave them lodging. It will cost us something to pry loose their tongues."

It was warm and peaceful in the courtyard. Raquel had resolutely stayed away from Gilabert's room, sending Yusuf off to perform small services for him that her mother, all ignorant, had asked her to do. "Is Raquel well?" asked her aunt Dinah.

"Very well," said Judith. "My Raquel is strong and energetic, like me. But like you, sister, she has her moments of laziness. Yusuf is so glad to take on her errands that she sometimes allows him to do her work."

"She is young," murmured Dinah. "She will learn. I am weary, sister. I think I will go to my bed."

"And I, sister," said Judith. "It has been a long journey."

Everyone followed them, except for the physician and his brother-in-law. The night sky was faraway velvet pierced with bright stars, and in the distance the sea murmured relentlessly. "It feels like a clear night," said Isaac.

"It is," said Joshua. "It is beautiful. The sky is carpeted with stars. It makes me wonder if I could bear your affliction as calmly as you seem to, brother. To feel only, and not to see.''

"One bears what one must," said Isaac. "And although often I am not as calm as I try to appear, I might as well complain that the sea is wet as that I am blind. I can do nothing to change it. And many things are left to me. I hear, and smell, and taste as well as feel." He paused and sniffed the air. "Are we to meet your nephew, Joshua?"

"Ruben? I certainly hope so, brother. At the moment I believe he is in the house, but hiding."

"Hiding? What cause has he to hide, if I may ask?"

"Fear. He is terrified." Joshua laughed. "And before you can ask me what terrifies him, let me explain that it is not a what, but a who."

"Who could keep him from his family and his supper?"

"A potent combination, Isaac. My wife and your daughter."

"He, too, has no desire to be matched with an unknown distant cousin."

"Indeed. Ruben has fallen in love. She is a small, shy mouse of girl, with a very modest fortune. She comes from a respectable, but by no means distinguished, family. And my wife . . ." His voice trailed away.

"I understand," said Isaac, laughing. "After all, your wife and mine are sisters. Perhaps we should take a hand in the matter before the young man starves himself for thwarted love."

"It may not be that easy."

"I did not suggest it would be easy—only necessary." He paused, listening to some small night sound. "But you, Joshua, sound weary. I must not keep you from your bed because I am restless with the weariness of travel."

"I am an old man, Isaac. An old man married to a young wife. That in itself is cause enough to be weary, is it not? But it is not my good Dinah who saps my strength. These days, the very stones of the city are uneasy and keep me from sleep. While others rest I prowl about the house and the courtyard and listen for the blow that will tell us that the end has come. Then, when the sky begins to lighten, I

realize that my fears are—not groundless, but exaggerated—
and I go to my bed and sleep for a while.''

"Three men were killed yesterday morning," said Isaac.
"At a *finca* hard by the road to Tarragona. Among them
was Fernan, the uncle of young Gilabert whom you are now
sheltering. I am not sure that the death of Don Fernan and
his men signals the end coming, but it seemed ominous.''

"Why ominous?"

"Because, if the young man is to be believed, the assassins could pretend to no good in Fernan's death. No one
benefited from it.''

"Surely that could not be entirely true," said Joshua
tranquilly. "There must have been some who felt that they
would benefit.''

"Indeed? And why do you say that?"

"There are always people who feel that the death of a
landowner might bring them an advantage. Perhaps they
have tried to discredit him, or even destroy his reputation
at various other times already," said Joshua.

"I would be very interested in knowing what you know
of the affair," said Isaac.

"Of this particular one, nothing at all. What do I know
of Christian landowners who live miles away from here? I
spoke in generalities only.'' He paused, and poured a little
wine into both their cups. "It did bring to mind another
case, however, one that I was more familiar with.''

"I would like to hear it, if you are not too weary."

"Not at all. This particular landholder's name is—no, I
will not tell you his name. Let us call him Don Fernan as
well for the moment," said Joshua. "We had extensive
business dealings over the years—extensive, profitable, and
very amicable. He did not own his holding, but had the
management of his brother-in-law's estate. His young sister
was a very worthy woman, one hears, who lived quietly
surrounded by household and family, greatly loved by all.
I believe she had a son, and perhaps one or two daughters,
but I cannot be sure of that. I never met the woman. Then,
some years ago, six perhaps, the brother-in-law died—''

"Of the plague?"

"In the plague, perhaps," said Joshua, "but as I remember, not of it. Even in that terrible year, people died of other causes."

"They did," said Isaac. "I remember that, too."

"After his death, a document was produced by his neighbor, a deed of gift of all his land, house, and the possessions therein, in return for a debt owing. Now, Don Fernan looked at the document and swore straightaway that the signature was not that of his dead brother-in-law. Other men came forward to attest to the same, I believe."

"But that should have settled the affair, should it not?"

"Ah well, as you know, Isaac, when a greedy man makes a claim of this sort, he usually takes care to have a powerful person or two behind him. The objection was disputed. Various witnesses came forward to attest that the brother-in-law was never in debt, and certainly not to the value of his house and land. The neighbor was challenged to produce the witnesses to the deed of gift. I do not wish to bore you with a long history of claim and counterclaim, but in the end, after three years of wrangling, Don Fernan won. He was now acting solely on behalf of whatever he possessed in nephews and nieces, for his good sister had died, worn down, they said, with grief for her dead husband and worry that she and her child, or children, would be cast out on the road penniless."

"A terrible story," said Isaac. "But all too common."

"It is not finished," said Joshua, rather grimly. "Next, someone—probably the neighbor—denounced my good friend Don Fernan as a heretic, and a shelterer of known heretics. He produced a document that he swore a servant brought to him, just before fleeing the area. The *finca* was in the diocese of Barcelona, where the denunciation caused a ripple of trouble, but was soon dealt with. Disappointed, the informer went to the Archbishop. He got nowhere with Don Sancho, but he did manage to interest the Inquisitor. The Inquisition was showing signs of renewed life in Tarragona then, and Don Fernan was seized while on a business trip here. There was a brief jurisdictional dispute during which his young nephew, a lad of sixteen or seventeen, I believe, disappeared. Don Fernan, who had both intelligence and friends, extricated himself from this new difficulty.''

''Why did the nephew abandon his uncle?''

''Everyone assumed it was because he was the cause of the rumors about heresies and sheltering heretics. But to know the truth, one would have to ask him. If one could find him. And he might answer. But I suspect that by now he has learned that not all men are to be trusted.''

''I'll warrant he has,'' said Isaac. ''Else he would not still be alive.''

''Of course, brother, it is likely that he is now far away from Tarragona, since he is wanted for who knows what and how many heinous crimes.''

''And the man who sheltered him would be in grave danger, would he not?''

''Oh, if I were that man, I would not be particularly concerned. The charges are false, and need only money and a little help to be put forever to rest.''

''A sad tale, Joshua. I pity the young man and I hope that you are right,'' said Isaac. ''But in my experience the falseness of charges is no guarantee that they will not be prosecuted.''

''Perhaps with the help of friends,'' said Joshua in gentle tones, ''not simply Jewish merchants who wish him well, but Christian friends, who have the ear of the King, the matter will not come to the pursuing of charges.''

Isaac chuckled. ''I always remembered you as a cunning man, Joshua. All your talk of gloom and sleeplessness and worry has led us into some interesting paths. As, no doubt, it was intended to.''

''I am glad I have not lost the skill. But it is true that I sleep badly these nights.''

''I shall give you some drops of a mixture I have prepared. Where is Yusuf?''

''He was somewhere about,'' said Joshua.

''I tax his strength by keeping him awake,'' said Isaac.

"Or rather, keeping him from his bed. He seems able to sleep anywhere. Yusuf!" he called softly.

"Here, lord." And the boy stumbled slightly as he came out of the darkness into the light of the lamp.

# THREE

**Friday, May 2**

It was early the next morning when Isaac and Yusuf walked up to the Archbishop's palace in response to Berenguer's summons. Suddenly a hand grasped his arm. "Master Isaac," said the Bishop.

"Your Excellency," said Isaac. "I did not expect to find you up so early."

"I had to speak to you, Master Isaac, and face-to-face, without interruption. It cannot be done this way," he said firmly. "You and Yusuf must move into the palace. Leave your wife to gossip with her family, and attend to me. Last night I could not sleep, and that fool Bernat—"

"I do not think Father Bernat a fool, Your Excellency," said Isaac.

"Nor do I," said Berenguer. "That's why he annoys me. They will drive me mad over this, Isaac—Francesc telling me what is right; Bernat telling me what is clever, and then the two of them joining together to keep me from doing what my own nature counsels me."

"And what is that, Your Excellency?"

"By now, Isaac, I am no longer sure. Last night they

insisted on forgoing their own rest to plot strategy. If you
had been there, we could have played chess. And I need
you. Every time I exchange a few words with Don Sancho,
my knee begins to ache.''

''Perhaps I should examine it—''

''My presence is required in the cathedral. Mass is about
to begin. You may go home and break the news to your
family, but I expect to see you after mass, and to have you
installed in your quarters before supper. They are ready for
you.'' And once more the bell called the bishops together.

''I am concerned about Gilabert,'' said Isaac. The morning
was half over, and he and Berenguer were walking toward
the ramparts, where they could have a quiet and private
conversation.

''Has his health suffered?''

''No. He is—as he insisted all along—a remarkably
strong young man. He suffered a setback the day you left
us, but is quickly recovering. Something else bothers me.
First, let me tell you of a small incident that occurred the
next morning, at an inn not far from the city.'' He described
what the child had said. ''I believe he is being followed by
Don Gonsalvo.''

''It sounds possible, Master Isaac,'' said Berenguer.

''Yes, Your Excellency. Then my brother-in-law told me
a curious tale about a family that he has done business with
for some time.''

''Tell me your curious tale. I fear I shall find it only too
fascinating.''

''And that is it, Your Excellency. The uncle, the neighbor,
and the nephew.''

''You make a most persuasive case, Master Isaac,'' said
the Bishop.

''My brother-in-law and his wife are quite capable of
sheltering Don Gilabert. He needs little care, and they seem
pleased to do it. But I am concerned about their safety, if
you understand me.''

''Perfectly,'' said Berenguer. ''I am also concerned

about his safety. Even if he were not the nephew of your brother-in-law's tale—and I believe he is—a man whose only living relation has been butchered recently seems to me to be living in peril. He would be better off behind stout walls, stouter even than those of the Jewish Quarter. Perhaps with the monks, or even with—'' He rose to his feet and walked restlessly about the room. "Is he well enough to travel?" asked the Bishop. "I mean to ride, not to be carried on a litter, or in a cart. That would be too noticeable."

"Yes," said Isaac. "But I would not like him to go alone. He cannot defend himself if trouble appears."

"I will send the captain of the guard," he said. "And one of his men. They have nothing to do but eat and grow fat and lazy, the captain says. Can he leave at midday?"

"Certainly."

"Bernat!" called the Bishop.

The secretary opened the door to the adjoining room. "Your Excellency?"

"I need you to write a letter and have it sent off at once."

"Yes, Your Excellency," murmured Bernat.

"And we shall need a habit—not yours, Bernat, you are somewhat on the small side for him—a larger one, but not one cut for one of your well-fed brethren."

"A Franciscan habit, Your Excellency?"

"Franciscan, Dominican. It matters not, although I like the idea of dressing him to look like you, Bernat."

"I shall go back to my kinsman's house and prepare the young man," said Isaac.

"And take leave of your wife and kin," said Berenguer. "Don't forget that I expect you here after dinner, bag and baggage."

"But, Isaac, you cannot leave. Not today. Everyone will be gathering here for the Sabbath."

"My dear Judith, I came to Tarragona, not to visit family, as pleasant as that may be, but as the Bishop's physician. He requires me. I am going. You will represent me as best you can, I know. Now I must dress Don Gilabert's hand. He is leaving at once to go to a kinsman's house.''

"I thought he had no family," said Judith suspiciously.

"No close kin," said Isaac. "But more distant cousins who will take him in until he recovers completely." He kissed her affectionately and turned to go. "And you might allow your sister the use of her marital bed once more," he said. "Now that I will not be in it. Good-bye, my dear. I am close by, and can be summoned—if there is need, and only if there is need—at an instant."

"Isaac—"

"Good-bye for the moment, my dear." And calling Raquel, he swept up the stairs toward the chamber where Don Gilabert lay brooding.


"The flesh has healed," said Isaac, after the cautious unbinding of the young man's left hand. "That was what concerned me. The bones will take more time to knit together and must continue to be protected."

Raquel retied the bandages covering the hand. "It is done, Papa."

"Good. As soon as we look at the wound in your leg, you may assume your new guise."

"And what is that?" asked Gilabert.

"A friar. The habit is arriving shortly. You will put it on, and then ride out with two stout guards to protect you to the castle at Altafulla, where you will be hidden as long as necessary."

"And what cause has the castellan to risk himself for me?"

"He owes His Excellency a great debt, although of what nature I could not say. Perhaps of friendship only. Rebandage the leg, Raquel," said her father. "I must speak to your mother again."

"I have no desire to leave here," said Gilabert, once the physician had left the room. "But now I realize I jeopardize your life and safety by staying. How fitting that I should skulk away dressed as a friar. Will you bring me that small box from the table?" he added without a pause.

Silently Raquel carried it over.

He opened it and removed a gold chain. "Take it," he said hurriedly. "This binds me to you, whatever happens to us. I know that you must marry, and so must I. If I don't, my lands will have no heir. But even so, our souls are one, and this chains soul to soul in love. Wear it in your hair and remember me from time to time."

Raquel took it and ran from the room.

But as Gilabert mounted his bay mare outside Joshua's house, Raquel came out after him. "Don Gilabert," she said. "I fear your wrist is not well enough bound for all this exercise. Give it to me."

He pulled his arm from the sling and held it out. With quick fingers she took a beautifully worked chain from its hiding place in her sleeve and wrapped it around his wrist. "May this protect you, my lord," she murmured, looking up. "My prayers go with you."

And in the heat and bustle of midday, a Franciscan friar on a bay mare, with a pack slung behind the saddle, rode through the gates of Tarragona, exciting no interest at all. Behind him two soldiers, dusty and relaxed, rode side by side, deep in conversation. As soon as the crowds had thinned out, the friar coaxed his mare to a trot, and then a canter. The soldiers, apparently realizing that they, too, had appointments to keep, spurred their horses to keep up

*Saturday, May 3*

Throughout the long unhappy night Raquel did not sleep more than a few exhausted minutes at a time. Mercifully, she was not sharing a chamber or, even worse, a bed; there was no one to witness her tears. When the tears stopped, the birds were awake and the sun risen. She rose from her bed, hesitant to leave the chamber while the household slept, and yet unable to stay in it any longer. She washed her salt-stained face, and then sponged the rest of her body, as if misery could be wiped away with water and towels, and dressed in her plainest gown and surcoat. She combed her hair back severely, twitched the covers on the bed into place to disguise her restless night, and headed down the stairs.

The quiet of the Sabbath could be felt everywhere. In the empty dining room, the table had been laid the day before with dishes of cold rice and lentils, cheese, and bread, all covered with linen napkins, and two large pitchers of cool *tisanes*. Raquel helped herself to a mint drink and carried her cup over to the shuttered window. Suddenly she felt as if she could not breathe in this dark room. She set her cup down and began to struggle with the shutters.

"Let me help you," said a cold male voice behind her.

She whirled around and faced Ruben. "Thank you," she said. "It is so close and airless in here, I could scarcely breathe."

"The courtyard is pleasant at this time of day," he said, pushing back the shutter. "I am going to eat my breakfast out there in peace."

"I'm not hungry," said Raquel, with a shudder.

"You are the physician more than I," he said. "I would think you should eat something, but it is no concern of mine."

Nettled, she picked up some bread and her *tisane*. "We have things to talk about, you and I," she said. "Perhaps I will join you. If no one else is out there."

"I'm not sure we have anything to talk about," said Ruben, his face turning red. "But you may, of course, join me."

"What is Aunt Dinah up to?" asked Raquel abruptly.

"Plots," said Ruben gloomily. "I don't want to sound rude—I mean any man would be happy to have a wife like you—but . . ."

"You don't want to marry me."

"Well . . ." He turned scarlet with embarrassment. "That's right. I don't want to marry you. If I had to, I suppose you'd make a good wife . . ."

"I don't want to marry you either," she said. "And it's

not because you don't seem pleasant it's just that . . ."

"Then you, too, must be in love with someone else," he said, sounding much more cordial.

"Why can't you marry the woman you want?" asked Raquel.

"She's not as rich as you are, and she's not family. She's not as beautiful as you are, either, but they didn't know that, and I think she looks just right, and she loves me. Which you certainly don't."

"How could I?" asked Raquel. "This is the first time I've spoken to you. Anyway, I'm sure I'd make you miserable."

"What should we do?" asked Ruben helplessly. "Aunt Dinah's absolutely set on this match."

"Is Uncle Joshua?"

"I don't think he cares."

"There you have it. I'll tell Papa, and you tell Uncle Joshua. Otherwise those two women will have the settlements drawn up as soon as the Sabbath is over. I lived all my life with Mama, and I love her, but I don't think I want to marry and move in with another just like her."

Lady Elicsenda, Abbess of Sant Daniel, disciplined daughter both of the Church and of a rich and powerful family, waited at the door into the Archbishop's study, looking as unmoved as a marble statue. The Reverend Mother, Sor Marta, and the bursar of the Tarragona house stood beside her. Behind that inexpressive face, the Abbess was silently calculating how far she must humble herself. Beyond that, she was not prepared to go.

The Archbishop's young page ushered them in with a practiced bow. "Reverend Mother, Lady Elicsenda, Sisters," said Don Sancho. The women walked halfway across the richly furnished room and bowed their heads in acknowledgment. "How fortunate at last," he added, "that we may meet to speak of the difficulties that have arisen at Sant Daniel."

"Fortunate indeed," said the Reverend Mother, rather

acidly. "Your Excellency, Lady Elicsenda begs permission to speak."

The Archbishop waited expectantly. He smiled. "Lady Elicsenda," he said at last, "you may speak."

Again she fell to her knees and lowered her eyes. "Your Excellency, I have been most grievously at fault. I am guilty of disobedience in not obeying Your Excellency's commands as soon as I heard them. I can only say, not to excuse, but to explain myself, that I placed the trivial concerns of the convent before my greater duty to the Church, to my order, and to my Archbishop. I beg Your Excellency to believe me when I say I never condoned Sor Agnete's transgressions, but prayed daily for her spiritual amendment."

"Were you successful in your prayers?"

"No, Your Excellency, in spite of all my prayers, and all my exhortations, she clings to her sin."

"God does not listen as readily, perhaps, to a disobedient nun," he pointed out.

"Your Excellency is very wise. I did not intend disobedience, Your Excellency, but I was remiss in not guarding against it."

"That will do," said the Archbishop. "Rise, Lady Elicsenda. You are free to return to Sant Daniel. Confess your fault to your sisters, and you may resume your duties. Except that Sor Marta will be responsible for fiscal order in the convent. She is wise and capable, and I am sure has already taken over much of that task."

"Long since, Your Excellency," said Elicsenda.

"And she shall report twice a year to . . ."

The pause was so long that all four nuns feared he had forgotten what he was talking about.

"To whom, Your Excellency?" asked Elicsenda at last.

"To His Excellency the Bishop of Girona, of course." He smiled. "And Sor Agnete will stay at the Mother House, living under whatever terms of penance you see fit, Reverend Mother, until her trial."

• • •

"Ellesenda, my daughter, you have escaped lightly," said the Reverend Mother as soon as they were safely inside the convent walls and away from prying eyes and gossiping tongues.

"I have, Domina," said the Abbess, her face as white as the linen that surrounded it. "Very lightly. I was prepared for the worst. I am grateful to His Excellency," she added dutifully, although it cost her a great deal to say it.

"I shall convey your gratitude to him at the proper time. And I, too, am pleased."

The May morning was warm and quiet, filled with the heady scent of roses. Joshua's household dozed in the Sabbath calm. Isaac, not needed for the moment at the palace, had walked the short distance to eat a late breakfast with his family, and then gone out with his brother-in-law. Ruben had disappeared. Dinah and Judith were gossiping and Raquel was in the courtyard again, sitting under an orange tree, enjoying the luxury of being alone. She leaned back against the tree and looked up, wondering if she could climb it and hide there for the rest of the day. Perhaps with the help of a bench—

Her musings were interrupted by someone pounding heavily on the gate, and then ringing the bell beside it so fiercely it clanged. Whoever it was, she decided immediately that she was unlikely to enjoy his company. Let someone else open the gate and entertain him.

Behind her was a narrow staircase leading to a low doorway. There was nothing beyond it except a small garret where food was stored. She darted up, pushed open the door, and stooping to enter, found herself in a room under the eaves, filled with racks of dried fruits and vegetables, cured meats and fish. The windows were covered with slats instead of shutters, with flaps of leather above them to let down in case of heavy weather. Raquel picked up an apricot and, nibbling on it, crouched low enough to approach the windows over the courtyard. Kneeling, she peered through the slats to see what was happening.

One of the menservants came out and opened the gate.

Six armed men burst into the courtyard and spread out as if they expected a troop of cavalry to oppose them. "Where is your master?" asked their officer.

"He is not at home," said the servant stoutly.

The officer drew his sword. "Don't play the fool with me. You know where he is. Go and fetch him."

"Why do you threaten my servant?" asked Dinah, coming down the stairs from her chamber, arranging her veil as she moved. "He cannot produce my husband from under his tunic. If you will be patient, he will no doubt return soon."

"Madame," said the officer, "your husband is sheltering an infamous young man, long wanted by the authorities. The penalties for aiding such a person are heavy."

"There is no such person in this house," said Dinah, with steel in her voice.

"We shall decide that," said the officer, and nodded at his men.

They fanned out to cover the whole house room by room and began to search. Through the window, Raquel could hear her aunt being sweetly helpful, opening up small chests and offering them a chance to look through. As they came across people, they herded them down into the courtyard, until it seemed filled with women—her mother, Naomi, housemaids, the cook—and two boys.

"Where are the men hiding?" asked the officer.

"They aren't hiding. They are out," said Dinah. "At their prayers. Paying visits to friends, perhaps. They did not know you gentlemen would wish to see them."

"Where is the sick man?" he said, suddenly, directly at Naomi.

"Sick man?" she replied. "There is no sick man here."

"Then what happened to him?"

"Did anyone look up here?" asked a voice. A man was standing at the foot of the staircase that led to Raquel's hiding place.

There was silence.

"There is nothing up there but the remains of last year's harvest, dried and stored," said Dinah. "Go and look, if you wish. The almonds are particularly good, I think."

The officer glared at her and started across the courtyard. As soon as she heard footsteps clattering on the stone stairs, Raquel crawled to the far side of the room, where it was possible to stand upright under the highest point of the sloping roof. She began to brush dust and cobwebs off her gown with frantic haste. If she was going to be dragged out there with the others, she didn't want to look as if she had been hiding. She picked up an empty basket and began to fill it randomly with dried things.

"What have we here?" asked a tall man, whose bulk filled the open door.

Before she could speak, a voice yelled up at him. "Here they come, sir."

"I must go," he said. "But that is an odd dish you are going to cook," he added. "Salt fish with apricots and walnuts."

"It is excellent if it is well prepared," said Raquel coolly. "You should try it. Especially with ginger."

"Is there anyone in here with you?"

"As you see, Officer," said Raquel. "You are welcome to come in and look."

"Nay, mistress. I am not fond of such cramped spaces. Besides, the man I seek is tall, and confined to his bed. Badly wounded."

"There is little room in here to keep anyone but the smallest sick person."

"As you say, mistress." He bowed and returned to the courtyard.

Joshua, Isaac, and Joshua's neighbor, the silversmith, were walking slowly toward the house, deep in conversation, when they were spotted by the guard posted outside the gate. He slipped into the courtyard ahead of them, unnoticed except by Yusuf. The boy was not interested in the details of politics and commerce that made up their discussions, and had fallen behind, but not so far behind that he could not smell out a guard.

He drifted up and touched Isaac's arm. "Officers, lord," he murmured.

"Then disappear, lad. If there's trouble, get the Bishop."

When the group entered the courtyard, the guard had a vague sense that something was missing. But the three men were there, and that was all that concerned him. He shut the gate and called for the others.

Yusuf stayed out in the street long enough to see the arrest. Within minutes he was at the palace; he was explaining the situation to the Bishop before the arrest party reached the gates to the Jewish Quarter.

"Thank you, Yusuf," said Berenguer. "Come along and let us see what the noble Don Sancho has done. You are sure those men were his officers?"

"Quite sure, Excellency," said Yusuf. "They mentioned the Archbishop as they were arresting my master and his two companions."

The Archbishop was not in his study, said his secretary. Under no circumstances would the Archbishop be available to anyone. The Bishop of Girona's question would be dealt with, but he could not see him now. Pale with anger, Berenguer strode out of the palace with Yusuf at his heels, followed by Bernat, Francesc, and the assistant to the Archbishop's secretary. Berenguer ran down the steps and headed for the gate to the Jewish Quarter. At that point he came face-to-face with the officers of the guard escorting their prisoners through the street.

Both groups stopped. "Where are you taking my personal physician?" said the Bishop in a voice that could have quelled a riot.

"To the Archbishop's prison," said the officer, looking around for someone to back him up.

"You cannot," said Berenguer.

"I have my orders, Your Excellency. From the Archbishop," he added desperately, not sure what he would do if the Bishop decided to free his physician then and there.

"Your Excellency," said a voice from behind him.

"Please, Your Excellency, I am sure that the Archbishop will be pleased to discuss this matter as soon as he is available."

"And when will that be?"

"Very soon."

An interested group of spectators was gathering, fascinated by the sight of a bishop locked in combat with the Archbishop's guard.

"They're taking the Bishop off to prison," said a voice.

"You can't do that. No one ever took a bishop off to prison except the Pope," said another. "It's not allowed."

"What do you know about it?"

"My sister works in the kitchen at the palace, and she knows," said a woman. "It's the Jews they're taking off to prison."

"What for?"

"For being Jews."

"The Bishop's trying to convert them," said another.

"Let me in. I can't see," said a third, and a chorus of voices echoed his words, pushing closer and closer to the center of the action.

The officer of the guard was growing scarlet in the face. He had been pushed right up against Berenguer, and was losing the slender authority he still possessed.

By then, Francesc and Bernat had elbowed their way through. "The crowd grows ugly, Your Excellency," murmured Bernat. "All of us are in some danger. Especially the Jews. It would be best to get safely to the palace."

Berenguer looked around him and concurred. "Come, gentlemen," he said in a clear voice, "let us return to the palace. All of us. Good people, let us through, I beg of you." But he said it, not in the tones of one who begs, but of one who knows that whatever he commands will happen. As if magically, the crowd began to melt away like unseasonable snows under the hot sun.

"And I shall stay here until I can speak to His Excellency, the noble Don Sancho," said Berenguer loudly.

The door to the study opened, and Berenguer went in.

"Your Excellency," he said. "Don Sancho. I had hoped to leave this for a more convenient hour, but the events of this morning make it necessary to act now."

A flicker of surprise darted over the Archbishop's face. "Act now?"

"His Majesty is most disturbed at recent events affecting the Jews of the city. This morning's—error—that led to the arrest of a merchant, and a craftsman, men of substance and of good repute, along with my physician, may make the situation worse."

"Which recent events, Don Berenguer?" asked Don Sancho cautiously.

"Attacks on Jews, and destruction of their property. I believe His Majesty's treasurer has written to you about it, and will have explained the situation better than I can. But since the problem now involves my physician, then I respectfully remind Your Excellency that if there is a complaint against Isaac, physician of Girona, or Joshua, merchant of Tarragona, that the only person who has jurisdiction in the case is the bailiff general."

"Ordinarily, yes," said the Archbishop. "But—"

"All Jews are of the King's chamber, as you know, Don Sancho," continued Berenguer relentlessly. "They are the King's treasure. Any case involving them must be heard by a royal official. Whatever jurisdiction I hold over Isaac, since he is one of the bishopric's Jews, I cede as I must to the bailiff general. And right now, while His Majesty prepares for war—with the generous assistance of the Jews of Tarragona, you will remember—you can be sure that he is taking a keen interest in their welfare."

"There has been a terrible misunderstanding, Don Berenguer," said the Archbishop smoothly. "The only arrest order I signed this morning was for a Christian who had been convicted of heresy and related offenses. As I remember it, one of his neighbors has sworn that he had seen the heretic in the city and knew where he was hiding. No one mentioned arresting Jews." He rang the bell on his desk, and in a moment his secretary appeared through a small door to his left. "Where are the Jews who were most unfortunately arrested this afternoon?'' he asked coldly.

"They are waiting in a room near the guards' quarters, Your Excellency," said the secretary nervously. "Since His Excellency the Bishop of Girona kindly pointed out that one of them was his physician—and at present living in the palace—we hesitated to place them in a cell.''

"Surely it would have been better to seek me out, and verify the order, would it not?''

"Indeed, Your Excellency. Much better. I should have thought to do that," said the wretched man, reaching for the responsibility and heaping it on his slender shoulders. But then, thought Berenguer, he lives a very comfortable life in return for being the Archbishop's scapegoat.

"See that they are freed at once," snapped Don Sancho.

"At once, Your Excellency," murmured his secretary.

"There will be a thorough investigation into this matter. You may assure His Majesty of that.''

When Berenguer left the Archbishop's study, he was waylaid once more by a young page. "Pardon me, Your Excellency," said the boy, "but I have a message for you from a noble friend who wishes to speak to you.''

Berenguer thought for one regretful moment of the sumptuous dinner that would no doubt be laid out for the conferees at the council, and turned to his small entourage. "Francesc, Bernat. I shall be with you later.''

"I apologize for asking you to come here once more,'' said Santa Pau. "And wrapped in that poor cloak. But you look so very like a bishop I did not want people noticing you.''

"My dear Santa Pau—I *am* a bishop. One grows to look like one very quickly. It is difficult not to. Do I see a pitcher of wine on that sideboard?" he asked. "And a tempting loaf? You have caused me to miss a banquet in coming to see you, but I confess I can happily dine on what I see in the room.''

"Excellent," said Santa Pau. "It is not much, but it is all good of its kind," he said, pouring wine and cutting off a piece of the loaf for each of them. He raised a cloth and revealed a fine dried ham from which he carved a pile of slices. That, with a bowl of fruit, he placed in front of Berenguer, along with the bread and a cup of wine. He gave the page a piece of bread with ham on top and an apricot, and told him to find someplace comfortable to wait. The boy took his bounty and left.

"You carve and serve expertly, Santa Pau," said Berenguer.

"I have been page, squire, and soldier," he said. "One learns. Now, you must wonder why I sought you out again so quickly, and at such an inconvenient hour. There were reasons."

"I assumed as much," said Berenguer.

"The first one touches you," he said, "because it touches your physician. A new municipal ordinance has been brought into effect, which demands a license and levies a large fee for any Jew wishing permission to enter the city."

"That will be a nuisance, but it is hardly a tragedy, Santa Pau."

The young man shook his head. "Consider, Your Excellency. Your physician and his family came into the city very recently; they do not have license to do so. They can be imprisoned, and fined heavily for transgressing. Once they are in prison, it will take time, money, and a great deal of influence to get them out again."

"But this could also happen to any of the merchants who are here on business, buying or selling."

"It could, and it might."

"Do they realize the effect that this will have on trade?"

"Oh—it will occur to them, and like other similar ordinances, they will withdraw it, or there will be a complaint from the Crown, and they will scramble to say it was all an error. But at this moment it is in effect because someone is aiming at a particular person."

"Isaac? Why?"

"It may be your physician. I am not sure, nor do I know why it would benefit anyone to attack him. There is a rumor, one of many conflicting ones, that the person who stirred up the councillors—speaking to them of Jews streaming into the city until there were more of them than Christians—was a representative of the papal nuncio."

"But again. Why?"

"I can think of many reasons. He may have a cousin who benefits financially from this legislation. His Holiness may have decided to support the Sardinians."

"That will please His Majesty," said Berenguer dryly.

"Of course, the simple presence of the nuncio is sufficient to create rumors that he is behind everything that happens in the city."

"That is very true," said Berenguer.

"Or someone may wish to raise difficulties for you, Don Berenguer."

"For me? Do you mean Don Sancho?"

"No. He was annoyed because you created a good deal of work and trouble for him, but he is not your enemy."

"You know my physician was arrested this morning."

"Yes," said Santa Pau. "I had assumed it was for failure to obtain an entry permit to the city, but they tell me it was not."

"No—it was because he was with his brother-in-law, who was arrested for harboring a fugitive. A heretic who had been condemned—*in absentia*—and must have returned to the city."

"And was a fugitive discovered?"

"No."

"From whom did you hear this, Don Berenguer?"

"From the Archbishop, who initialed the order at someone's request, and from Master Isaac. It was what he was told at the time of his arrest."

"Don Berenguer, if you will excuse me, I must make further inquiries. My page will take you back to the palace. I don't suppose your physician was actually assisting his brother-in-law to harbor a notorious heretic, was he? If he was, of course, no doubt he had an excellent reason to do so, but at the moment I prefer not to know what it is."

• • •

The little page knocked on Berenguer's door before the rest of the delegates had finished their dinners.

"My master says it would be wise for you and your party to leave the city now. You may tell the Archbishop His Majesty has commanded you to wait upon him in Barcelona."

"I may, may I?" said Berenguer, in amusement.

"Yes, Your Excellency," said the page in all seriousness. "And it would be wise, said my master, not to tell anyone else you are leaving."

"We must leave very quietly," said the physician. "And without notice. I apologize for snatching my family away, Joshua, when they have scarcely arrived, but we have no choice."

"I think," said Joshua, "that nothing should be mentioned of this. Do you hear, Dinah? Nothing, to anyone."

"Even here?" said his wife.

"Even here there are informers, as you know well," said Joshua. "Greedy wretches and miserable creatures who will betray their brothers for a penny or two. No one must know, not even the servants."

"It is the Sabbath," objected Judith.

"And we have so much to talk about, Judith and I—" said her sister.

"My dear," said Isaac, "we are in danger. And so, kind sister, are you, your children, and your entire household. We must get ready to leave."

Raquel and Judith packed and said muted good-byes to Joshua and Dinah. Naomi and Ibrahim had already left with the boxes of clothing—to deliver them, they said, to Master Isaac, since he was living in the palace now.

The Bishop's servants began to leave, two a time; then one wagon headed for the gate, followed sometime later by the second.

By the time the city of Tarragona stirred itself from its after-dinner lethargy, the Bishop and his entourage were on their way to the castle at Altafulla.

⋆ ⋆ ⋆

"There are so few of us now," said Raquel. "What has happened?"

"Sor Agnete won't be coming back," said the sergeant. "The other nuns leave next week with the Bishop of Vic's party. His Excellency left two guards behind to conduct them safely on the last stage of their journey."

"But where are our musicians?"

"Who knows where they might be? They earn a living where they can, and no doubt decided to stay until the crowds left the city."

"I shall miss them." She paused. "And of course, Don Gilabert is no longer with us."

"We'll miss them all, Mistress Raquel. Especially the musicians. They were a merry pair."

A fast-moving horse and rider coming up from behind them interrupted their idle conversation. The rider slowed his mount to a walk beside the sergeant and held up a leather bag. "If you please, sir, I seek the Bishop of Girona. This is his party, is it not?"

"It is," said the sergeant. "And up there is the Bishop himself."

Berenguer was deep in conversation with his physician when the messenger found him. "Your Excellency," said the newcomer. "I carry a letter for you from the Archbishop, with his compliments."

"From the Archbishop?" said Berenguer. "Open it, Bernat."

"The envelope sent by Don Sancho encloses another letter, Your Excellency," said his secretary. "On it Don Sancho writes that the enclosed just arrived from Girona."

"Then you need not wait for a reply," said Berenguer to the messenger. "Please convey my thanks to His Excellency."

When the messenger, duly rewarded, had gone, Bernat broke open the seal and laughed.

"Is the letter so amusing?" asked Berenger coldly.

"No, Your Excellency. Forgive me. It is from Don Arnau, enclosing a third letter. On the envelope Don Arnau writes that all is well, and that the enclosed arrived Wednesday." He broke the seal of the inner letter. "This one is from Empuries, Your Excellency, from your friend."

"He is prompt in his reply," said Berenguer. "Read it to us, Bernat."

"As Your Excellency wishes. He says, 'I regret that no one among my acquaintance, in or out of holy orders, has the name Norbert de C., except for an aged and degenerate cousin of the Cardona family, who does not fit your requirements. As you requested, I asked Rodrigue de Lancia if he knew a friar named Norbert. First, he claimed to remember no one of the name. Then he recalled that a boorish, unpleasant gentleman named Gonsalvo de Marca, whom he had had the misfortune to meet, had greeted a drunken friar named Norbert with hearty enthusiasm at an inn where they were all staying. There was little else that he could or would say of this Norbert. Either he knew nothing about him, or he had no wish to say what he knew. And on my part, my dear Berenguer, I would like to know—' and he asks about Your Excellency's current situation," said Bernat.

"I will answer him later," said Berenguer. "My friend spreads gossip like a village midwife, Isaac. But he says much of interest, does he not?"

"A murdered friar, and an injured young lord," said Isaac. "And Don Gonsalvo connected to both."

"I would not have picked Gonsalvo as a vicious torturer," said Berenguer.

"I, too, find it difficult to believe. His manners hide more than his noble ancestry, if it is true."

# PART FOUR

# ONE

## The Road Home

"Do you see where it sits, Mistress Raquel? On the hill over there?" said the sergeant. "Altafulla."

"That's a steep road," she said uneasily. "Is there another way up?"

The sergeant grinned. "Easier than the road? No."

"The castle looks very . . ." She paused, staring at the thick walls that seemed to hang threateningly over them. "Safe."

"With the portcullis lowered, they can withstand a big army from the north or the east," said the sergeant. "From that tower you can see troops approaching a half day's march away. It will never be taken by surprise."

"If the enemy approaches from the right direction," Raquel pointed out.

"Very true, mistress. In theory, other castles to the west and south will have stopped hostile invaders from those directions long since."

"And in practice?"

"In war, mistress, anything can happen. My experience is that the enemy always comes from the direction you least expect. And so—"

"That is the direction you prepare?"

"Right. Look around. Anyone attacking our party should come from ahead and to our left," he said, pointing to positions suitable for an ambush.

She nodded. "How else could they set up a trap to catch us?"

"Then why are we being followed?"

"Followed?"

"Two horses behind us, taking good care not to be seen."

"I don't know," she said uneasily.

"Nor do I." And he rode off to speak to the captain.

The lord of the castle and his lady descended to the court-yard to welcome the travelers. The lord seized on Berenguer at once, carrying him off into the tower, while his lady and the steward arranged accommodation. In a moment of quiet, a page boy approached the physician. "Excuse me, señor," he asked, "but are you Master Isaac?"

"I am."

"My lord and His Excellency the Bishop would like you to join them in his lordship's study."

"Certainly. But first tell me, lad," said Isaac, "do you have a friar staying at the castle still?"

"Father Gil? Yes, we do, Master Isaac."

"I would like you to take me to him after I speak to his lordship."

"He, too, is in the study, Master Isaac," said the page.

When they arrived, Berenguer and Gilabert were alone. "Gilabert must return to Girona, Master Isaac," said the Bishop. "He plans to leave tomorrow and ride there in three days. Alone, dressed as a friar."

"The habit disguises me well," said Gilabert. "I will be quite safe."

"A friar, alone, galloping over the mountains like a royal messenger?" asked Isaac. "You will be remarked upon by everyone who sees you."

"I mentioned that," said Berenguer. "Without a doubt, he would be much safer with us, traveling at a sober pace."

"I agree. Is your errand so urgent, Don Gilabert?"

"It is, Master Isaac."

"Is it better to arrive three days later, or not at all?" asked the physician.

"You think there is that much danger on the road?" asked Gilabert.

"We are being followed," said Berenguer. "But we have guards to deal with threats. Even my priests and I are equipped to defend ourselves. You will be alone and hard-pressed to defend yourself against a single foe."

Gilabert raised his hands helplessly. "I am defeated by the wisdom around me," he said. "I will join you. With pleasure."

"Even traveling with us, you should stay in that sober habit. I assure you, Isaac, it changes his appearance profoundly. But if you are to be convincing, those curls must go."

"I was afraid you would want to shave my head," said Gilabert.

"We won't shave it," said Berenguer. "Many a tonsured friar neglects to keep his crown clear of hair for months, no matter how many statutes I draft on the subject. With hair clipped short over the crown, you will look like a traveler, of whom much is forgiven."

"I am in your hands, Your Excellency," said Gilabert.

"Good. But I must also insist that you stay close to Father Bernat or Father Francesc. Then, if someone calls for you to hear his confession, you may send one of them instead."

"Yes, Your Excellency, but—"

And the Bishop broke into peals of laughter.

Conversation over the supper table ranged from talk of war to scurrilous tales about his fellow bishops from Berenguer, aided rather too freely by Bernat. Gilabert, now looking very like a friar, listened quietly, as did the women.

"Tell me, my lord," said Berenguer, during a quiet moment, "who is this Gonsalvo de Marca? We have chanced upon him several times on this journey."

"Don Gonsalvo," said his host. "A strange man, is he not?"

"He is a friend to all," said his lady bitterly, "who loves his neighbor like a brother, as Cain loved Abel."

"I am acquainted with him, as are most people in the vicinity," added her husband, "but I cannot say I know him well. Nor do I wish to."

"We only noticed that he is a bore, whose rich estates and ancestry do not compensate for his country manners," said Berenguer.

"All that is true enough. He is also a greedy, stupid man, fond of going to law."

"He spoke of a lawsuit."

"He is a dangerous opponent. Too lacking in wit to drop an action before it harms him as much as his victim. Is that not true, Alicia?"

"Yes," said his lady, bitterly. "He went to law against my cousin over a property and lost a great deal. But in doing so he almost ruined my cousin and caused great suffering to his family. I will never forgive him."

"He is not welcome in this house," said the lord, and then paused to consider his next remarks. "They say, Your Excellency, that he is involved in many doubtful ventures. He has a gift for convincing people—for a time at least—to throw their lot in with him. And their fortunes. I hope you were not considering a business arrangement with the man."

"Certainly not," said Berenguer. "I cannot imagine any circumstance in which I would trust him with something I valued."

"I am relieved to hear that," said his host.

As Isaac followed his wife and daughter from the great hall of the castle, Berenguer fell into step beside him. "This being Gonsalvo de Marca's country, Isaac, I was hoping our host could enlighten us more."

"A fondness for the law courts and for doubtful business transactions does not necessarily mean that a man enjoys murdering harmless friars."

"If he was a harmless friar," said the Bishop. "There is much we do not know."

The travelers gathered in the courtyard to take their leave long before the sun was high enough to chase the mists away from the hollows. The draft mules were already hitched; while the horses and riding mules were being brought out, Gilabert whistled.

The big black tossed his head, broke away from the lad holding him, and trotted over to Gilabert. "You may take my mare, Yusuf," he said as he mounted the black. "She's a good animal, and more your size."

"Why the pretense that you had never seen that beast before, Don Gilabert?" asked Berenguer casually. "He is yours, isn't he?" They were passing through the long arched portico that pierced the wall on the north side of the castle, and their words were lost to those behind in a confusion of echoes. "It's always been evident that he was."

"He is," said Gilabert affectionately. "His name is Neron."

"Then why this elaborate game?"

Gilabert waited until they were in the open again, scrambling down the slope to the road. "Because, Your Excellency, I was—I am—puzzled over his presence in your retinue. I was attacked not far from Girona—unhorsed, wounded, bound, and carried away. I saw my attackers. They spoke to me; I spent some memorable hours with them. One of them told me with great satisfaction that whatever else happened, they would at least have my excellent horse." He stopped for a moment. "At some point in our discussions my body sought refuge in oblivion. When I came fully to my senses, I was in that field, twenty miles from the city, snatched from death by a kindly bishop and a skilled physician. It seemed a heaven-sent miracle until I saw that my rescuers had my horse."

"And you concluded that you had been attacked by my minions?"

"Perhaps I am too suspicious, Your Excellency, but I was torn between throwing myself on the mercy of the monks of Sant Pol, and clinging to you and your retinue until I discovered the reason why. Hence my rather inventive stories of my background.''

"Do you still think me a villain, Don Gilabert?''

"I decided some time ago that you were an unlikely assassin, Your Excellency. But how *did* you get my horse?''

"I didn't. He found us. As soon as the wagon you were on started to move, he came galloping after us. We made inquiries, but found no one who admitted to losing him. The captain and I suspected he was yours and kept him, assuming he had escaped your attackers and followed you.''

"As simple as that?'' said Don Gilabert. "How far do we travel today?''

"To Vilafranca, all being well.''

The sun was casting long shadows when the stone walls of Vilafranca, shimmering in the heat of the plain, rose up in front of them. As they approached the gate to the royal palace, a page ran up to Gilabert. "Are you Father Gil?'' he asked.

"Yes, lad,'' said Gilabert.

"I have a letter for you. The bearer regrets he could not stay.''

Gilabert looked at the writing on the outside sheet. "And who was the bearer?'' he asked.

"Another gray friar, Father. But he did not give me his name.''

"No doubt he reveals it inside. Thank you.''

Gilabert dismounted before breaking the seal and unfolding the letter. He stopped in the courtyard, read it through, thrust it into his tunic, and went up to the gallery with a puzzled frown on his face.

Raquel gave her mule to a stable lad, watching intently as Gilabert mulled over the document, no more able to ignore his presence than one can ignore a sore in the mouth that the tongue constantly touches and aggravates.

# TWO

## The Mountains

Once more the mountains reared up in front of them, still steep and dark, but now too familiar to be remarked on. The mules plodded steadily upward, neither requiring nor appreciating direction from their riders. When they turned onto the track to the keep near Castellvi, Raquel looked around in astonishment. "We're there. I hadn't realized it was so close."

"And how is my brave little patient?" asked Isaac, as soon as they entered the keep.

"You must see for yourself," said the castellan's lady. "I beg your pardon, Master Isaac. It was thoughtless of me—"

"In my own ways, my lady, I do see. You must not worry about choosing your words," he said gently.

"Then come with me, Master Isaac, you and your daughter. Please."

The baby was playing with a carved animal; when he saw his mother, he clambered to his feet and tottered inexpertly but fearlessly over to her.

"Those are his footsteps?" asked the physician, sounding as astonished as he could manage after a long day's ride.

"They are," said his mother, gratified. "He is as strong as he ever was. And he has a new nurse. We are forever in your debt, Master Isaac."

"I think that we are also in yours, my lady."

"And in short," said the Bishop, "because your lady's happiness was a matter of some importance to those women, they took us over the ridge by a small road and we avoided the ambush."

"I do not know what to say," said the castellan. "My woods are not filled with outlaws, Your Excellency, although it is possible that one or two of the men are not as honest as they ought to be. But this is poor country right now, and there are some who could be tempted to waylay a traveler for a few pennies."

"You are rich in timber, cousin."

"But poor in skilled woodcutters to bring it in. Many died in the plague; some who survived went elsewhere, looking for an easier existence."

"In defiance of the law," the Bishop pointed out.

"One cannot blame them entirely," said the castellan.

"If the profit from selling our possessions was their only motive for the attack," said Berenguer, "it does not concern me. Their wives kept us from harm and I suspect they will not try it again. But I would like to know if an outsider suggested it. Or worse, paid them for it."

"We can find that out," said the castellan, leaving the small room that served him as study.

He returned with a nervous-looking maidservant, who curtsied and stared resolutely at the stone-flagged floor. "This is my wife's maid, who warned us there might be trouble on the road. And it is a very good thing you did so, my dear," said the castellan. "For you may have saved many lives, and kept men from being hanged for a serious crime."

She didn't seem to enjoy her role as general savior of the village. "Well—I hope they don't find out what I did," she said. "Except Papa. He knows already, and it was him that told me. But it wasn't right, to have your guests killed and robbed after the physician was up all the night with the baby and saved his life after what Lluisa did. So I told my lady.''

"Did he tell you why they would do such a thing?" asked Berenguer.

"No, Your Excellency. He never did. I thought it would be for the money and the horses and mules, and the fine clothes.''

After dismissing the maidservant, the castellan started for the door. "There is another we should speak to," he said. "Come with me, cousin."

"If you have a skilled woodcutter," said Berenguer as they walked around the outside of the keep to a large shed that served as a workshop, "why is he occupied in mending wagons?"

"Because it takes a team of men to bring down a big tree, cousin. You should know that. I don't have any more like him."

"Of course," said Berenguer. "I was not thinking."

"Hola," called the castellan as they neared the shed. "His Excellency the Bishop of Girona wishes to meet the woodcutter who saved his life."

" 'Tis nothing, Your Excellency," said the woodcutter, whose dark eyes were assessing Berenguer shrewdly. "I had my own reasons. Doesn't help a village if all the men are hanged."

"I wondered, my friend, if an outsider had come by, and put this idea into their heads."

The woodcutter set down his adze and ran his hand over his head. "Would someone in Your Excellency's party have an enemy?"

"It could be," said Berenguer. "We think it might be so."

"Well—as I remember, Your Excellency, there was a man by." He picked up a piece of shaped wood and held it up to the light. "Said he represented the King, and had been sent to capture a villain who had tried to kill His Majesty." He picked up his polishing stone and started to work on the piece in his hand. "Said we'd know the man because he was recovering from wounds he got while escaping.''

''This is most interesting,'' said the Bishop. ''Go on.''

''The murderer was traveling with a band of cutthroats led by a rebel disguised as a Bishop,'' said the woodcutter serenely. ''There was a great reward for their deaths, and he was to pay it as soon as the deed was done. Each of them had two pennies to start, with the rest to come later.''

''But not you?'' said Berenguer, savoring the thought of himself as a leader of cutthroats.

''I didn't like the sound of it. By then we had heard you might be coming, and I knew you for one of my lord's kinsmen.'' He set the piece of wood in the wagon and began to fit it in. ''I saw Your Excellency at his lordship's wedding. It didn't seem likely an impostor could visit without someone noticing. So I left. And told my daughter.''

''And she told her mistress.''

''Not at first. She was frightened. But later she did.''

''Do you know who this man was?''

''Do I *know*? I don't,'' he said cautiously. ''He *said* his name was Lup, from Sant Sadurní.''

''Was he a big fellow, red of face, who talks overmuch?''

''Nothing like, Your Excellency,'' he said. ''I didn't see him close to, but he was a handsome sort of fellow. And too prettily dressed for the King's sergeant, or messenger, or whatever he was supposed to be. He looked like a squire, sent on his lord's bidding.'' He turned back to his work. ''But which lord, I could not say.''

''Thank you, good man,'' said Berenguer, and reached for his purse.

''If you've anything to give, Your Excellency,'' said the woodcutter, ''I don't need it for telling what happened and no more. Give it to my girl to put for her marriage portion. Times are hard for the young up here.''

''He's a remarkable fellow,'' said Berenguer as they walked away.

''He is,'' said the castellan.

''And tell the physician, Your Excellency,'' the woodcutter called after them, "that crazy Marta's son is running around, like to live to plague his mother for many years yet."

"And so, Isaac my friend," said Berenguer, when he had delivered the woodcutter's message, "I doubt the attack was planned by our Gonsalvo. Unless he has a 'prettily dressed squire.' Because the woodcutter seems a shrewd observer of men. He is much trusted by my cousin."

"And any man could be that squire's lord, Your Excellency."

"Anyone."

"Then we are not much further ahead."

When the party was gathering in the courtyard, saying their farewells, Isaac turned to his apprentice. "Tell Don Gilabert, Yusuf, that I would be honored if he would ride with me part of the way this morning."

"Yes, lord," said Yusuf.

"And then return here, and take the lead rein."

And Yusuf promptly disappeared.

"And Raquel, be so good as to ride with your mother, and occupy her with your conversation."

"What is wrong with Mama?" asked Raquel.

"Nothing at all, my dear," said Isaac.

"Good morning, Mistress Raquel, Master Isaac," said Gilabert. "Shall we ride out? I see that Yusuf is to take the bay mare and your mule."

"For a time at least," said Isaac.

"I must join Mama," said Raquel, whose face was now scarlet. She turned her mule and rode off.

"Mistress Raquel has learned great skill in handling the reins," said Gilabert.

"I'm glad to hear it," said Isaac. "She has had little else to occupy her recently. I'm pleased she has turned her time to good use. Tell me, Don Gilabert," he went on without a pause, "why are you the target of assassins? What do they want from your death?"

"Am I?" he asked cautiously.

"Oh yes," said Isaac. "The ambush that failed to trap us here was laid for you alone. The rest of us were spoils for the benefit of the mountain men paid to carry out the act."

"You know that?"

"We are certain of it. One of the men decided against joining in. He warned us something was afoot."

"Master Isaac, I have lain awake many nights trying to puzzle this thing out. No one benefits from my death. I have no heirs. My lands—if they are my lands—"

"And why do you doubt that they are?"

"They are subject to confiscation, but the order has been challenged and we await a decision now," he said impatiently, as if this was a detail he had no time for at the moment. "If they are mine, they would have gone to my uncle, I suppose, in default of anyone else. Except that my uncle is dead. The men who killed him have paid the price—"

"They have?"

"My loyal friends Andreu and Felip have seen to that."

"Ah," said Isaac. "I thought that for a pair of strangers, they were uncommonly interested in your welfare."

"Yes," said Gilabert. "They have been the best of companions to me. If we had we stayed together, I am sure I would have escaped my attackers. But I had a task to carry out that had to be done alone, and we separated. You came upon the results," he added dryly. "My friends searched for me, and then stabled their horses and joined your group, since we had agreed to meet on the road to Barcelona if we lost contact—as we did."

"They cannot have expected us to find you near death in a field."

"Perhaps not. But little that happens to me surprises them," he said. "I received word from them at Vilafranca that the villains had admitted they were hired, and described their master as best they could. He sounded like a man I may have seen, but whose connection to me I cannot imagine."

"Might you have a brother of whom you know nothing?"

"A brother? No. I have no brother. I am sure of that."

"How can you be? He could be the son of your father's mistress—many respected gentlemen have more sons than are commonly spoken of."

"You will say, Master Isaac, that I speak with the voice of a naive child, but I cannot believe it. My parents were besotted with each other. As I remember them, they were rarely out of each other's sight. They married young and clung to each other like a pair of vines."

"And had only one child?"

"Only one sturdy enough to live," said Gilabert. "The others all died in infancy. My mother was perhaps over-young to be bearing children—so the gossip in the house was."

"That is sometimes the case," said Isaac. "You have no cousins who might hope to lay claim to the estate in the event of your death?"

"No. My mother had two brothers—Uncle Fernan, who was childless, and one who died in childhood—and a sister, a nun. None of my father's brothers or sisters lived past childhood, except one stepsister; his father married a second wife, a widow with a daughter. She had no more children."

"Had the stepsister any children?"

Gilabert paused. "Not in wedlock," he said. "If I am to believe servants' gossip, she had a bastard son, Master Isaac. He was put out to nurse and she entered a convent. This may not be true, you understand. My nurse was a fountainhead of information and rumor. And misinformation."

"So there could be a man who believes that his connection to the estate is close enough that in the absence of other heirs, he might inherit. How old would he be?"

"He is no blood connection to me, but otherwise, he could exist. As for his age, that I do not know. I believe his mother was young when it happened, but that was only my childish impression. She must be over forty if she lives still, and I can't remember if I was ever told her name."

"Did rumor give the name of the father?"

"No, curiously enough," he said. "I'm sure there was much speculation. My nurse said he was likely some handsome groom or forester, without a penny, and that her property all went to the convent, and the child was left to starve. But my tutor claimed that her lover was a rich man, who settled enough on the child to raise him. Which does one believe?" he asked. "My tutor and my nurse were both fond of convenient lies. We would have to go back and ask the rest of the servants, who no doubt would give us several more versions of the poor woman's history."

Isaac shook his head. "What can you tell me of Gonsalvo de Marca?"

"You heard what people think of him," said Gilabert. "At Altafulla. It is true enough. Otherwise, I can only say he is a neighbor who is after my lands."

"Does he have a squire, handsome and elegantly dressed, in his household?"

"Don Gonsalvo? A squire? He is no great lord, Master Isaac. He is a rustic boor from a good family, who rides about with a pair of country louts for protection."

"Thank you for your frankness, Don Gilabert," said Isaac. "It is a welcome change."

"Since it seems likely that I may live after all," he said, "it would be more comfortable to do it at my own hearth. And I have had enough of assassins."


"I had an interesting conversation with Don Gilabert," said Isaac.

"What did you discover?" asked Berenguer, and listened intently to a detailed account of their conversation.

"True. It is interesting," said the Bishop, "but I am disinclined to believe in shadowy heirs when we have a substantial villain with an excellent motive for murdering both the friar and Don Gilabert."

"Don Gonsalvo?"

"Who else? For it is Friar Norbert who asked for my help. And how would the death of the poor friar help an heir to Don Gilabert's property? Unless the friar's death has something to do with the terrible events at the *finca*, then let us leave vengeance for his uncle's murder to Don Gilabert, who seems well able to deal with it. Just because I was lost in my own problems, Isaac,'' said Berenguer, ''and forgot the murdered friar until that letter came, does not mean we should forget him now.''

''You had no leisure to think of it until now, Your Excellency. But I do not think your friend's information enlightens us much.''

''It provides the connection between the friar and Don Gonsalvo,'' said the Bishop. ''He wanted the letters the friar was carrying. The friar is murdered.''

''That is like saying, Your Excellency, that if I admire your horse, and state that I want him, and subsequently you die, I murdered you. I must object on logical grounds. We don't know what those letters were.''

''One of them was the written judgment in the case of Huguet de Lancia Talatarn,'' said Berenguer.

''Only Rodrigue de Lancia and his cousin want that one,'' said Isaac.

''That is also true. The other could concern the lawsuit that Gonsalvo pursues. As tenuous as the link may be, I still find it interesting.''

''If it were the judgment on the lawsuit, Your Excellency, and Don Gonsalvo had murdered the friar for it, he would have it. And he would not be pestering the canon vicar of Barcelona for it, would he?''

''You are relentless, Isaac.''

''And why should he wish to murder Don Gilabert?''

''Because he wants his lands—you told me that yourself.''

''And is he Don Gilabert's heir, Your Excellency, that the young man's death puts him in possession of his lands?''

''I think it is time we stopped for dinner,'' said the Bishop.

•　　•　　•

They crossed the Llobregat with the afternoon sun warm on their backs, and headed up out of the valley to Terrassa. This time they stayed with the Carthusians, who could afford more lavish hospitality than the impoverished Augustinians, but even so, one monastery guest house blended into another until they all seemed to be the same guest house. The next day, they ate their soup in another monastic refectory at Granollers. And suddenly Girona was within reach. Mountains gave way to hills and valleys, rocks and pines to fertile fields. They had long since passed the road to Barcelona. Once they reached Hostalric, home was less than a day's journey away.

Isaac now spent the hours on the road lost in his own thoughts. He no longer attempted to puzzle out the enigmas of the trip; with deliberation, he cleared his mind and let all that had happened float freely, stripped of theory, or emotion, or the prejudices of others.

Before they expected it, the massive stone presence of Hostalric rose up ahead of them. It was a market day, and the town was lively with buyers and sellers. Taverns rang with laughter, and there was a comforting bustle everywhere of business as usual. Cooking smells drifted through the air, children played in the streets, and the travelers' spirits lifted.

The next morning, Berenguer took a place beside his physician as he and his family sat at breakfast. "I received a message from your patient this morning," he said. "He has left with friends, he says, and bids us farewell for the moment, excusing himself on the grounds that there is something that he must do that he cannot leave to others to do for him."

"So Don Gilabert is gone?" asked Isaac. "I am surprised he stayed with us so long. He was very intent on carrying out some task. But then he was also intent on staying alive long enough to do so."

"Apparently he rode off at dawn, in hood and habit, and was joined by a pair of gray friars. The stable lad followed them out to the street, and watched them leave at a gallop," said Berenguer. "And now, after thinking over your arguments of yesterday, Master Isaac, I am distressed that I have not been able to assist Don Gilabert."

"How had you expected to help him?" asked the physician.

"I think we must believe that he is the nephew of your kinsman's tale—the one who has been harassed and persecuted through the ecclesiastical courts. We had enough evidence of that in Tarragona."

"I would agree with Your Excellency," said Isaac. "There cannot be two young men with quite that same history."

"Had all his troubles happened in my diocese, Master Isaac, it would have been possible to prevent a great deal of his suffering. But to discover now what was going on, and who was responsible—"

"Have you changed your mind about Don Gonsalvo, Your Excellency? You do not believe him to be behind the young man's misfortunes? Don Gilabert would agree with you, it seems."

"Some of them, yes, Master Isaac. But I cannot believe that anyone driven only by stupidity and greed could create quite that much havoc."

"But greed has brought down empires, Your Excellency."

"It has, Master Isaac. When combined with sharp wits. But laying false charges in ecclesiastical courts is too precarious a route to wealth for your ordinary greedy villain. To discover why Don Gilabert is being pursued, I fear that one would have to return to the *finca* near Vilafranca. And I have had enough of travel for now."

"Gilabert is going to Girona, Your Excellency?"

Berenguer paused. "That is what he said. He had business to take care of in Girona."

"Have you considered, Your Excellency, that Friar Norbert was killed the day we left? And that Don Gilabert was seized that same day? Both near the city? A great deal happened close to home. As soon as you had left."

"Are you suggesting that the solution to Don Gilabert's difficulties is to be found in Girona?"

"It may, Your Excellency. His enemy seems to have strong connections with Girona as well as with the south. If you could find such a man—"

"And how do I accomplish that? Post a proclamation that anyone with family or business in the southernmost part of the diocese of Barcelona is to declare himself? The canons would be convinced that I have gone mad."

"No doubt, Your Excellency. That does not mean you should dismiss the possibility," said Isaac seriously. "But I have a better suggestion."

"I would like to hear it," said the Bishop.

"Send a reliable messenger to Girona to announce our early arrival tomorrow."

"Tomorrow?"

"Yes, Your Excellency. And then he is to tell anyone who is curious enough to listen the following interesting bits of gossip."

# THREE

## Girona

Galceran de Monteterno greeted his nephew on the steps
of the Bishop's palace with a warm clasp to his bosom.
"My dear Fortunat," he said. "I am delighted to see you.
You must tell me your news."

"I shall, Uncle. And do you still wait for the Bishop to
return from the General Council?"

"A messenger just arrived to tell us that he comes tomorrow. The meetings do not end until Tuesday," he said,
frowning. "Something has happened to send him home
early."

"What?"

"I cannot say, but since the diocese is running smoothly
in his absence, nothing here has drawn him back. Shall we
walk in the gardens? Or down by the river?"

"Down by the river, if it is to your liking, Uncle. There
are fewer distractions and interruptions there."

And while the Bishop's party moved at a brisker pace than
usual, with the scent of home in their nostrils, life carrried
on as usual in and around the city. In the palace kitchens,
young Enrique, the guard, was enjoying a substantial early
repast to compensate him for his hasty breakfast. "It has

been a terrible journey," he said, his mouth stuffed with ham and bread.

"What happened?" asked one of the kitchen helpers.

"Everything—we were attacked twice, you know, but first we found an injured man by the road, and everyone had to look after him day and night, and now he and that Sor Agnete from Sant Daniel are both locked up tighter than wild beasts in the prison in Tarragona. And half our company hasn't returned with us . . ."

And all the servants and hangers-on who congregated in the kitchens during the mid-morning lull listened avidly to every word.

Upstairs, Don Arnau, canon vicar of Girona, the only canon to be unaware of the news as yet, sat closeted with his secretary and longed for the Bishop's speedy return. Galceran and his nephew, Fortunat, apparently weary of looking at the river, were strolling through the crowds of shoppers at the market, chatting and examining goods for sale. Fortunat winked at a handsome woman standing by baskets heaped with nuts, picked up a handful of almonds, and walked on. She frowned, looked at the canon, and decided against complaint. "Thieving priests," she muttered, and moved in front of her wares.

"But, Uncle," Fortunat was saying, "things are going very well because of your generous assistance and advice. Five *maravedis* more and I will be in a position to support myself, and repay you all you given me."

"Repayment is not necessary, Fortunat. You know that. It will be sufficient that you are no longer in need of my purse. Whatever you may think, it is not a magic kettle that cannot be emptied. And I wish you would curb your habit of petty thievery. The merchants assume that I condone it, and it occasions discontent."

"Certainly, Uncle," said the young man sullenly, cracking almonds with his teeth and discarding the shells as he went.

"Fortunat," said Galceran, "I would like to know more about—"

But his nephew wasn't listening. He had approached a

table where a sweetmeat seller had laid out his wares. Five
or six children were crowded around it and the stallholder
was fully occupied in keeping their grasping hands away
from his goods. At the back of the display were his choicest
and most expensive delicacies—dates soaked in brandy,
stuffed with chopped fruit, honey, and almonds, and rolled
in ground nuts. Fortunat's hand darted out between two of
the children, caught one up, and popped it in his mouth
before he could be seen.

But the stallholder was not as slow as the young man
had counted on. "There, you!" he yelled. "That thief in
the blue tunic! Stop him!"

"Are you calling me a thief?" said Fortunat, whirling
around. "I'll have you before the judges if you're not careful."

"I know your kind, you thieving little cur," he said.
"Slinking around the market looking for what he can take.
Look at him! Threatening me with judges when his teeth
are black with my honey and dates."

"Watch what you call me, you miserable son of a whore!
I wouldn't touch your foul goods—"

"Look, Uncle Marc. It's the sweetmeat seller! The one
who sounds like the friar." The little girl was dancing in
her excitement and impatience. "And that other man. The
one who stole the date. He sounds just the same. Quick,
Uncle Marc, before they go away."

Then her eye fell on the familiar figure of the guard who
had accompanied her to the market the week before. "Señor," she called out. "Here's the man. And another just
like him. Hurry!"

"Help me with those two men," said the guard to his
partner. "And quickly!"

"What's going on?" asked his partner.

"Father Arnau wants to talk to them," said the guard.
"Don't ask me. Ask that little girl."

It was almost the dinner hour before Don Arnau had Fortunat, the sweetmeat seller, the little girl, Pere Vitalis, and
Ramon de Orta gathered together around a table. "This is

a truly unfortunate misunderstanding," Galceran murmured, coming in and taking a seat beside his nephew. "I
only wish to help straighten it out if you will allow me to
stay."

"What misunderstanding, Galceran?" asked Don Arnau.

"My date confection was no misunderstanding," said the
sweetmeat seller belligerently.

"Ah," said Don Arnau. "We are here about something
else. We will settle your complaint later, whatever it is.
Now tell me, my good man, where are you from?"

"I have a license to sell in Girona," said the sweetmeat
seller.

"I'm sure you do. Our officers are most vigilant in these
matters. But where are you from?"

"A village near l'Arboç," he said. "In Penedès."

"And you speak like one who comes from there?"

"I speak like everyone else at home," he said. "Not like
the people up here."

Don Arnau's secretary entered the room and murmured
something in his ear. "Everyone is waiting, Don Arnau,"
he said, loud enough to be heard.

"Oh dear," said the canon vicar. "This is difficult. It is
the dinner hour, and we have guests who ought not to be
neglected. What shall I do?" he whispered to the secretary.

"Let everyone go, Don Arnau," suggested Galceran,
"and ask them to return before vespers. We can deal with
it all then."

"I can't do that," said Don Arnau, who had now heard
of Berenguer's return. His mouth settled in a thin, stubborn
line. "This is too important. No. We shall all dine." His
eyes swept about the room. "Since there are not enough
places laid at table for everyone," he said, "then I and the
other canons will join our guests and everyone else may
dine in here. We shall meet again when the meal is over."

"And my nephew?" said Galceran.

"Perhaps he had best dine with us for the time being.
We do not wish this good man's meal to be spoiled by
acrimony." He smiled benignly on the sweetmeat seller,
whispered something to the guards, and left.

• • •

Isaac and his family had been the first of the travelers to reach their own gates. They scarcely had time to send one of the astonished sevants to the house of Ephraim and Dolsa to fetch the twins when the bell warned them their first visitor had arrived. "I shall be in my study," said Isaac quickly, "and am not to be disturbed unless it is a matter of life and death."

"It is, Master Isaac," said a voice from the other side of the gate. "My life and death, I'm afraid. If someone will let me in, I will explain."

"Ibrahim, let him in."

"Thank you, Master Isaac. I shall not keep you more than a minute," said Gilabert, coming in. "Is there somewhere we can speak?"

And Isaac led him into his study.

"Master Isaac," said Gilabert rapidly. "I have in my hand two sealed documents that I should not carry with me. Will you keep them until I can arrange to have them sent to Barcelona?"

"I would, gladly, Don Gilabert. But I think these documents should be in the hands of the Bishop. Let us take them to the palace before anyone realizes you have them. Are you still robed as a friar?"

"I am."

"The whole world is accustomed to seeing me visit the palace in the company of friars and priests. We will not be noticed."

"Thank you, Master Isaac."

As the sumptuous meal was coming to a close, a gray friar, looking shabby with dust, entered the reception room where the sweetmeat seller and the others were finishing dinner. He stayed close to the wall away from the windows and sat down in the darkest corner of the room. Two servants came in after him and whisked away the plates and bowls in time for the reappearance of the clerical party.

Don Arnau smiled his tight-lipped smile and turned to the child. "We were talking before about the sweetmeat seller, weren't we? And then you told your uncle and the guards that this gentleman spoke the same way? Is that right, my dear?''

''Yes, I did,'' said the little girl. ''That's what I said, because it's true.''

The sound of running feet, of doors closing, and of spurred boots on the tiled floor of the entrance hall stopped the discussion. Then a familiar voice roared, ''Where is this meeting that concerns the friar?'' And the door was flung open.

Everyone rose.

''Pray, be seated, gentlemen,'' said Berenguer de Cruilles. ''And young lady. And Father Gil. You are here as well. Good,'' he added cheerfully, nodding at the friar lurking in the shadows. ''I am most interested in the results of your inquiry, Don Arnau. Do not let me hinder your progress. I shall sit here quietly and listen.''

And one by one, everyone was seated again.

''And who is the child, Don Arnau?'' asked Berenguer in a whisper that could be heard throughout the room.

''She discovered the unfortunate friar, Your Excellency,'' replied the canon vicar. ''She recognized his accent as being the same as that good man's. He is a sweetmeat seller from Penedès.''

''Clever creature,'' said the Bishop, and smiled benignly at her.

''And where are you from, señor?'' asked Don Arnau, turning to Fortunat as if there had been no interruption.

''An estate not far from Granollers,'' said Fortunat.

''And Granollers is several days ride from l'Arboç,'' said Galceran.

''He doesn't sound like it when he's just talking,'' observed the little girl. ''Like now. Only when he's cross. When that man called him a thief, and he yelled back at him, they sounded exactly the same.''

''You know,'' said the girl's uncle, ''begging your pardons, sirs, for interrupting, but she's right. He did. I noticed it, too.''

The sweetmeat seller had been staring at Fortunat as if

he were some kind of fabulous beast—a unicorn or a hip-pogriff. "I know who he is!" he said. "I remember him. He's the bastard Magdalena was rearing. Sneaking, thieving little wretch he was then, too."

"Be careful what you say, my man," said Galceran. "This is my nephew."

"That may be, Father," said the sweetmeat seller cheerfully. "But he's also the bastard son of the lady over at—"

"I think we should settle this after we have time to consider a few other things," said Berenguer, rising from his chair. "If you will forgive this interruption, Don Arnau. You have gone a long way toward solving some very vexing questions. The Archbishop will be pleased. Very pleased." Don Arnau gave him a frosty smile. "Now—tell me more about this most excellent witness," he said, looking down at the little girl.

Berenguer listened with attention and patience to Arnau's long account of the little girl's accomplishments. "She is an observant and honest child indeed," he said. "What was the delicacy that this man created that tempted you so at the fair?"

She explained as best she could, but the sweetmeat seller looked puzzled. "It was the one in the middle of the very back," she said impatiently. "And it had preserved cherry stuffed with something right on top. It was beautiful."

"Ah, you have excellent taste. It is called 'Aunt Felipa's Delight.' But I'm afraid that it and my brandied dates are my most expensive confections."

After a brief discussion with the Bishop, the little girl, with coins clutched in her fist, was sent off with her uncle to purchase a Delight from the sweetmeat seller's wife.

Berenguer looked around the room. "We will need all of you later. Don Arnau, let us talk about this for a moment. I am still woefully ignorant of many things. And then I must speak to the good Friar Gil over there."

Berenguer entered his study, followed by Francesc, Bernat, and a scribe. Gilabert and Isaac were already there, waiting. The sergeant entered and took his place standing by the door. The Bishop sat in his accustomed chair with a sigh of relief. "It is good to be home," he said. "Please, gentlemen, sit down."

"Your Excellency," said Gilabert, "I have here the documents that the unfortunate Father Norbert was carrying. He wished you to send them to the proper persons." He bowed and handed two sealed documents to Berenguer. "One, I believe, relates to me. I have not violated His Holiness's seal."

Berenguer looked at them, handed them to Francesc, and remained in silent thought for a moment. "How did you come by these documents?" The scribe began taking down the questions and responses in a rapid hand.

"I had heard that Father Norbert was at Avignon," he said. "And that he was on his way south again, on foot. We knew he would be somewhere between Girona and Figueres at that point. We were traveling north to meet him on the road."

"Why?"

"I thought he would know the results of my case. I did not want to make direct inquiries—there is a price on my head and I had no desire to be seized. I simply wanted to know if it was safe to go home, or whether I should flee— perhaps to England—to escape hanging for a crime I had not committed."

"How did you find him?"

"On the road. Some five miles from Girona. I knew him, you see," he said hesitantly. "I had expected him to be reluctant to speak—"

"Because he had testified against you?"

"You know that?"

"He left a letter as well."

"I see. But he was eager to talk. It seems an act of perjury that led to a man's death was too much even for his conscience. I was disappointed to learn he had fled Avignon before the decision was handed down," said Gilabert, "but then he told me that the messenger carrying the documents relating to my case had caught up with him at an inn a few miles up the road. During the evening the messenger was struck down with a terrible sickness and

called for a priest. Never again will I say that God does
not punish evildoers, Your Excellency. The dying man
forced Father Norbert to swear he would deliver those documents to the canon vicar of Barcelona. Norbert was a picture of terror. He believed the messenger had been poisoned
for them, and that carrying them would lead to his doom,
one way or another.''

"He would be killed on the road, or clapped in prison
in Barcelona for perjury," observed the Bishop.

"Precisely. He gave them to me and I promised to bring
them to you, at least. Then he tried to give me the money
he'd received to perjure himself," he added bitterly.

"In his letter Friar Norbert said that two men at the inn
that night had reason to kill for those documents. Were you
one of them?"

"No, Your Excellency. I spent the night with a family
nearby."

"Near Girona?"

"Yes."

"Their name?"

"I cannot say, Your Excellency. Not until I know what
is in that document. If it clears me, I will give you the
name, and they will vouch for my presence. If I am condemned, it does me no good to be cleared of poisoning the
messenger—I will still be hanged—but they can suffer for
harboring a criminal.''

"Do you know a Rodrigue de Lancia?" asked Bernat
suddenly.

"I don't believe so," said Gilabert. "Who is he?"

"A seafaring gentleman," said Berenguer. "And you
still do not know what is in that document?"

"No."

"You did not open it?"

"I had no time. I reflected that he—"

"By 'he' do you mean Gonsalvo de Marca?"

"Possibly. I don't know. But he would still be looking
for it, and so I concealed both of them in a safe place. It
was not until we were in Terrassa that my friends told me
that the unfortunate friar was murdered."

"Do you know a small village near l'Arboç, called Santa Margarida?"

"Yes. It's hardly a village, though. Just a few houses on the Foix. Some ten miles from the *finca*. Perhaps less."

"Then let us speak to this sweetmeat seller again," said the Bishop. "Ask him to come in, Sergeant," he said.

The man in question appeared with commendable promptness.

"Tell me, do you know this gentleman?"

"I do, sir," he said. "It's the young lord, Don Gilabert, who was in such trouble. You may not know me, señor, but—"

"I do indeed. You helped out at harvests when I was just a boy, and you can't have been more than fourteen. Your name is—" He thought for a moment. "Tomas. That's it, isn't it? Tomas. And what brings you to Girona?"

"When my parents died, my uncle, who was a confectioner of sweetmeats, took me into his business. He taught me the trade, and now, part of each year, I travel from market to market with my wife, selling our wares."

"And do you know one Norbert, from the same vicinity, perhaps?" asked the Bishop. "He became a friar."

"Not well, Your Excellency, but I have heard of him," he replied.

"Then let us see young Fortunat," said Berenguer. "Perhaps he can clear up some things that puzzle us. Do you know Fortunat, Don Gilabert? He, too, comes from your part of the world, if Tomas is to be believed. Have him come in."

The door opened and the sergeant ushered in Fortunat. His uncle followed, as if by right, and no one turned him back. "This is Don Fortunat," said the Bishop. "Don Gilabert."

Fortunat paled slightly, smiled, and sat down. His uncle leaned over to speak to him, and then, appearing to change his mind, straightened up.

"I know him," said Gilabert, the color draining from his face, but in a steady voice, "I am unlikely to forget him. Ever. While his friends held me down, he ground his boot heel into my hand, and told me what pleasure it gave him to feel the bones break under his foot. And how much he would enjoy the feeling again if I refused to speak. I spent many, many hours with that man.''

"He lies," said Fortunat. "I have never seen that man before. My uncle can attest that I was with him, here, when this liar was injured."

"How do you know when he was injured?" asked Isaac suddenly.

"It is the talk of the palace," he said carelessly. "Every bootboy knows when it happened."

"I know that voice," said Isaac. "And like the hiss of a venomous snake, it makes my skin tighten in revulsion. Do you remember, Your Excellency, a man who paid a purseful of money to a diocesan messenger to tell his servants in Tarragona that he was coming home? There he is."

"He raves," said Fortunat. "I have no servants in Tarragona. Do I, Uncle?"

"Do you know what that message meant, Your Excellency? Master Isaac?" asked Gilabert. "I can tell you, because my friends, Andreu and Felip, pursued the two villains who received it. It meant that I was dead, and they should kill my uncle. There was no point in taking the trouble if I still lived."

Galceran was staring at Gilabert in horror. "But you were dead," he said, and turned to his nephew. "First, you told me he was dead," he repeated in a shaken voice, "You swore he was dead. You said you had seen his body. And then you said he was safely locked in a prison in Tarragona, about to be hanged. How could you have been so stupid?"

"Did you hope, on the strength of your mother's tenuous connection to our family, to claim the estate after my death?" said Gilabert, looking at Fortunat. "And of course, my uncle's death, since he had a better claim. Why were you so anxious to get the documents? They couldn't help you one way or the other."

"That fool Gonsalvo wanted them," said Fortunat. "It

was worth five *maravedis* to me to get them from you."
He shrugged his shoulders. "And I have often wondered
how difficult it would be to make a man talk. I thought it
would be easier. But I have not the skills of a professional
torturer."

"You were going to give him the documents, take the
money, and then claim the whole estate?"

"It was no more than he deserved," said Fortunat. "And
if you had died when you were supposed to, it would have
worked. My uncle assured me of that."

"I did not," said Galceran. "I would never have suggested such an evil course of action."

Tomas the sweetmeat seller had been silently watching
everyone, when he suddenly thumped his fist down on the
table. "I know where Norbert went," he said. "He became
the young lord's tutor."

"Is that true?" asked Berenguer.

"It is, Your Excellency," said Gilabert. "My loyal and
trusted tutor."

"And if this priest is his uncle," added Tomas, "then
he must be your uncle, too, Don Gilabert. For Fortunat is
the son of your poor aunt—everyone at home knew that.
She paid Magdalena in our village to look after him. The
priest must be another of her brothers."

"She had only one brother," said Gilabert. "My father.
And Don Galceran is certainly not my father. I could hazard
a guess about whose father he is, though. He and my tor-
mentor are as alike as two pebbles from the same stream."

"That is not at issue here," said Berenguer. "We will
look into it in due course."

"You have been betrayed indeed, Don Gilabert," said
the Bishop. "But we have heard enough for now. Young
Fortunat and his uncle will be tried tomorrow for crimes
against the Church, and then Fortunat will be turned over
to the secular arm for his crimes against the Crown. Everything else will come out then."

"Once I realized that Norbert thought his letter was going
to the canon vicar of Barcelona," said Berenguer, "the entire letter began to make sense."

"And the confession to murder?" asked Isaac.

"Someone paid the poor wretch to perjure himself in the papal court. Probably Gonsalvo de Marca, although it will be difficult to prove."

"Perjury in a case where the accused will hang if convicted. Most justly did he consider himself guilty of murder."

"The seal on that document was unbroken," said Berenguer. "He assumed he was carrying Gilabert's death warrant."

"But the document could be exactly that, could it not?"

"I have availed myself of doubtful episcopal privilege, Isaac, and broken the seal. The case against him was never strong, and Norbert's testimony was so at variance with the sworn depositions of other witnesses that it was discounted."

"And Gilabert is cleared?"

"Yes. For the third and last time. The case has no higher court to go to."

"And what of your canon? Is his only crime that of committing a youthful indiscretion which has returned to haunt him?"

"They are certainly father and son," said Berenguer. "They have admitted the relationship. They are alike both in appearance and in claiming to be the innocent victim of the other's vile machinations."

"What reason had they to create such havoc?"

"Greed. And bitterness. One gathers that Galceran has a younger son's insufficient portion. If Fortunat had chosen the Church, he could have used his influence to steer him toward prosperity, but the boy had no liking for the life. He wanted worldly fame and a fortune. There have been many families lately that are lacking in heirs, and the flimsiest claims to inherit have gone unchallenged. Theirs seemed to be as good as any."

"Except that two men had better claims than young Fortunat."

"Yes—but thanks to the greed of his neighbor Gonsalvo

de Marca, the principal heir was hunted, unsettled, and un-
married. Who easier to kill?''

"Like a rabbit surrounded by hounds,'' said Isaac. "An
extremely resourceful rabbit.'' He stood. "It must be approaching sundown, Your Excellency. Now that we are at
our own board, my wife's law once more rules the household, and I must return in ample time for the Sabbath. I
trust Your Excellency's health has not suffered from this
journey.''

"I will demonstrate it by walking down with you to the
plaza,'' said Berenguer. "To taste the pleasure of using my
legs again. I wish to thank you for suggesting that I send
a messenger with false news.''

"You made an excellent choice. I gather that young Enrique convinced everyone that Gilabert was hanged or as
close to it as could be.''

"He was the sergeant's choice. He said if we needed a
convincing young liar, Enrique was our man. But what
made you think of it?''

"I had an odd feeling that our lost heir was here, in
Girona. Nothing more than that.''

"I see that Don Gilabert waits for us at the foot of the
stairs,'' said Berenguer. "I give you my leave to take off
that habit now, Don Gilabert,'' he said. "Although it be-
comes you well.''

"I would make a poor friar, I fear. And after all this
trouble, I believe I'm expected to marry and provide my
estate with an heir,'' he said.

"I suspect you are right.''

"I am here to take my leave of you,'' he said. "Master
Isaac, I lack words eloquent enough to thank you for saving
my life—and my poor maltreated hand. I shall be grateful
to all of you for as long as I live.''

"Let me examine that hand once more before you leave
us, Don Gilabert,'' said Isaac. "Unwrap it.''

"Lord,'' said Yusuf, "the sun is low in the sky. The
mistress—''

"Watch, Yusuf, so you can help him bind it up again.''
Isaac took the hand delicately in his and felt the injured

bones. "They are knitting together well," he said. "Be gentle with them for a few weeks and you will have use of that hand again."

"Master Isaac, in His Excellency's stable is my uncle's bay mare. She is a good creature, and I leave her for young Yusuf here. And for Mistress Raquel I leave my—" He paused. "My gratitude and my hopes that she will know happiness in her life in the future."

"I will tell her when she is ready to hear it. Not now. It is too soon."

"You are a strangely perceptive man, Master Isaac," said Gilabert, and hastened away.

"Lord, we must run."

"Then let us hurry, Yusuf."

Raquel stood in her chamber, her head aching, too weary for useful work and too restless to lie down. The room, usually a refuge in moments of turbulence, felt narrow and oppressive. Abandoning her unpacking, she made her way down to the empty courtyard and wandered aimlessly until the bell warned of another visitor. Quickly, she sat down on the edge of the fountain and waited for Ibrahim to deal with the intruder, whoever he was.

"Mistress Raquel is in the courtyard, master," said Ibrahim, all helpfulness. "Over by the fountain."

"My aunt thought you might not have time for Sabbath preparations," said a familiar voice. "She sends you a dish of something. I don't know what it is, but it has a tempting smell."

"Daniel!" said Raquel, and stood up.

He placed a covered earthenware dish on the table and turned toward her. "Mistress Raquel," he said with a formal bow. "I hope you are well."

"We are all very well. Please, sit down," she added, seating herself hastily on a bench.

"But you must regret the sudden end of your journey," he said. "I can understand that. We were surprised—pleasantly—to have you back early. It is good for us, but perhaps not for you."

"Daniel, I couldn't be happier that it's over," she said, her eyes filling with tears. "I am so relieved to be home."

"What's wrong, Raquel?" he asked, sitting down next to her, then abruptly standing again. "Has something terrible happened?"

"I don't know what you mean, Daniel," she said, staring down at her hands. "But a great deal has happened. We've been away."

"I know you've been away. I could not help noticing," he added, with a tightening of his jaw. "Tell me about the trip."

"What is there to tell? It was long and tedious. We were attacked twice, once by bandits and once by mountain folk, but the guards protected us. I'm sick to death of sharing filthy bedchambers with my mother and the nuns. I liked Uncle Joshua, who is a charming old man, but my aunt Dinah is a lazy version of Mama. What else do you want to know?"

"And your cousin Ruben?"

"Oh—Ruben. He's shy and awkward, and rather homely. And terrified of women. He hid whenever I was around. He wants to marry some girl who loves him madly, but Aunt Dinah thinks I'll have more money. Papa said she also thinks that other girl would try to throw her out of her house when Uncle Joshua died. But I trapped him over an early breakfast and told him I had no intention of marrying him. He was very relieved."

Daniel laughed. "Shy and homely? And I had imagined him rich and handsome."

"If you don't believe me, ask Yusuf. He'll tell you how handsome he is. And I doubt if he's rich. Most of Joshua's money goes to his daughters."

His face changed, serious once more. "None of this explains why you're so unhappy."

"Why do you insist that I'm unhappy?" she said, standing up. "I'm weary, and sick of travel, nothing more." She went over to an apricot tree and inspected the fruit, before sitting on the edge of the fountain again.

"There's more to it than that," he said, "I can see it on your face."

"This journey changed me, Daniel," she said impatiently. "Or if I didn't change, then I saw myself for the first time."

"Why has that made you unhappy?"

"I don't know. It's too difficult to explain. I liked my life the way it was, busy and useful. I knew who I was. But I was wrong. I saw it was all going to end, and I didn't know what to do. I learned too much about myself on this journey. I want to be the person I was before I left, but I can't. I must be a woman and give up everything." Tears trickled down her cheek and she mopped them up with the end of her sleeve.

"At least you must give up doing that," said Daniel, picking up her damp sleeve tip.

She looked up with a very uncertain smile. "I don't trust myself anymore," in a low voice. "Not that I did anything wrong, but I used to believe I would always do what I thought was right. Now I'm not sure."

"Whatever happened, and I have no idea what it was, Raquel—and I'm not asking you to tell me—but I do know by now that no one trusts himself. I found that out the first time my life took a strange turning. Look at today. I came here full of anger, determined on a bitter quarrel. Instead I saw you in misery and changed in a moment. Do you see? I don't know myself, nor do you, I expect. Perhaps you should marry me," he said, gently picking up her hand, "and we can trust each other instead of ourselves."

"What an odd way to look at it," she said doubtfully. "But if I did, what would Papa do? His Majesty wishes Yusuf to go to court in a year or two."

"What he always does. We could live here, and you could do what you always do. I don't want you to change."

"Oh, Daniel. Think of it. In the lions' den with Mama hanging over our shoulders? I'm not sure I could bear it, and I know you couldn't."

"Then come live with us, with my aunt and uncle. You'd

be only two minutes away from your father. Think about it, Raquel. But don't think too hard," said Daniel with a rueful smile. "I won't be able to stand much more of this, you know."

# EPILOGUE

"And what does His Holiness wish to tell us?" Don Pedro asked his secretary, drumming his fingers on the carved wood of his chair.

"Shall I read the entire letter, Your Majesty?"

"It would be best."

"It is dated at Avignon, last month, Your Majesty. It says, 'To King Pedro the Ceremonious. The Holy See prays, on the petition of Tomàs de Patrinhanis, ambassador of the city and people of Ancona, that he force his subjects, the pirates Ian de Pródica, master of the galiot *Santa Eulalia,* Pedro Bernardo, of the *San Salvador,* Huguet de Lancia Talatarn, Guillermo Pedro de Raxath, and Francisco Alberich, of the *San Juan,* to restore the ships, provisions, money, and other goods robbed from Nicolas Polluti near the island of Rhodes, and from other merchants of Ancona in the port of Le Palais, on various occasions.' With the usual compliments, Your Majesty," said the secretary, laying the letter down on the table.

"Under what compulsion?" asked His Majesty.

"None, Your Majesty."

"How very interesting," murmured Don Pedro.

"Will Your Majesty do as His Holiness requests?" asked Doña Eleanor. "And confiscate the ships?"

"Unfortunately, we cannot confiscate their galiots. Not now."

"Cannot?"

"They no longer have them. We confiscated them when we first heard that a decision had been reached." Doña Eleanor laughed her infectious little laugh and His Majesty smiled. "They are even now being refitted for war. But when we were first told of His Holiness's disposition in this matter, it laid heavy penalties on ourself and our people if we did not comply. Olzinelles, what is your opinion on this shift? Does it indicate a change in policy?"

And the business of the court continued.

The Archbishop of Tarragona was seated with his secretary, the secretary's assistant, and a scribe. On the table in front of him was a letter from the Bishop of Barcelona, along with several other documents. Standing on the other side of the table was Don Gonsalvo de Marca. He smiled, a big, friendly smile, and sweated in spite of the pleasant breeze that cooled the room.

"Don Gonsalvo, I have here a copy of the judgment in the case of the accused heretic, Don Gilabert de—"

"Yes, Your Excellency?"

The Archbishop frowned. "As I suspected would happen when you pursued this case beyond our jurisdiction, Don Gonsalvo, Don Gilabert's appeal has been heard and granted. He is cleared, without a stain upon his character."

"I am happy to hear it, Your Excellency," said Don Gonsalvo uneasily.

"Are you? I, too, am pleased, Don Gonsalvo. Since we have indications that a witness was suborned."

"Indications?"

"He confessed it, in writing. I have a shrewd suspicion that I am now talking to a man who suborned perjury."

Don Gonsalvo said nothing.

"And I am forced to wonder whether I am talking to a man who was involved in the brutal murders of Don Gilabert's uncle. After all, Don Fernan was the principal force behind clearing his nephew's name. Did you find him so inconvenient, Don Gonsalvo?"

"No, Your Excellency," said Gonsalvo, sweat pouring down his face and his voice trembling. "I never touched Don Fernan. I swear. Nor asked no one to touch him. I couldn't have been more astonished when they told me about it. I tripled the guards around my house—ask anyone—because I thought there were bandits in the neighborhood. I would never have thought of killing Don Fernan."

"Strange as it may seem, Don Gonsalvo," said the Archbishop, "I believe that you wouldn't have thought of it. And no one else thought of it for you?"

"Pardon, Your Excellency?" he said, looking confused.

Don Sancho raised his head and looked straight into the landowner's eyes. "Don Gonsalvo. Should there ever be another case like this in the diocese of Barcelona, or any other diocese within the archdiocese of Tarragona, then officers will be sent to Avignon and to other relevant places to discover further proof—should it be needed—of your involvement in Norbert's perjury and the deaths of Don Fernan and the others. I suggest that from this day forward you stay at home and look after your herds and vines instead of bothering your neighbors. Do you understand me?"

"I do, Your Excellency."

The Archbishop turned to his secretary, and Don Gonsalvo left the room as rapidly as possible.

"Now, what were we working on?"

"I was going over the final details of the council records before placing them in the library, Your Excellency," said the secretary. "There is one problem. What am I do about Girona?"

"What do you mean, what are you to do about him?"

"Pardon, Your Excellency, I was not clear. But His Excellency the Bishop of Girona was here when the roll was taken, and he was here for some parts of the council, but then he rushed off when His Majesty summoned him and he wasn't here.''

Don Sancho thought for a moment. ''Then list him neither among those present, nor among those absent,'' he said. ''As he was not one or the other.''

''A judicious solution, Your Excellency,'' said the secretary, and the scribe put down his pen.

And thus is explained the extraordinary circumstance that the records for the General Council held at Tarragona in 1354 fail to mention the noble Berenguer de Cruilles, Bishop of Girona.